INGENUE

Also by Jillian Larkin

VIXEN

INGENUE

❖ ❖ ❖

Jillian Larkin

DELACORTE PRESS

Text copyright © 2011 by The Inkhouse

Jacket art copyright © 2011 by Zhang Jingna

Songs quoted: "Downhearted Blues," lyrics and music by Lovie Austin and Alberta
Hunter, 1922; "St. Louis Blues," lyrics and music by W. C. Handy, 1914; "Second Hand
Rose," lyrics by Grant Clarke and music by James Hanley, 1921; "Nobody Knows You
When You're Down and Out," lyrics and music by Jimmy Cox, 1922.

All rights reserved. Published in the United States by Delacorte Press, an imprint of
Random House Children's Books, a division of Random House, Inc., New York.

Delacorte Press is a registered trademark and the colophon
is a trademark of Random House, Inc.

theflappersbooks.com
www.randomhouse.com/teens

Library of Congress Cataloging-in-Publication Data is available upon request.

ISBN: 978-0-385-74036-4 (trade)
ISBN: 978-0-385-90836-8 (lib. bdg.)
ISBN: 978-0-375-89911-9 (ebook)

The text of this book is set in 12-point Granjon.
Book design by Trish Parcell Watts
Printed in the United States of America
10 9 8 7 6 5 4 3 2 1

First Edition

For my parents.
If you hadn't given me the courage to take New York
by storm, Gloria, Lorraine, Vera, and Clara
never would've gotten the chance.

ACKNOWLEDGMENTS

The 1920s were all about independence, but writing about the 1920s would be impossible without a whole lot of fantastic support. Thank you to Ted Malawer and Michael Stearns at the Inkhouse for your keen eyes and even keener senses of humor. And thanks to Wendy Loggia, Beverly Horowitz, Krista Vitola, Barbara Perris, Trish Parcell, and everyone at Delacorte Press and Random House Children's Books for making what could be hard work fizzy and fun. My special thanks to Meg O'Brien and Emily Pourciau—my publicity extraordinaires, who could pull off bobs far better than I ever could. Thank you to my mother for being the best first reader I could ever ask for, and to Daniel DaVeiga for your support, insight, and tolerance of a constant soundtrack of Bessie, Duke, and Louis in our apartment this summer.

Money.

It was worth so much, but weighed so little.

She placed the satchel on the table, opened it with a soft click, and flipped back the top. It was filled with dozens upon dozens of thin, green bills, rubber-banded in fat stacks. Hundreds.

Then she picked up the list. Three names, all practically kids: Sebastian Grey, Carlito Macharelli, and Jerome Johnson.

She reached for her gun. It was an automatic she'd bought in downtown Chicago specifically for this job. Once she was done, she'd lose it somewhere. It was a .38, a good gun to kill with.

She unwrapped it and worked the slide, made sure all the parts were clean and functioning. It smelled of oil and cordite and had a reassuring weight in her hand. Effortlessly she snapped one bullet after another into the chamber.

There was a fashion among the younger people she knew for revolvers, but she'd never been comfortable with the turn of the cylinder. And besides, the problem with letting young people into the business was that they made messes. But that was why she always had work—no one liked to clean up messes. So they always had to hire a cleaner.

She slid the gun into its holster and the list into her pocket.

Now she was ready. Or almost: First she had to wash her hands.

She hated being dirty.

PART ONE

FOOLS IN LOVE

❖ ❖ ❖

"I hope she'll be a fool—
that's the best thing a girl can be in this world,
a beautiful little fool."

—Daisy Buchanan, in F. Scott Fitzgerald's *The Great Gatsby*

VERA

Fashion kills.

Crouching for long periods of time was never fun, but doing it in patent-leather T-strap heels was murder. Vera usually tried to wear more comfortable shoes when she was following someone, but there'd been no time to change. She'd been working at the Green Mill when she'd overheard Carlito Macharelli mention a meeting on the docks with Sebastian Grey.

She'd immediately called a cab.

"Follow that car!" she'd ordered the driver.

A normal cabbie would never put himself at her disposal for this sort of activity—a black girl? Telling a cabdriver to follow a wealthy white man?—but Wally was not a normal cabbie. He was that rarity: a black man with his own taxi and license. He was a family friend and happy to help her clear her brother's name. "Jerome is like the son I wish I'd never had," Wally liked to say. Most nights, he waited outside the Green Mill until she was done with her shift to take her home.

Tonight they followed the taillights of Carlito's Rolls-Royce all the way through downtown and to the docks—a place Vera usually avoided. This area was dangerous. Vera already worked in a Mob-run speakeasy; she didn't need the added threat of being around when the gangsters unloaded the hooch.

She asked Wally to let her out a block behind where Carlito parked the Rolls in the vacant lot. The hulking shadows of ships loomed to the east, but here the docks were still and silent.

Vera edged close to the Rolls, dodging from shadow to shadow until at last she found a hiding place behind a stack of tied-up crates. Already, there was Bastian Grey—she could see his smug features as he lit a butt from his silver cigarette case. He ambled out on the pier and stood smoking, staring out at the water.

She was sweltering on this warm summer night, thanks to her black, knee-length trench coat, but Bastian looked at ease in the heat, irritatingly handsome in a brown suit, his cheeks freshly shaven, his dark hair slicked back and parted. He was a looker, that much Vera couldn't deny.

"What do you want?" Carlito called out as he walked up, the lights from the pier warehouse catching his gray pin-striped suit and black fedora.

Carlito was her boss and had once employed her brother, Jerome, as the piano player at the Green Mill. But then Carlito and Tony Pachelli, one of his goons, had tried to kill Jerome. And Gloria, Bastian's high-society fiancée, had shot Tony dead. And then Gloria and Vera's brother had had to flee Chicago to save their lives.

And it was all Vera's fault.

Vera had been the one feeding Bastian information about Jerome and Gloria. Vera had been the one determined to break up their secret affair. Just because Vera hadn't known that Bastian was telling everything to Carlito didn't mean she was any less guilty.

That was why Vera was here, crouched behind a stack of crates, hoping to learn something incriminating about Carlito and Bastian—something she could use to barter for her brother's life.

"What do *I* want?" Bastian flipped his cigarette in a bright arc across the lot. "*You're* the one who told me to meet you here."

Carlito stepped backward. "No, I didn't."

"Secret notes and midnight meetings." Bastian walked a few steps away. "I'm tired of your little games, Macharelli." Only a young man as despicable as Bastian Grey could work with mobsters *and* show a proud distaste for them at the same time.

"This isn't a game," Carlito said, casting a quick glance over his shoulder. "And I didn't send you a note. That means someone else did."

"Don't be absurd," Bastian said, lighting another cigarette. "Why would anyone go to the trouble of dragging us out here?"

Vera was leaning forward to hear better when she felt a hand crawl over her mouth. "What are you playing at?" a woman's voice whispered.

She wanted to struggle against the stranger's hold, but she couldn't give herself away. She felt herself being turned around to face her attacker.

Vera stared into the eyes of Maude Cortineau, Carlito's moll. When Maude had been a flapper, she'd barely paid attention to anyone outside her glamorous inner circle. Since she'd gotten with Carlito, she stuck to his side and spoke only when she was spoken to.

"I'm *trying* to eavesdrop," Vera whispered back. If Maude had been planning to bust her, she would've done it already.

"Shut up, Vera," Maude hissed. "I was waiting in the car, and I saw you running around behind these crates like you didn't have a care in the world. If Carlito sees you, you're in deep trouble. Don't be an idiot. You don't want to end up like me."

After dropping out of her bluenose prep school, Maude had become the queen of the Chicago flapper scene. Sequins, feathers, gold lamé—she wore it all. Her makeup was always flawless and her headband always settled perfectly over her blond bob.

But now her beaded red dress hung over her bony body

like a burlap sack. Deep shadows lurked underneath her kohl-rimmed eyes. Carlito had sucked the life out of her: The flame that Maude had once been famous for had been snuffed out.

"Maude! Where the hell are you?" Carlito called from the other side of the crates.

"Just be smart and hide," Maude said, clacking away in her heels, back to Carlito's Rolls. Carlito was pacing by the car as Maude ambled up, smoking a cigarette. She was the perfect portrait of boredom.

Carlito banged his fist on the hood. "I told you to stay in the car!"

Maude dropped the practically new cigarette. "I wanted a ciggy," she replied in a soft, defeated voice. "I know how you don't like anyone to smoke in your car, Daddy."

"Get in," he said. "We gotta go, and fast. This is a setup."

"You're being silly, Macharelli!" Bastian shouted. "No one is after us!"

But Carlito ignored him. He slid behind the wheel, cranked the engine, and sped off with a squeal of tires.

Vera let herself relax against the crates, leaning out to check on Bastian. How could she have been so stupid as to ever trust him? *Those eyes,* she thought. When she'd first met Bastian, his green eyes had seemed sincere—swoony, even. Arrogant, of course, but that was to be expected from a rich white boy like him. She hadn't realized the heartless steel his irises really concealed until she'd accused him of sending a man to kill Jerome and he'd just smiled and called her "silly, stupid Vera."

And in all honesty, that was exactly what she was.

Vera opened her purse and felt the comforting, cool metal of Bastian's pistol inside. She'd carried it often since she'd found it at Gloria's feet that night. Bastian certainly didn't know it was his own gun that had killed the gangster, that his own fiancée had pulled the trigger.

Vera had never used a gun before, but if a dame like Gloria could use one, then so could she. Vera loved Jerome every bit as much as Gloria did, and would go just as far, if not further, to protect him.

She snapped the purse shut and looked back toward the docks.

Footsteps, approaching from the other side of the dockyard. The figure wore a long black overcoat and a hat with a wide brim. Vera watched the person walk down the pier.

"Sebastian Grey?" Vera was shocked to hear the voice of a woman.

Bastian turned from the water. "I don't believe I've had the pleasure—"

"Skip the formalities. I'm looking for Macharelli. And the piano player, Jerome Johnson."

"Do I look like their keeper?" Bastian breathed out a cloud of cigarette smoke, and then his face brightened. "You're too pretty a woman to be chasing after trash like Carlito. But if you must know, he took off a minute ago."

The woman made a swift movement, and Bastian raised his hands in surrender. "Where to?" she demanded. "And where's the piano player?"

"No need for guns," Bastian said, slowly backing up. "Carlito went home. And Johnson? No one knows where he disappeared to. He sent his kid sister a postcard from a post office box in New York, but that's been a dead end so far."

"Thank you," the woman said. "You've been most helpful."

Then Vera heard the unmistakable sound of a gunshot. Two.

Instinctively, she cowered, knocking her heavy purse against the crates.

The killer turned at the noise, her features hidden by shadow. All Vera could see was the silver pistol, pointed directly at her.

The third gunshot in as many minutes rang out over Lake Michigan.

The bullet slammed into a wooden crate so close to her head that Vera felt splinters hit her face. She didn't wait for another bullet. She just turned and ran.

It wasn't far to the edge of the dockyard, and the wall of crates was between Vera and the shooter. But Vera was wearing heels, and she'd never been able to run in heels.

Until now.

She waited for the crack of the gunshot and the bullet in

her back as she crossed the lot, as she turned and ran the block to Wally's cab, as she banged on the window to wake him from his nap.

"What's the rumpus?" he said as she clambered into the backseat.

"Drive!" she said. "As fast as you can."

Wally didn't need to be told twice. He turned the key, gunned the engine, and took off.

When he dropped her at the club, it was already locked up for the night, but that didn't slow her down: She fumbled through her purse, found Jerome's old keys, and slipped the brass master into the lock.

Whoever the killer was, she wouldn't miss the next time.

◆ ◆ ◆

All that had been hours ago.

Vera had made a pot of coffee. She'd sat down in a booth to try to figure out what to do next. And once she'd been sure she was alone, she'd cried. She'd cried for vile Bastian Grey, and for her brother, and for herself. She was only seventeen. She was supposed to be in school, not fleeing killers. Her mother had been dead for years, and if her father found out about the mess she'd gotten herself into, it would probably kill him, too.

The only reason this place was a safe haven right now was that it was morning, much too early for anyone—the band, the girls, the owners—to be there. That would change in a few hours. Vera needed to gather her things, figure out a plan, then scram.

But she couldn't stop shaking. Maybe she could wait just a little longer. Just until her nerves settled.

Then she stiffened in her seat: a jangle of keys outside the door. She needed to hide.

But by the time she'd slid out of the booth, the door was already open.

"What are you doing here?" a man's voice exclaimed.

Vera's heart slowed. The voice wasn't the cool steel of a thug's, but warm, buttery, and familiar: Evan. The trumpet player in the band and an old friend of Jerome's.

Despite the early hour, Evan was already dressed for the day in a soft white dress shirt and brown slacks. He looked the slightest bit amused, thanks to the way his lips naturally turned up at the corners. His face was smoothly shaved, his cheeks and jaw incredibly angular. He removed his brown derby hat as he flicked on the light and walked into the room.

"What are *you* doing here?" Vera asked, shutting her purse. "What time is it, five in the morning?"

"Five-thirty," Evan replied. His eyes widened as he took in Vera's appearance. She was still wearing her sleeveless gold dress, though it was a wrinkled mess. Evan picked a splinter of wood out of her hair. "What happened to you, Vera?" He pointed at the booth. "Take a load off, girl." He went behind the bar and ran the tap.

When he came back, he handed Vera a tall glass of water. She held it out in front of her: Her hand wasn't shaking.

"It's water," Evan said. "It's for drinking."

Vera smiled for the first time that night and gulped down the entire thing.

"Thank you." She leaned back in the booth, feeling a bit more herself. "Now, I think you were just about to tell me why you're here about ten hours earlier than usual."

"You're welcome," Evan said. He sat down opposite her and ran a hand through his sleek dark hair—Vera could smell the Brilliantine. "Truth is, Vera, I'm taking off."

"You were just going to ditch the band?"

"Aw, it ain't much of a band anymore. Tommy's been talking about joining up with a piano player at another club, and Bix never wants to practice. Without Jerome or a decent singer, this ain't a good gig anymore. I just came by to get my trumpet."

Vera couldn't help feeling hurt. He'd been planning to leave without saying goodbye?

Evan reached out to pat her hand. "I was going to tell you. I just wanted to sneak my horn out of here early, before anyone was around. Or at least it was *supposed* to be before anyone was around." He gave a wry grin. "Now, what are *you* doing here?"

Before Vera knew what was happening, words started spilling out of her. She told him how she had betrayed Jerome and nearly cost him his life. How Bastian and Carlito had been lured to the docks, and how the killer had shot Bastian dead. And she told him how she'd nearly caught a bullet herself. "And the woman asked about Jerome," she said. "Bastian knew about Jerome's post office box in New York City. He knew Jerome had sent me a postcard."

"He sent you a postcard?"

"Months ago. I—I carried it around like a dog with a bone. Someone must have gone through my purse when I was working. Someone must have told—" She swallowed heavily. "And now the killer knows he's in New York."

Evan reached over and tilted her chin upward, forcing her to look at him. "That is not your fault. But don't you worry—I'll help you sort this out."

She turned away from his hand. "I'm dealing with it all right on my own."

Evan raised his eyebrows at her torn dress and dirty face. "Yep, you're doing just fine."

Despite herself, Vera laughed, and then she stood. "I'm gonna go clean myself up a bit."

She washed the grime off her face in the ladies' room. Now she'd gone and involved Evan. He was the one person besides her father she really cared about in Chicago, and she'd repaid his friendship by putting his life in danger, too. In the dressing room at the end of the hall, she stuffed her makeup kit, red hairbrush, and silver clutch into a large black shoulder bag she found on the floor.

Then she looked at the clothes rack and winced.

She couldn't very well run away with only a bag full of sparkly flapper dresses. Still, she chose three of her favorites and packed them. And then, murmuring an apology, she swiped a few of a fellow cigarette girl's simple day dresses, including a pale yellow number that she slipped over her head. It was a little tight, but not in a bad way. Finally, she slipped her feet into a pair of black ballet slippers. With her T-strap heels packed in the bag, she slung it over her shoulder and said goodbye to this place.

She found Evan behind the bar. His beat-up trumpet case and a tan briefcase sat on the floor near the booth.

Two glasses of water sat on the table. Evan carried over a pair of plates from the bar and set them down. "Isn't that Betty's?" he asked, glancing at her dress.

"Not anymore," Vera replied as she sat down.

"Fair enough," Evan said, taking a seat. "I figured you might be hungry. Sorry it's not the greatest breakfast—I worked with what was available."

Vera looked down. A ham and cheese sandwich. There was even a pickle next to it. Evan was kind as well as handsome. And unlike her, he remembered the importance of things like drinking water and eating regular meals.

She grabbed the sandwich and devoured it.

Evan cleared his throat. "So, what's the plan now? Send a note to Jerome?"

Vera pushed the plate away. "There's no time for a note. Somebody's got to stop this woman." She opened her bag and pulled out Bastian's gun. "I'm going to New York."

Evan dropped his sandwich. "What the hell are you doing with a gun, Vera?"

She sighed. "Long story, and I'm not particularly in the mood to tell it."

"Then save it for the train ride to New York," Evan said. "No way am I letting my best friend's sister head into danger by herself. I'm coming with you."

GLORIA

"Extra! Extra! Harry Houdini, King o' the Cuffs, will break out of a straitjacket right in Times Square!" A dark-haired boy offered a paper to Gloria with a hopeful look in his big brown eyes.

She smiled at the boy, at his dirty face. The fact that she couldn't spare him a penny or two made her heart ache. But there was a different ache Gloria had to deal with this Tuesday morning—the growling in her stomach.

She wandered through the open-air market on First Avenue, pretending to shop. The large wooden pushcarts offered everything a fashionable New York City girl could desire: cloche hats in every shade from midnight blue to the palest rose, tiny silver compacts, endless tubes of lipstick. Soft silk stockings, along with the new artificial silk ones that, while cheaper, were still way out of Gloria's price range.

Gloria stopped and ran her fingers over a long string of white beads. She glanced down at her pale pink dress with its delicate lace embroidery. A narrow belt settled low on her hips, with a large cloth flower in the center. She couldn't help thinking how the necklace, wound twice around her neck, would really complete the outfit.

A woman with frizzy gray hair, standing behind the push-cart, cleared her throat. "You better buy those beads if you're planning to paw 'em much longer," she snapped.

The woman's gaze was focused on the gaping hole in the palm of the white glove on Gloria's left hand. Despite the rest of her rich girl's outfit—the pink scarf wrapped around her hat, the pointy-toed black heels—that one hole gave Gloria away for what she truly was: a woman who couldn't afford to replace even a torn glove.

A desperate woman. A woman who would steal.

Gloria gave the pushcart woman a polite smile. "I was just browsing." She would have to remember to keep her palms out of sight.

Gloria weaved away through the crowd and finally reached her destination—the food stalls.

Her stomach rumbled loudly at the sight of the shiny red apples and creamy hunks of cheese on display. A rainbow of vegetables decorated the stalls—green peppers, orange carrots, and yellow squash. Platters of sugar cookies were laid out, and hints of brown sugar and cinnamon wafted up from fluffy apple pies. She followed closely behind a young couple sharing buttery popcorn. Just watching them eat was the most delicious thing Gloria had done in a while.

She removed the oversized black purse hanging over her shoulder and slung it back on under her thin coat, then slid it behind her back.

It was now or never. As long as she hid her hands and kept calm, this was going to be duck soup.

She edged toward the baker's stall. Standing in front, looking over a platter of muffins, was a man in his early twenties, cute, wearing a plain blue shirt, knickerbockers, and a newsboy cap.

He would do.

Gloria let out a helpless cry. "There he is!" She pointed at the man with a trembling finger. "The man who stole my purse!"

The man looked up from the muffins. "Hey now, girlie, I ain't done nothing!"

But a balding man in an apron had already grabbed the so-called thief by his collar. "You think you can steal from a nice young lady outside *my* stall?"

"*All* my *money*!" Gloria wailed.

A group of men closed in on either side. "We'll get your money back for you, miss, don't you worry," said a man with a dark mustache as he joined the baker.

"But I don't *have* her purse!" the accused thief cried out. Gloria could no longer see him over the shoulders of the men around him.

Gloria dove toward the baker's stall. She snatched the closest loaf of bread within reach and stuffed it inside her coat, then inched behind the pushcart. She backed away through the crowd, pointing, saying, "Those men caught a pickpocket!" until she'd reached the mouth of a nearby alley.

And then she turned tail and ran.

Once she was in the alley, leaning against the brick wall, she caught her breath, composed herself, and strolled to the other end of the alley and out onto Second Avenue.

A successful steal.

She began the long walk home.

These days, Gloria barely gave thievery a second thought. Going hungry had changed her. She and Jerome had burned through the last of her family's money sometime in April, and now it was June. Gloria had to rely on her wits—and her looks—so that she and Jerome wouldn't starve.

She passed a gray, blocky high school and felt a brief pang for her old life at Laurelton Prep. Back then, a tardy slip from a teacher could seem like the end of the world. She should be sneaking notes in class, not stealing loaves of bread.

What would her mother think if she knew her daughter was stealing bread? What was her mother doing now, anyway? They hadn't had any contact in months, not since Gloria had fled town. Gloria would have liked to be in touch, but she worried that her mother would track her down.

Silence was safer—at least until she had her future figured out.

She turned onto 110th Street, and the already shabby brownstones became even shabbier. Paint peeled off the buildings in giant brown scabs, and many of the yards were just hardpan dirt. There was a church on the corner, but it looked as run-down and miserable as the homes around it. She glanced away from the church and noticed a flyer tacked to a lamppost.

Gloria swallowed hard. She was staring at herself.

It was an old photograph. She was smiling shyly in a conservative frock, looking exactly like the perfect debutante and bride-to-be she had been a year before. The innocent, apple-cheeked girl in this photo never would have disobeyed her Prohibition-loving fiancé and sneaked out to the Green Mill. Or snagged the job as the Green Mill's singer with Jerome, the joint's black piano player. Or fallen in love with Jerome and killed a man to save him.

It was a Missing Persons notice:

LOST GIRL
Gloria Carmody, 18
SUSPECTED KIDNAPPING!
Mother Worried Sick!
If spotted, contact:
Cooper Station Post Office
Box 1281
New York, NY

Gloria reached up and ripped the flyer off the lamppost. How long had it been up? How many others were there? And—most importantly—who was hanging them?

It could have been her mother. Or Bastian could have been looking for her, considering they were supposed to be married by now. But the person most eager to find her was Carlito Macharelli, and it certainly wasn't because he was "worried sick" about her.

For a moment Gloria was back on the snowy pavement outside Jerome's apartment. Tony's gun was pointed at Jerome, and without even thinking, Gloria took Bastian's pistol out of her purse and shot Tony dead.

Gloria shuddered. She could still see Tony's blood seeping into the white snow.

She folded up the flyer and stuffed it into a pocket.

At the next corner, she climbed a small flight of stairs to a tall brown apartment building. She held the door for a woman and her two young children and waved her hellos to the few mustachioed men sitting in the dilapidated lobby. At first Gloria's red hair had drawn stares in the predominantly Italian building, but the residents were used to her by now. She ducked into the stairwell.

But instead of going up, she went down.

In the dank basement, she opened the door to the boiler room. She avoided the large white pipes—they were hot, she'd learned the hard way—and made her way to the far corner. There, from behind the water pump, she dug out a canvas bag.

She dumped out its contents, removed her white gloves and cloche hat, and replaced them with long black gloves and an oversized hat that sloped down over her eyes and covered her features. She slipped her arms into a black wool coat that came down to her ankles. Then she placed her earlier accessories in the canvas bag, returned it to its usual hiding spot, tucked the bread under her coat, and exited through the back.

The wool of the coat was itchy and awful against her skin as she walked out into the hot sun.

A few sad patches of grass were dying in the dirt yard behind the building. Gloria walked to the left corner of the wooden fence, searching for the board with the dark brown scar at the bottom. She found it, pushed the loose board aside, and climbed through a gap just large enough for a person. For a made-skinny-by-hunger person, at least.

On the other side was a yard much like the one she'd left, only with even less grass. A few women with dark skin were sitting on chairs outside the back door, fanning themselves and shooting the breeze. The women glanced up as Gloria climbed the steps to the door but didn't say anything.

Inside, a few black children careened down the staircase as she went up, but they barely paid her any attention. Gloria unlocked the apartment door and closed it behind her, then flung the coat, hat, and gloves away. This routine was becoming more and more irritating. And dangerous. The yards had been empty during winter, but now people were all over the place, and this disguise wasn't going to fool anyone. What sort of nut wore a long black coat in New York in the middle of June?

But this was the only way Gloria and Jerome could stay together. They were living on the lam—they certainly didn't need the kind of extra attention that an unmarried white woman and a black man living together were bound to receive.

"Jerome?" she called softly, but it was obvious he wasn't home.

Their place wasn't exactly large enough to hide in. There was a tiny kitchen with a lovely oak table and chairs that Gloria had spent a half hour haggling over at the flea market. There was a comfy overstuffed chair they'd found on the street. And there was Jerome's secondhand piano, an old upright they'd found at an estate sale. The wood was scratched all over, and Gloria was convinced the thing had never been completely in tune, but she knew that a life without some sort of piano would be like a life without air to Jerome.

It was a far cry from her family's mansion on Astor Street. Back home in Chicago she'd drunk out of crystal; here she and Jerome got excited when they found two mismatched but unchipped glasses they could afford. But so what? While she and Jerome didn't have much, at least everything they had was *theirs*.

They'd gotten lucky when Jerome found an abandoned Victrola on the street. With a little fine-tuning it worked swell, and now it sat in the corner of their bedroom along with their collection of records—Bessie Smith, a couple of Gershwins, the Jelly Roll Morton she'd bought Jerome to replace the one he'd left in Chicago.

Gloria set the loaf of bread on the kitchen table, then dug down into the bottom of the laundry hamper and retrieved a heavy canvas sack, which she set beside the loaf. Newspapers were spread across the tabletop, all of them open to the classifieds. Several ads were circled in ink.

Gloria pushed the papers aside, opened the sack, and removed a pile of textbooks. European history, algebra, biology—all her old friends. She fished out her notebook as well as her math workbook and, tearing off the heel of the bread and gnawing on it, began working on a problem set.

She'd been studying secretly for several months now. Not even Jerome knew.

But it was the only thing that kept her sane. After weeks in New York and dozens of failed auditions, Gloria had started to worry. Maybe she *wouldn't* make it as a jazz singer. Then where would she be? No inheritance, no high school degree, no real qualifications for a job.

So she had written a letter to her old English teacher, asking for help.

Miss Moss had always been Gloria's favorite teacher, and Miss Moss had agreed to keep Gloria's address a secret and to help her graduate from high school. Soon textbooks began arriving at the post office box Gloria and Jerome shared. Miss Moss instructed her long distance, through the mail, and as long as Gloria kept up with her lessons, she would be ready to take her exams at the end of the summer. Provided she could sneak back to Chicago. Provided she wasn't arrested for murder. Provided—

Oh, it was too much to think about! She took another bite of bread and chewed thoughtfully.

After she finished her homework and stashed her book bag, she put the rest of the bread on a plate. She should have stolen some cheese to go with it. Maybe tomorrow.

Then Jerome walked through the door.

In a tan suit and an Optimo Panama hat, he looked handsomer than ever. Gloria had always figured that over time, she would get used to seeing his beautifully sculpted face. But her passion only grew every day. Those long, elegant fingers felt even better clasped behind her back than they looked when he played the piano. And she always felt a flutter in her stomach when his lips broke into that easy, enormous smile at the sight of her.

Gloria went to him. "Well, hi there. How was your day?"

Jerome took off his hat and settled it on her head. "Better now."

As he pulled her into a kiss, Gloria forgot all about her hunger and her old society life. She could hardly believe she'd spent so much time engaged to Bastian, suffering through his chaste pecks, never realizing how glorious a kiss could truly feel. Jerome *was* the right man, the only man for her. He was kind, funny, smart—Bastian's polar opposite.

That Jerome happened to be black and she happened to be

white seemed so inconsequential when they were alone in the little world of their apartment. They were just a boy and a girl in love.

After a minute, Gloria pushed him away. "As much fun as this is, there's something I need to show you."

At the table, she pulled the flyer from her coat pocket.

His brow furrowed as he read it. "Where did you get this?"

"Found it stuck to a lamppost on Third Avenue." She sat and took off Jerome's hat. "Bastian or Mother could maybe have had someone put them up—they've got connections in New York. . . ."

"And so does Carlito," Jerome finished. "But it's a big city, sweetheart. They're gonna have to hang a lot of flyers if they want to find you."

Gloria caught sight of her reflection in the mirror on the opposite wall. "I doubt anyone would recognize me, anyway." Her hair was long and flowing in the photograph on the flyer. But that wasn't how she looked now. Her bob had grown out a little since the last trim, but she still looked the part of the daring flapper, in a jaw-length shag of red hair that nearly disappeared under the right hats. And hunger had added its own styling: Her cheekbones seemed to jut out a bit more now; her jaw looked longer, sharper.

"Yeah, but those eyes of yours are unforgettable." Jerome kissed her on the forehead as his stomach growled. "Now . . . have we got anything to go with this?" He produced a wedge of bright orange cheese from his coat. "I might have stumbled into a cart on the way home."

Gloria sliced the grainy loaf of bread while Jerome cut up the cheese, and asked, "So, any promising leads today?"

He shook his head. "Charlie at the Marble Room just hired a singer, and they're going to bring back their old piano player."

Jerome's buddy Lenny had promised Jerome and Gloria a gig at his piano bar in Greenwich Village, but by the time they showed up in New York, Lenny had changed his mind. He said that maybe having a white singer and a black piano player wasn't the greatest idea—too risky. He'd been wide-eyed and terrified. Someone had put the scare in him. "Someone threaten you?" Jerome had asked quietly.

Lenny had mopped at his face with a bar towel. "Shouldn't have advertised who my new piano player was."

After that, Gloria and Jerome used aliases for their auditions. Jerome worked through the names of the guys in his old band—"Easier for me to remember who I'm supposed to be," he explained—while Gloria took names from novels she'd read.

But it didn't matter what they called themselves: No one was hiring. Every club owner they went to assured them that they were a little too *different,* a little too *radical* for the club's usual audience.

Jerome cleared his throat. "I was thinking, Glo. Maybe we should try splitting up. I look for gigs uptown, you look downtown?" He loosened his bow tie. "Just until something better comes along, you know?"

"Sure. We could try that." Gloria fiddled with her napkin. "We could also try talking to my father," she said quietly.

Lowell Carmody had been living in New York since he'd sent Gloria's mother a telegram informing her that he was leaving her for a dancer named Amber. Gloria could have reached out to her father at any time, but the only things Lowell Carmody cared about were himself and his money, and a scandalous daughter would be bad for business. Gloria was worried that he would ship her right back to her mother in Chicago. And to Bastian. He *certainly* wouldn't approve of Jerome. But at this point Gloria was willing to risk it.

Jerome looked down at his plate and chewed quietly.

"After everything he put me and my mother through, he owes me, don't you think?"

"Yes, I do. And that's why I would never accept any help from him." Jerome patted her hand. "I said I'd take care of you, honey, and that's exactly what I'll do. End of story."

Jerome got up and went into the bedroom. When he returned, Duke Ellington's smooth piano wafted through the apartment. Jerome held out his hand. "May I have this dance?"

Gloria grinned and stood up into the circle of his arms.

And then they danced. It was easy to forget their worries when his hand was at the small of her back and he was spinning her slowly around the small apartment, their bodies pressed oh so close together. So close that nothing could ever separate them. He was as exquisite a dancer as he was a piano player, and the two of them moved with a liquid grace that had her smiling until her cheeks hurt.

"Pretty good dinner tonight, don't you think?" Jerome asked.

She looked up at him, and for a moment her mind spun with everything that was wrong—money, hunger, constantly hiding from gangsters *and* the police. And none of those concerns was even the most obvious one. But as Jerome gazed at her, as if she were the only person in the world who mattered, the soft tones of the piano and the copper flecks in his eyes took over her thoughts once again.

And so she simply leaned her cheek into his chest and let him sweep her away.

LORRAINE

Lorraine was peeved.

She crossed her arms over her silky blue Lanvin dress. "Jimmy, put the rosewood wardrobe with its back facing *away* from the wall. How are we supposed to get at the gin?"

A young man with shaggy dark hair smacked his head with his hand. "I'm sorry, Miss Lorraine. We'll get that fixed up right away."

Once the wardrobe was turned, the two men felt around for a small catch on its side. A door embedded in the back of the wardrobe sprang outward, revealing a hollow space behind the false back. Dozens of bottles of clear liquid were stacked within. Jimmy and another man began removing the bottles and placing them in an already half-full crate.

The back room of Saunders' Furniture on West Tenth Street in Greenwich Village was buzzing with activity. Lorraine strolled around with her clipboard, watching the men sweat under the bare lightbulbs overhead, and eyeballing the ugly furniture that filled the space.

A shipment of bureaus, desks, and wardrobes had recently come in. As always, the Opera House crew dealt with the shipment the night before Saunders and his sons brought the pieces to the front of the store. Much of the furniture would then be shipped off to waiting customers—some still with concealed liquor bottles and some without.

This deal worked out well for everyone—Puccini De Luca, the owner of the Opera House, had an easy way of getting eel juice into the joint and a respectable front for the speakeasy if the cops came sniffing around. And crotchety old Saunders was able to move some of his plug-ugly furniture at crazily marked-up prices.

Lorraine ticked off items on her list. "Twenty-four bottles Kentucky mash whiskey—check. Watch that you pack those with straw."

Both men nodded, saying, "Sorry, Miss Lorraine!" and "We didn't know!"

"That's why I'm here, boys," Lorraine said, and swept past. Power was exhilarating. She was eighteen and beautiful—in the right light, anyway—and these men feared her.

All the liquor had come in; she'd leave it to the boys to crate the bottles and lug the crates through the halls and down the stairs into the Opera House. Heavy lifting was men's work! Lorraine pushed through the storeroom's back door and out into the hot summer night.

The dim alley was lit by a lone bulb sticking out of the wall above the door. Though it was only nine-thirty—a good couple of hours before things got busy—a line of hopefuls had already formed along the alley wall. At a second door, a muscle-bound man with a mustache stood guard. Beside him was a shorter and less muscular man (but still huge by any standards a girl could think of).

Lorraine walked down the alleyway toward them and tapped the taller man on the shoulder. "Hey there, Vin."

"Well, hello there, Rainy Day." Vinny Roberts was a big teddy bear and one of the few employees at the Opera House whom Lorraine genuinely liked. "To what do we owe the pleasure?"

"Just loitering." She leaned against the building. "God, how I love leaning against a nice brick wall. Really straightens out the spine."

Vinny just laughed. "Rainy Day's still silly as ever."

The eyes of the men and women in line kept flicking toward her—in admiration and jealousy, probably. Lorraine had always worn the most fashionable outfits, but when she moved to New York, she'd raised the stakes: She'd had her dark bob cut into the newly fashionable shingle style. Now her hair was even shorter and tapered to a V at the nape of her neck. "How is Reggie settling in?"

Vinny clapped the smaller man on the back. "Oh, just fine. Ain't that right, Reg?"

Reggie crossed his arms, making his biceps bulge. "Yes'm, settling in great."

Lorraine met his brown eyes. "What's the password tonight?"

Reggie glanced at the line of customers and lowered his voice. "Applesauce."

She gave one nod. "And you never let anyone in without the password."

"Never ever!" Reggie affirmed.

"Unless?"

He gave a wry grin, tipping his hat. "Unless I see a dish that looks good enough to send Puccini's way."

Lorraine patted his arm. "Attaboy. I'm heading down for the night. Shipment came in late, so they're gonna be bringing booze down after the first rush of customers."

Lorraine opened the steel front door and turned left down the hall, following the sounds of Rob tuning his upright bass and Felix doing scales on the piano. The hallway ended in red velvet curtains and, just beyond them, an open area and the rickety spiral staircase that led down into the speakeasy known as the Opera House.

To the right of the stairs was the club's long bar; to the left was a row of red leather booths, and stretching away across the golden hardwood floor was a sea of small tables, votive candles set square in the centers of the black tablecloths. At the far end was the stage, which was dimly lit as the band got ready. Red-tinted images of New York City landmarks—Times Square, Central Park, the Woolworth Building—covered the walls. It was a heckuva swanky joint.

The place was pretty deserted still—only a few regulars

sat alone at the small tables, nursing drinks in mugs. A group of businessmen filled one of the booths, having bought early admission with a fat roll of cash. Bernice and Hazel, two cigarette girls, said hello, but Lorraine pretended they didn't exist. It was important that they remembered *she* was the boss.

"Well, *lo* and behold, have we got a looker here," a gravelly voice said from behind her.

Lorraine turned to see Dante Vega, a close friend and business partner of Puccini's. Dante was a bit of a piker, always coming in to mooch free booze, scaring the customers with his dark buggy eyes, his enormous nose, and the jagged scar running down his left cheek. Dante always said "*Lo* and behold" when he saw Lorraine. He thought it was hilarious.

She forced herself to smile. "No small thanks to you, sweetheart."

Dante had given Lorraine the blue Lanvin dress the day before. Dante was Puccini's best friend. So if Dante gave a girl a gift, she'd better be wearing it the next time he saw her.

"Shipment come in okay?" Dante asked, leaning away to light his cigar. "Greasy Fred's gonna have a real problem if he keeps dawdlin' with our product."

Lorraine nodded. "The boys are crating up the last of it now."

"Good. And you check on the band?"

"I was just about to, but then you had to go and start distracting me."

Dante knocked back the shot of Scotch that Cecil the bartender had placed in front of him. "Well, I certainly wouldn't want to do that." He leaned closer, his breath reeking of cigars and something less pleasant. "Unless of course you *want* to be distracted."

Lorraine gave him another smile. "Not while I'm working, honey."

He waved her off with a fat hand. "Aw, such a hard worker! Bet you got straight As back in that fancy school of yours in Chicago. Hard work and smarts'll take you a long way." Dante picked up his brown derby from a nearby table and put it on. "I'm gonna tell Vinny to start lettin' the birds in, so be ready." He ambled away toward the stairs.

The only place Lorraine wanted her "smarts" to take her was the Barnard campus in September. Working at the Opera House was a nice little summer job, but it wasn't what Lorraine Dyer was about, no sir. It was just a sweet gig at the cool and sophisticated kind of place where Lorraine was sure she belonged.

But it turned out that working in a speakeasy was still *work:* checking on the band, making sure the hired boys mopped up the alcohol-coated floors, keeping track of all those tiny red chips that the dealers used on poker nights. And even the merest *thought* of the club's bathroom made her want to run back to Chicago as fast as her legs could take her.

Not that anyone would have welcomed Lorraine if she had.

Her parents had barely spoken to her since the night she'd exposed that lying tramp Clara Knowles. Just like everyone else, Lorraine's parents had blamed Lorraine for the scandal that erupted. They'd proposed that she could "mend her ways" by spending her summer doing charity work. But Carlito Macharelli had proposed something else, something much more interesting than spending her days chaperoning filthy little orphan children in Chicago's Astor Square Park. And Lorraine had leaped at it. Her folks were only too happy to have her packed off to college early—or so they thought—and no longer their problem. "The university will instill in you a more refined morality," her mother had told her.

Instead, she'd ended up here, working for a gangster.

It wasn't as if Puccini were the worst boss in the world. Just last week, he'd given Lorraine the night off for her eighteenth birthday. Not that she had anything to do or anyone to do it with, but still, it was a nice thought. She had spent the evening alone, listening to records and rearranging the two chairs and couch—she called it a davenport, because that just sounded better—in her new apartment on East Twelfth Street.

Lorraine looked up and saw Cecil smiling at her from across the bar. "Dante giving you much trouble?"

"Nothing I can't handle." There had been a time when Cecil's flirtatious attention would have had her dashing out to the alley for some necking. But since that fateful night at the Cloak & Dagger months earlier, Lorraine was swearing off bartenders *jusqu'elle . . . jusqu'à nouvous . . .* however that went. She was swearing off them *until further notice.* She maybe shouldn't have tossed her French textbook in the trash on graduation day. *Tant pis!*

"So, we ready to open officially for the night?" Cecil asked.

"Yep. I've just gotta make sure the village idiot is ready, too."

"Hey now, Spark's a good egg. His mama just dropped him on his head one too many times when he was a kid."

"You ask me, his mom should've dropped him a few *more* times and done us all a favor."

A group of giggling women with feathered headbands descended the stairs. "Here we go," Cecil said as he poured vodka into two shot glasses. "Time for one quick belt, if you're up for it."

Lorraine stared at the shot glass, filled to the brim with throat-burning, world-fuzzying, wonderful, beautiful liquor. A drink would be pos-i-lute-ly lovely, but . . . she couldn't risk even the slightest bit of foggy-headedness at this job. If she messed anything up, it would get back to Puccini. And then Puccini would send a telegram to their mutual friend back in Chicago. And then Carlito would come to New York and teach Lorraine a lesson.

Cecil could drink and work, but not Lorraine. She pushed it away. "Don't tempt me."

Cecil threw back both shots, one after the other. "I guess you'll have to be responsible enough for the both of us."

Lorraine remembered sitting next to Carlito in his reserved booth when he'd told her his plans for her. It was a
few weeks before graduation, and Lorraine had become a
regular at the Green Mill. Carlito paid her to hang around
and be a pretty face for the male patrons to look at. It was
easy peasy work, made Lorraine feel desired, and gave her
something to do after all her so-called friends had abandoned
her. And she kind-of-sort-of *liked* Carlito.

The thing she'd tried to explain to anyone who would listen was that Carlito was very attractive. Not just handsome—
though his slicked-back hair and dark eyes were good-looking
enough—but powerful and fearless. She had no idea
whether Carlito was actually strong, but everyone treated
him as if he could break a person with a snap of his fingers.
It was a little bit frightening and a lot sexy. Lorraine had
never met someone so young who seemed so confident and
dangerous.

"So," Carlito had said, shuffling a few poker chips through
his fingers, "you're leaving for New York and Barnard soon,
isn't that right, Lorraine?"

She narrowed her eyes. Maybe she mentioned Barnard a
lot—it was a big-deal school, and people needed to know
that she was a smart cookie—but she didn't think she'd said
anything to Carlito. And why would she have? Her deal had
been to work for him at the Green Mill until graduation.
And then she could go back to how her life was supposed
to be.

"Maybe at the end of the summer," she said.

Carlito laughed and draped his arm around her. "I've gotten very attached to you these past few months, doll. You work hard, and you're feisty. Perfect for a position I'm looking to fill over the summer."

"No thanks, Carlito, I—"

He patted her thigh. "So I guess you *don't* want Jerome Johnson and what's-her-face, that Gloria dame, to pay for what they did to you?"

She almost sprayed her drink all over him. Gloria. She hadn't heard that name since Jerome had run off with Gloria months earlier. There were rumors about what had happened—one of Carlito's goons had gone missing around that time, and no one seemed to wonder where he'd disappeared to. Which meant he was dead. A tiny part of Lorraine worried that Gloria had been involved in the gangster's murder, but a much larger part hated Gloria for abandoning her, and that part won out every time.

"What exactly do you have in mind?" she'd asked Carlito.

Six weeks later she was here at the Opera House, living off her paycheck and her allowance from her parents (to whom she'd promised "progress reports" from the summer classes she was taking before Barnard started in the fall) and stopping Spark from abusing the musicians. "The bass goes *behind* the piano, not on top of it," he was saying to Rob. "You think you're fronting this band?"

"Leave him be, Spark," Lorraine said, striding toward the stage.

Spark was a skinny man who liked to wear brightly

colored bow ties and vests. With his wispy brown hair and stupid straw boater hat, he looked like a child playing dress-up.

"Why, hello, Raine," Spark said, removing the boater and pressing it to his chest. "Whatever did I do to earn the privilege of your attention? I figured you were just gonna stay at the bar and let me do all your work for you."

Spark was supposed to be Lorraine's comanager, but they both knew that Lorraine gave the orders and Spark took them. He was ten years older than Lorraine, which sometimes seemed to make him think he was smarter than she was.

Lorraine looked at the band on the stage. "They all set?" She got her answer when the band launched into an upbeat tune. The blond piano player, Felix, was hitting on all six, his fingers flying over the keys. He was one of the best piano players Lorraine had seen, second only to . . . well, Felix was definitely the best piano player Lorraine knew who wasn't also a murderer.

Carlito had told her that Jerome had stolen money from the Green Mill, and when Tony had tried to stop him, Jerome had taken out a pistol and shot Tony in cold blood.

Lorraine hadn't even had to fake her shock. Jerome was even worse than Bastian. Murder! Gloria had thrown away her friendship with Lorraine for a poor black piano player who went around *killing* people? "It's just not right," she said aloud.

"I dunno," Spark said. "I think they sound pretty good. But of course, I don't have your educated ear, Lorraine."

She looked at Spark. "Your ears are so tiny it's a wonder you can hear anything at all." Then she turned on her heel and walked back through the swiftly filling room to the door marked EMPLOYEES ONLY beside the bar.

She didn't look back to see whether Spark was following—she knew he was.

Through that door and then another door was the Opera House's tiny office. Dante, Lorraine, and Spark all made use of the place, and it was in a constant state of messiness—sticky rings on the oak desk left by glasses of Scotch (Dante), discarded headbands and gloves lying on the file cabinets (Lorraine), crumpled sheets of paper in the trash can and on the floor (Spark), and overflowing ashtrays on every possible surface (all three).

Lorraine sifted through the mess and unearthed a folder. "I made some changes to our ad. Make sure to take it over to the *Times* first thing in the morning."

Spark sat down in the desk chair, propped his feet up, and opened the folder. He read through the advertisement. "This is *a lot* more specific," he said.

"We want a certain type," Lorraine said.

"But what was wrong before? Just saying we're looking for a young, pretty singer with experience?"

"I have a look in mind. A vision, if you will."

"Why's she gotta be a redhead?"

Good question. Lorraine bit her lip. " 'Cause we want her to look Irish. Ireland is known for its jazz singers."

"Since when?" He shook his head. "Never mind. And she has to be five-three? What's that about?"

"Acoustics," Lorraine said quickly. "That's the perfect height for a singer to . . . project effectively. Everyone knows *that*."

Spark snorted. "Uh-huh. And what's this business about her having green eyes?"

"Spark!" Lorraine snatched the folder from him. "How about we just do what we were hired to do? I was hired to think, and you were hired to . . . why *did* Puccini hire you, anyway?"

Spark stood up from the chair and bowed. "Why don't I go and make sure Cecil isn't giving away free hooch to his buddies again?"

After he was gone, Lorraine looked at the ad one more time. It was the perfect bait. Gloria had been in New York for half a year; she had to be running out of money. Sure, an ad like this probably would've seemed fishy to the old Gloria. But desperation put a whole new shine on things.

Carlito's plan was simple. "There are two different ways to catch a bird," he'd said. "Beat the bushes so it flies out. Or lure it into a cage. We're gonna do both. My guys are gonna beat the bushes. You're gonna build a gilded cage so that the birds fly right inside. You manage one of my clubs in New York, and you hire Gloria and Jerome. Then I show up to collect a debt. It's that simple."

"What are you going to do to them?" Lorraine had asked.

"Nothing to the girl. I don't hurt women, it's not my style," Carlito had said. "As for the piano man, well . . . I'll rough him up a bit and send him on his way. Teach him a lesson." He'd leaned in a bit closer to Lorraine. "*We'll* teach him a lesson."

Lorraine had liked the sound of that.

Now Lorraine shivered a little and slipped the folder into Spark's absurd yellow briefcase. She went back out into the bar.

It was just the usual chaos. Sparkling young women and dapper young men, the girls sporting their sultry flapper best—all drop-waisted, shimmery, sleeveless evening dresses, and hair crimped and bobbed and caught in beaded headbands. They constantly checked their cigarettes and their cocktail glasses for lipstick marks, and they constantly laughed—they were desperate to be witty. The men were the same way, only without the lipstick and headbands. Lorraine could barely stand any of them. Had she been as dizzily vacant as the flappers who filled the club and cut a rug on the dance floor?

She let out a heavy sigh. She missed the days when a speakeasy seemed like a rebel's paradise, full of sparkling diamonds glinting in a smoky pool of soft jazz and even softer laughter. Now it was just a whole lotta hard work. She felt as if she was somewhere between being a waitress and a maid. Although she was pretty sure Marguerite had never had to scrape vomit off the floors of the Dyer residence. (Not that Lorraine did the actual scraping. But watching over Jimmy's shoulder while he did it to make sure he didn't leave any specks was almost worse.)

But it was only for the summer.

Once Gloria fell into Lorraine's trap, Lorraine would tell Carlito where Gloria and Jerome were hiding. And Gloria would suffer. She would have to watch Carlito and his goons rough up her boyfriend. She'd have to go along as they ran him out of town. Then Gloria would wander back to her sad little New York life, broken and alone. Eventually, she would come crawling back to Lorraine, begging for forgiveness.

And Lorraine would laugh. No, she would cackle! Like a witch!

Gloria had made a huge mistake when she'd crossed Lorraine Dyer. Now Carlito would come and take Jerome away, just as Gloria had taken everything from Lorraine—Bastian, Marcus Eastman, the flapper lifestyle Lorraine had introduced her to—without a thought for anyone but herself.

Once *l'affaire Gloria* was all wrapped up, Lorraine could start her real life in New York. She would have some positively scandalous stories to tell to her spectacular new Barnard friends about how she palled around with mobsters and ran their gin joints and how it was all so old hat for someone as worldly as she.

Lorraine was almost done making nice with gangsters and doing actual *work*—her revenge on Gloria was so close she could taste it.

So why did she feel so awful?

CLARA

Looks ain't everything.

Clara's black feather fan *looked* like the perfect accessory to go with any slinky flapper dress—dark, intricate-looking, sexy. But as a fan, it didn't work so well. She was no cooler after ten minutes of flapping, and now her arm was tired.

She dropped the fan into her purse and pulled out her copy of the *Illustrated Milliner* magazine. She liked it for the pictures and the articles, which weren't too literary but were engaging enough. She'd wanted to be a writer back in the old days, when she was living in New York with Leelee and Coco. Poetry mostly, but writing for a magazine seemed fun. Glamorous. A way to set trends and impress people.

Clara laughed a little to herself. Who cared if she wasn't a trendsetter anymore? The only person she wanted to impress was Marcus, and he'd fallen for her when she'd been stuck wearing dresses that were about as attractive as potato sacks—let alone anything that would be featured in a magazine. She shook the Cartier bracelet on her wrist and smiled. *That* was far more gorgeous than any stupid dress in the *Milliner*.

But what Clara loved most about the glittering diamond and platinum bracelet was what it meant. Marcus had first given it to her when he still believed she was Country Clara, Gloria's innocent cousin from a small Pennsylvania farm. And then even after he had learned the truth about Clara's turbulent past, he had again clasped the bracelet on her wrist and asked her to move to New York with him for the summer.

Clara hadn't taken it off since.

She knew that Marcus had imagined that she would be living in Upper Manhattan, close to him and Columbia, where he would attend college in the fall. Instead, she had chosen to live in Brooklyn Heights. She just couldn't go back to Manhattan, not yet. She didn't want to run even the slightest risk of falling back in with her party-all-day-and-all-night crowd—or into the lifestyle that went with them. For right now, Manhattan was like a giant neon LOOK BUT DON'T TOUCH sign blinking at her from across the East River.

Aside from Marcus, there was only one reason to visit Manhattan—to find Gloria.

Clara knew that her cousin was in New York City somewhere. Gloria had promised she would send Clara a telegram in Pennsylvania once she and Jerome arrived safely in New York, but the telegram had never come. And now Clara herself had come to New York, and Gloria was no closer to being found.

Clara leaned back on her bench and looked down the street, past the line of elegant brownstone town houses. She could just make out a tiny part of the Brooklyn Bridge. It was beautiful, just like everything else in Brooklyn.

Her folks hadn't been so enthusiastic about her returning to the very place where she'd lost her virtue. In fact, they'd forbidden it.

But then her aunt Bea had stepped forward on Clara's behalf and persuaded them to give Clara a second chance. "The mistakes Clara committed in the past," she wrote, "have made her a better person." Her aunt had testified that Clara had become a new woman in Chicago and a favorite of the smart set. And she'd praised the positive influence of Clara's beau, the upstanding young man Marcus Eastman, one of the most sought-after bachelors in the great state of Illinois.

So the Knowleses had grudgingly allowed Clara to return to New York. But she'd had to make promises: Not to fall back into her wild ways. Not to run with the same group of "dissolute girls." Not to drink. Not to dance. Not to set foot in palaces of sin (as they called speakeasies). They sent Clara money from time to time at her Brooklyn address, but it was the absolute minimum.

Clara had resorted to wearing dresses that had gone a little threadbare, and she couldn't afford to replace her worn-out black Mary Janes. Her apartment was spacious and cheap, but that was only because it was such a long hike from the subway stop. She was making ends meet, but just barely.

Clara jerked when she felt someone slide up close to her on the bench.

"You sit with such *style,* miss," a soft voice whispered. "You positively brighten up this dreary bench just by parking yourself on it."

She exhaled deeply and turned toward him.

Marcus's sky-blue eyes shone mischievously from under his hat—his eyes were the same color as her dress, only brighter. He was dashing in a tan suit and a light blue shirt. With each passing day, he looked less like an eighteen-year-old and more like a man. But then he'd smile, and his cheeks would dimple, and she'd see in his face the charming boy he would always be.

She scooted away from him. "I don't take kindly to strange men."

Marcus scooted right after her, wrapping his arms around her. "You'll find that few strange men are as devastatingly strange as I am."

She laughed. "You may have a point. You are *exceedingly* strange."

"I exceed in everything, darling." He kissed her softly on the lips. It wasn't much more than a peck—there were children walking by, after all—but it still left Clara a little off-balance.

Back when she was sixteen, she'd run off to New York in search of that intense, heart-wrenching, almost painful kind of love. She'd spun through parties, dinners, nights at the theater; dancing with men whose gorgeousness belonged within the pages of magazines. But only one thing was on those men's minds, and it certainly wasn't love.

Who would have thought that she'd end up finding true love in that stuffy, flat, snobby, high-society nonsense world that her parents had always pushed her toward?

"Were you waiting long?"

"Years and years," Clara replied, laying a hand across her forehead. "I was simply dying in the heat."

"Oh, that *would* have been tragic. I would have had to eat alone."

She pushed him away. "You're a beast."

Marcus stood and offered Clara his hand. "You could have gone ahead," he said. "I would've just met you at the restaurant."

"You know you would have gotten lost without me."

He grimaced at the street sign. "You may be right. Why can't they just use numbered streets here like they do in Manhattan?"

"They're trying to force you to use your head every once in a while."

He huffed. "Never. There will be more than enough for my head to deal with in the fall."

"Marcus, your parents practically built half of Columbia. You probably won't have to try too hard."

They walked arm in arm down Hicks Street and toward the Franklin Arms Hotel. A breeze stirred the treetops, but down here along the slate sidewalks the heat was stifling.

"I hope you didn't have *too* much trouble getting here," Clara said. "A little trouble, of course—you need to work for love or it's too easy. But not *too* much work, or it's like . . . work."

He sighed. "It's just so *far,* Clara. Why do you have to live all the way in Brooklyn? It's like another country. People even dress differently here. Look at that man in that horrible coat."

Clara rolled her eyes. "That's a woman in a maternity dress."

"You see what I mean?"

"You know why I live out here."

"But I don't know why you won't let me help you out. It would be a gift to me more than anything, to have you closer. No more decade-long subway rides."

She smiled but murmured, "I can't, Marcus."

Marcus gave her hand a squeeze. "Sorry to pester you about it. I just miss you."

The only way to reach the restaurant was through the hotel lobby. It was a grand old place, and bright with the golden light from a dozen wall sconces.

The restaurant was darker and more run-down, but the room felt plush anyway. The red wallpaper was richly textured, and the long mahogany bar was beautifully polished, and even at lunchtime, intimate candles lit each table. A man played a slow tune on a glossy-white baby grand in the corner. Clara adored this place—it reminded her of the speakeasy Marcus had taken her to in Chicago on their first date.

After the waitress took their orders, Marcus looked around. "We should come here at night sometime. The band's supposed to be the cat's meow."

Clara shrugged. "Maybe." She would have loved to go out with him in Manhattan—it wasn't as if her parents would ever find out—but a promise was a promise, and she was trying to be good. "I'm sorry I haven't been the most exciting girlfriend."

Marcus laid his hand over hers. "I can't think of anything *more* exciting than being here with you."

Lunch was lovely, but Marcus was in an odd mood. He seemed eager to finish as fast as possible. When Clara remarked on how quickly he was shoveling down his salmon, he grinned.

"I just want to get out of here and take a walk across the bridge. It's such a beautiful day."

Clara hiked an eyebrow. Sweet as Marcus was, he rarely gave a damn whether it was "a beautiful day."

The waitress returned and asked, "Dessert?"

As Clara said, "Yes!" Marcus said, "No, thank you, just the check."

She frowned as the waitress walked away. "A cake-eater

like you rejecting a slice of cake? I never would've believed it."

Marcus paid the check promptly, and then he grabbed Clara's hand and pulled her back outside.

◆ ◆ ◆

Marcus had been telling the truth: The day *was* beautiful, the sky bright and blue, and a nice breeze off the water chased away the heat. Clara's Mary Janes clacked on the wooden planks as they made their way across the bridge, her hand in the crook of Marcus's arm.

"You won't get a better view of Manhattan anywhere," he said as they strolled underneath the first arch.

The farther they walked, the more clearly Clara could see the aquamarine Statue of Liberty raising her torch to the sky. Wind dimpled the water and twined the smoke rising from passing steamboats.

When they came to the second arch, Marcus eyeballed the cart of a nearby vendor, one of the many who camped out on the Brooklyn Bridge every afternoon. "On second thought," he said, "I think dessert *is* a good idea."

"I'd kill for an ice cream," Clara said.

"No need for violence, Miss Knowles. If it's ice cream you want, then it is ice cream you shall have." He walked over to the vendor with two fingers raised. "I scream for— Oh, never mind. Two, please."

Clara turned away and leaned her elbows on the railing.

She had a swell view of the Manhattan skyline—the tall white Woolworth Building, the spires of Park Row. She'd almost forgotten how idyllic the city could look from a distance, the way it did to newcomers.

Marcus walked over with a cup of lemonade. "He was out of ice cream."

At times like these, Clara remembered that she really didn't know Marcus all that well. She'd only been in New York for three weeks, and she and Marcus had spent the previous months with a few hundred miles between them. They'd had a small amount of precious time together when Clara had stayed with Gloria in Chicago, but for much of that time Clara had believed that Marcus's interest in her was just a cruel joke he had cooked up with Gloria and Lorraine.

And it had been, at first.

But things had changed. She and Marcus had developed real feelings for each other. Clara had tried to tell him about her wild flapper life in New York and her affair with Harris Brown, but that desperate wench Lorraine had got there first: She'd drunkenly announced to the world the one secret Clara most wanted to keep hidden. Not only had Clara had an affair with an engaged man—she'd become pregnant. And then had lost the baby.

Clara had been sure Marcus would leave her after that, but he hadn't wavered.

But what would happen when he started classes at Columbia in the fall?

"Let's sit for a second." Marcus led her over to a metal

bench and sat next to her, taking hold of her hand. "So, listen. I have a surprise for you."

Suddenly his strange behavior made sense. "Oh? I love surprises."

"Right." He took a deep breath. "You remember how my father went to Columbia and my mother went to Barnard? Well, dear old Mother's been writing letters to her friends on the admissions board. And my father handed out some bribes—er, donations."

"Whatever for?" Clara asked. "I mean, you were already accepted."

"It's not for me, Clara. After all that and a little sweet-talking, they were able to pull some strings and get *you* into Barnard!" He pulled her into a tight hug and laughed. "Now you can go to school across the street from me! Your parents will be thrilled, you'll have a good reason to move uptown, and life will be just peachy! Isn't it wonderful?"

Clara pulled away. "They got me into Barnard? They can just . . . do that?"

"My dad's got low friends in high places." Marcus met her eyes, his smile dimming a little. "You aren't excited. That is not the face of a thrilled Clara Knowles."

She let out a forced-sounding laugh. "Of course I am! It's just— Wow, it caught me off guard. Barnard . . . wow."

"You don't need to be nervous, Clara. You're the smartest girl I know. Look at how easily you finished up your course work before you moved here. You're certainly smarter than the Unmentionable, and *she* got in."

Clara paled. She'd forgotten that Lorraine was going to Barnard as well.

"Sorry to remind you. Is that what's wrong?"

Lorraine's being at Barnard didn't help matters, but Clara would be able to avoid her easily enough. It was more that enrolling would force her to face her old uptown haunts and even older friends before she was sure she was ready.

And as awful as Lorraine was, at least *she* had gotten into Barnard on her own merit. "Getting me into Barnard . . . it's just a lot. I didn't even want you to get me an apartment, and you got me a whole college."

"I thought an apartment would be a little cramped," he said. "My parents wanted to do this for you, Clara. Actually, that's the other thing: My father's in town and wants to meet us for dessert at Le Royale Bakery. He's so eager to meet you."

Suddenly Marcus's refusal of dessert at the Franklin Arms and his random desire to enjoy the outdoors made sense. As he pulled Clara into a kiss, she tried to feel as happy as he obviously felt. *Barnard.* Her parents would be so proud. They might even start sending her more than nickels and dimes.

Clara wasn't sure she could accept Marcus's offer, but she did need to find the courage to face Manhattan—even Greenwich Village. Marcus had been kind enough to leave her past in the past.

It was time she did herself the same favor.

VERA

Vera yawned and watched the beams of morning sunlight stream in through the giant half-moon windows of Grand Central Station.

She had never been to New York before—never been anywhere outside of Chicago. If this had been a normal trip, she would have been marveling at the beautiful building's grand staircases and the starry mural on the ceiling, gold constellations connecting to create Pegasus and other signs of the zodiac against a blue-green sky.

But all she could think about was the killer coming after Jerome.

If the woman found out the address of his post office box in New York City, then eventually she would just come and wait for Jerome or Gloria to turn up. But she probably had her hands full with Carlito in Chicago, and that might buy

Vera just enough time to find her brother first and warn him.

Vera smiled as Evan appeared with two cups of hot coffee. She drank down a big gulp. "Now I feel human again." She looked at the map of Manhattan hanging on the wall. "His post office box is close to Harlem . . . so I guess we should walk to Times Square and take the train uptown. Not that I know a damned thing about the subway."

Evan reached over and squeezed her hand. "We'll find him, don't you worry. Here, I got you something." He handed her a small paper bag he'd been holding, which contained a single glazed doughnut. "A little something sweet for somebody sweet."

Vera started to laugh. "Excuse me?"

Evan's cheeks darkened. "Sorry. That was stupid."

Vera was about to laugh again but stopped herself. Was Evan flirting with her? It didn't seem likely—he was her brother's friend and former bandmate first. But did former bandmates hop overnight trains to cities halfway across the country?

No.

Could Evan . . . like her? She looked at him again, his high cheekbones, his dark and stormy eyes. Evan was gorgeous, and he played the trumpet like a dream.

But Vera wasn't here to fall in love. She was here to find Jerome.

That didn't mean she couldn't enjoy a doughnut, though.

"Thanks a lot," she said quietly.

Evan chuckled. "Yeah, I've given you a sandwich *and* a doughnut. Maybe I'll even throw in some fruit and vegetables sometime, though I don't want to spoil you."

After they'd checked the map once more, Evan and Vera walked outside into the bright sunlight. Vera marveled at the buildings they passed. They loomed higher than any she'd seen back in Chicago. Despite the early hour, men and women filled the sidewalks. The men mostly wore suits and straw hats, while the women dressed in smart-looking day dresses with skirts that came down only a few inches past their knees.

Cars of every make and model crowded the streets, as well as a few horse-drawn wagons. Hulking yellow-and-black Checker cabs tried in vain to weave through the stalled traffic. A wonderful smell of brown sugar pervaded the air— Vera realized that the source was a cart selling sweet, hot peanuts, cashews, and almonds.

"So you want to get off at a Hundred and Third Street," Evan said once they were on the subway and the train clicked into the Eighty-Sixth Street station.

"But you won't?" Vera asked, frowning. They'd just gotten here. She wasn't sure she was ready to face this strange city alone yet.

"Naw, I'm gonna stay on until a Hundred Forty-Fifth. I'm gonna start lookin' for a gig right away. A friend works up there at the Hooch Pooch."

"Meet back at the Hundred and Third Street station around four?" Vera asked.

"That should be just enough time . . . for a few clubs to kick me right back out the door." He let out a nervous laugh.

Vera nudged his shoulder with hers. "Don't be ridiculous. I bet you find something before I even make it to the post office."

◆ ◆ ◆

Vera emerged from the station and straightened her cloche hat.

The subway stop was only a few blocks from the post office, and it was a pleasant walk. This area was a bit like her neighborhood in Chicago. She passed tiny markets selling everything from newspapers to cigarettes and hot coffee. There were more white people than black. Vera decided to keep her head down so as not to raise suspicion.

The post office was like every other post office she'd seen, if a little dingy. A few people with packages in their arms stood in line in front of a bank of small wooden-framed windows. Others strolled in, went to the wall lined with the little brass doors of post office boxes, and opened them with tiny keys.

Vera selected a sheet of stationery and an envelope from a display, paid for them, and went to a table to dash off a short note to Jerome.

Dear Jerome,
There is too much to say and this note has to be short, so I'll get to the point: Someone killed Bastian Grey and is after you. The killer may have got this address from him, so you'd best stop using it. I am in the city, staying at

Then she realized she didn't know where to tell him to look for her; she and Evan hadn't found accommodations yet. She scratched out the line and began again.

I'm staying in the city, and I will go wait under the clock in Grand Central from noon to two every Saturday until you show up.
Your loving and worried sister, Vera

This was not the best plan for finding Jerome and Gloria. But it was the only lead Vera had.

She folded the note up and tucked it into the envelope, casually watching the customers in the post office. Who knew how often Jerome and Gloria checked their mail? Would they come together? Or would Gloria waltz in like the redheaded woman who'd just entered, glanced around nervously, and gone over to one of those tiny mailboxes—

Vera realized she wasn't looking at a Gloria look-alike: it *was* Gloria. She was a lot thinner and was wearing a cheap blue dress that old high-society Gloria wouldn't have touched with a ten-foot swizzle stick, but it was definitely her.

Vera was just about to call out Gloria's name when she saw that Gloria had been followed.

A woman in a dark gray dress and a large hat had entered the post office right on Gloria's heels and was standing at the bulletin board as though interested in the WANTED posters. But her head was clearly tilted in Gloria's direction. The woman wore large sunglasses and kept one hand hidden in her handbag.

Between the hat and the sunglasses, Vera couldn't see much of the woman's face. She was young, for sure, with slender legs and arms and a pretty bow mouth.

And then Gloria passed between them with a rectangular package in her hands and disappeared through the door.

A second later, Sunglasses followed.

And a moment after that, Vera followed Sunglasses. Gloria's bright red hair was about twenty feet away. That girl stuck out like a bonfire in the dark. Bobbing along ten feet behind her was Sunglasses' large hat.

The woman was definitely following Gloria. Vera's heart tightened. What should she do? If she yelled Gloria's name, would Gloria be happy to see her? Or would she run away?

Calm down, Vera told herself. Right now she needed to get this creepy woman away from her brother's girlfriend.

Vendors' stalls lined the sidewalk, selling cheap jewelry and hats and other things—the sorts of things that made walking fast difficult. Vera stepped into the street, put her head down, and rushed past the stalls. Within a few minutes, she had overtaken both Gloria and the woman. When she got to the corner, she doubled back.

A scarf vendor's tiny cart was parked right near the intersection. The vendor—an older black man with disordered hair—had stepped away and was busy smoking and talking with another man outside the delicatessen on the corner.

Vera pretended to study a set of sparkly headbands. Gloria passed, with Sunglasses a dozen feet behind. Vera slipped behind the cart, counted to three in her head, grabbed the cart by its bottom, and put all her strength into tipping it over.

It made a satisfyingly loud noise when it hit the ground. The woman's shriek that accompanied the crash was even *more* satisfying. The cart had found its target.

Vera ducked low behind an old Model T and hoofed it around the corner and out of sight behind a van on the far side of the street.

The vendor had set his cart upright again and was standing in front of Sunglasses, pointing his finger at her. "What, you think that's funny? Messing with a man's livelihood?"

The woman said something, and the vendor threw up his hands.

Vera looked in the direction that Gloria had been walking in. Gloria's bright red hair and bold blue dress were nowhere to be seen.

GLORIA

Gloria pretended to study a glass-topped table.

Had she gotten the address wrong? The sign read SAUN-DERS' FURNITURE, but that couldn't be right. Could it?

She should have known that this job—which seemed practically tailor-made for her—was too good to be true.

As she examined an ugly old maple bookcase, she felt a tap on her shoulder. She turned to see a balding older man with silver hair and horn-rimmed glasses. He wore a simple collared shirt and brown trousers and spoke with a slight Southern twang.

"Welcome to Saunders', young lady. You lookin' for anything specific today, or just browsing?"

Gloria tried to seem nonchalant. "Just browsing, thank you."

"Heading to a party later? I can't imagine you'd get so

dolled up just to visit my store, though I'd be mighty *flappered* if you did." He guffawed. "Get it?"

Gloria blushed, glancing down at her long emerald-green dress. It was one she'd brought from Chicago—a Chanel chiffon with a dropped waist. It had sheer, ruffled cap sleeves and a scoop neckline, though it didn't scoop so far as to be inappropriate for the daytime. It *was* a bit fancy for furniture shopping, but it was the most flattering dress she currently owned.

She pulled a copy of the *New York Times* out of her purse and flipped to the page she wanted. "Sir, would you happen to know anything about this? I called earlier and made an appointment, but perhaps I mixed up some information. . . ."

The man pushed his glasses up on his nose and looked at the newspaper, reading the heading of the classified ad:

WANTED: INGENUE TO SING AT HOT NEW CLUB!
Green-eyed redheads especially desired to sing bluesy tunes. Established talents need not apply; we want only fresh blood—preferably from out West. New to town? This could be the gig you came here for!

TEL. SPRING 4829
Call for an appointment between 12 and 5

Note: A singer taller than 5'3" will throw off our aesthetics.

He looked toward the back of the store and called, "Neal! Get out here!"

A young man with a long face and messy dark hair walked through a swinging door at the back of the room. "What's going on, Pop?"

The old man beckoned him to come closer. "This young lady would like to see the vanity we've got on hold."

Neal's eyes brightened. "Oh, right, the *vanity*."

. Gloria had no idea what was going on. "I really don't need a vanity."

"Follow Neal and you'll find what you're looking for, darlin'. Though I can't imagine what a sweet girl like you could want down there."

Gloria straightened her posture. "I'm not as sweet as I look."

Why hadn't she thought of it before? Even though the police usually knew where the speakeasies were (and even frequented them), clubs had to at least keep up the appearance of hiding themselves away. Most clubs had some sort of front—apparently this furniture store was one of them.

In her two-toned pumps, Gloria followed Neal around open crates and pieces of half-assembled furniture. At the back of the shop, Neal opened a door onto a narrow hallway that ended in red velvet curtains. Just past those was a spiral staircase.

"Well, this is as far as I go," Neal said. "Nice meeting you, Miss, uh—?"

"Rose. Zuleika Rose," Gloria said.

This would be the first audition she'd gone to without

Jerome accompanying her. She'd sung her song three times in front of the mirror this morning, making sure each phrase and each facial expression was just right. She was as ready as she would ever be.

As she descended the rusty-railed staircase, she noticed that the barroom was practically empty. Red leather booths lined the wall closest to the stairs. Spotted but grand mirrors hung behind each booth, giving diners the chance to subtly ogle the men and women along the bar. Across the golden hardwood dance floor was a sea of small wooden tables and chairs, where anyone who didn't have the face or the money for a booth could rest their gams.

But what made Gloria smile was at the opposite end of the barroom: the stage.

It was small but nicely decked out. Plush gold curtains hugged the sides, and the gleaming rosewood of the boards shone as if it had been polished. A light threw a glowing spot center stage, just waiting for Gloria to fill it. A good-looking young man with dirty-blond hair picked out a slow tune on the grand piano.

"It's a ducky joint, ain't it?" A lanky man stood at the foot of the stairs, holding a clipboard. He had a thin face with an almost comically long nose and small, muddy eyes. He was wearing an orange bowler and a red vest with orange polka dots.

He smiled with a mouthful of crooked teeth. "You're a little late, my dear."

"I'm sorry. When I scheduled the audition, the girl didn't say anything about the furniture store, or how this is—"

"A speakeasy?" The man tittered. "We try not to mention that if we can help it." He stuck out his hand. "You're . . . Zuleika, right?"

"I am," she said, shaking his hand. "Zuleika Rose."

"That's a helluva strange name," he replied.

"Why, thank you!" Gloria had chosen it from a novel she'd read. She hoped he hadn't read the same book. He didn't seem the reading type.

"They call *me* Spark," he said, doffing his hat and sketching a little bow. "Welcome to the Opera House." Spark sat down at one of the wooden tables. "The name's new—we used to be called the Kennel Klub and a couple of other things before that. Brings in more customers every time we shut down and reopen."

"I like the walls," Gloria said. Most of the clubs she'd visited didn't care about decoration. Patrons came for two reasons: jazz and booze. They didn't spend time studying the décor. But the murals here were totally jake—a reddened, stylized New York City, packed with skyscrapers and tiny figures rushing about. And the scarlet tint gave the speakeasy even more of a risky, dangerous feel. It looked like a swanky version of hell.

Spark looked around as he lit a cigarette. "Oh, yeah, that was Vito, Puccini's son. Puccini's the guy who owns the place, and his son thinks he's an artist, or some horsefeathers."

Spark picked up his clipboard. "I've gotta ask you a few questions before you go wail up there." He pulled a pencil out from behind his ear. "Address?"

"You can reach me care of Post Office Box One Sixty-Eight."

"I didn't ask where I could *reach you,* I asked where you *live.*"

"Actually, you said 'address.'"

That seemed to fluster him. "I meant, where do you live?"

Gloria forced a little laugh. She needed this job. "Oh, here in the city."

"Well, I didn't think you took a steamboat to get here," he said, tugging at his bow tie. He seemed nervous. "C'mon, darlin', it's not a tough question."

"I live uptown. Near Harlem," Gloria replied. "It's cheaper."

"That's awful close to all them Negroes. You don't mind? I wouldn't feel safe, personally, and you're just a little bit of a thing. Who knows, maybe you like the Negroes."

She could feel a blush spread over her cheeks. What kind of question was that? He was a creep. "Don't be ridiculous," she replied.

Spark shrugged. He seemed to be looking *behind* Gloria rather than at her. "Don't worry about it—no judgment here."

Gloria remained silent. There was something fishy about this guy.

"Anyways," Spark said with a frustrated groan, "Negroes make the best musicians. Duke Ellington and all that." He pointed at the handsome pianist up on the stage. "The ones I seen are a hell of a lot better than that kid, let me tell you." He cleared his throat. "You, uh, ever come across any fine black piano players?"

"Never," Gloria lied, hoping Spark didn't ask many more questions. Most auditions, she just sang and got sent on her way.

"Yeah, I guess you ain't had much time. You look like you're still in school. You strike me as the kind of dame who went to one of those bluenose prep schools."

"What makes you say that?"

He glanced over her shoulder again. Gloria turned, trying to see what he was staring at, but saw only her own image in the mirror behind the bar.

"Oh, I've just got a cousin, or a friend—a friend of a cousin, really—who went to a school like that." Spark took a few deep breaths. "You wouldn't know her. She lives in Chicago."

Gloria shook her head a little faster than probably looked natural. "Can't say I've ever been."

"That's too bad, it's a fine city. Windy, eh? So . . . windy. Anyhow, this cousin of a friend is a real pistol. I guess she got into a bad spot back there and pushed her friends away. Even stabbed one in the back."

"Well then," Gloria said brightly, "I'm glad she's not here!"

"Yeah! I hope she isn't! Would be a bad place for her to turn up."

Gloria nodded toward his clipboard. "Maybe you want to hear me sing?"

Spark gave one last glance at the back wall. "Sure, I think we're all set. Let's see what you can do."

As Gloria walked to the stage, she glanced again at the mirror behind the bar. Had someone been watching them? Watching her? No, that was silly. Spark was just a creepy older guy. Either that or fascinated by shiny things. Or . . . completely spliffed. Wouldn't be the first speakeasy worker she'd met who sampled the goods.

Gloria pulled her sheet music from her bag and handed it to the piano player. She tried to imagine she was handing the music to Jerome: the way his fingers would linger on hers for just a moment and how he would wink and give a smile meant just for her. But this man took the music without any ceremony, the way any stranger would.

"You ready?"

She nodded, exhaling as he began to play the introduction, and stepped close to the microphone. Back when she had auditioned at the Green Mill, she had refused to sing her favorite song: "Downhearted Blues," by Bessie Smith. She'd told Jerome that she didn't give away her best stuff for free.

But that had been before she knew what it was like to be hungry. And worse, what it was like to watch the man she loved go hungry as well.

Today she would give away the best she had, and she would sing as if there were a hep band behind her and a roaring audience in front of her.

Gee, but it's hard to love someone when that someone
*   don't love you.*
I'm so disgusted, heart-broken, too. I've got those
*   down-hearted blues.*
Once I was crazy 'bout a man. He mistreated me
*   all the time.*
The next man I get, he's got to promise me to be
*   mine, all mine.*

Trouble, trouble, I've had it all my days.
Trouble, trouble, I've had it all my days.
It seems that trouble's going to follow me to
*   my grave.*

She felt as if she were *in* her voice. It was the best she'd ever sung.

Until she realized the piano player was two bars ahead of her. Spark wasn't kidding: This guy was terrible. Why was he playing so fast? This was a *blues* song, for God's sake.

She rushed to catch up, but then he abruptly slowed down and she lost some of the lyrics. "But the day you quit me, honey" turned into "buday quimoney," and Gloria didn't even know where to fit in "it's coming home to you."

"Can we stop for a minute?" she asked.

She could hear Jerome's voice in her head: *I don't care if you forget the words. I don't care if you go off-key. I don't care if the building is on fire—you* never *stop in the middle of an audition.*

"Somethin' wrong?" Spark asked.

Yes, Gloria wanted to say, *everything* was wrong. She shouldn't have been there alone. It should have been Jerome playing for her instead of a man who played the saddest song she'd ever heard as if it were a party jig.

"Can we start over?" Gloria looked back at the piano player. "And can you go a little slower? It's a really sad song . . . I mean, have you heard it?"

The man gave her a smile that would've been charming if Gloria hadn't been overcome by the urge to roll up her sheet music and beat him senseless with it. "Sure, Mamie Smith, right?"

It took all of Gloria's willpower not to burst into tears right there on the stage.

"Yeah, give it another try," Spark said, his tone surprisingly kind. "Forgive Felix—he can play, but he's dumber than a box o' nails."

"Hey!" Felix called. But he sat up straight and watched for Gloria's cue.

Gloria launched into the song again. Felix played more slowly this time, though still too fast for her liking. She managed to get all the words out, but her heart wasn't in it.

She'd failed. No one in his right mind would hire her after this audition.

As soon as Gloria finished singing, Spark stood and clapped. "That's just great," he said. "You've got yourself a job, doll."

He couldn't be serious. Both of her attempts at the song had been disasters. "Really, just like that? Don't you have any other girls to audition?"

Spark lit another cigarette and shook his head. "We ain't gonna find another canary like you. That was real fine." He offered his cigarette case.

Gloria shook her head, still shocked. "No thanks."

With his cigarette dangling from his lips, Spark made some notes on his clipboard. Then he removed a few sheets of paper and handed them to Gloria. "Here's some paperwork. You can bring that along with you to rehearsal on Monday, one o'clock sharp. And in the meantime . . ." He took out his wallet and counted out a few bills. "Here you go."

Gloria stared at the cash in her hand. "What's this?"

"It's money. Legal tender. You trade it for goods and services."

She smiled. "I mean, why—? I haven't performed yet. Or even been to a rehearsal."

"It's an advance. And there's more where that came from." Gloria stared at the money in his extended hand, still unsure whether she should take it. Spark grabbed her hand and closed it around the cash. Then he gave her a little push in the direction of the stairs. "Go on, get something to eat. You look like you could use a sandwich. Or two." He turned away. "Have a nice weekend, kid."

Gloria clutched the paperwork in one hand and the money in the other. Then she folded the bills and gingerly placed them in her purse. It wasn't much—far less than her weekly allowance back at home. But New York was her home now—and this was more money than she'd had in weeks.

She smiled again at Spark, genuinely this time. "Thank you! You won't be sorry!"

◆ ◆ ◆

When Gloria walked out of the subway station, she made her way to the open-air market on First Avenue. She passed through the crowds with her head held high. Why? Because she had money in her pocket. She was a singer! Or at least . . . she was going to be. Zuleika Rose: the Ingenue of the Opera House.

A half hour later, loaded down with her purchases, Gloria turned toward Second Avenue and began the long walk home. It was wonderful to actually *buy* something instead of steal it. She felt happy and confident for the first time in ages.

And nervous.

Jerome would be happy for her, she was sure. He'd be proud she'd landed a gig so easily on her own. He'd be excited to see all the food she was bringing home and to know that the hard times were coming to an end.

She was about to cross Lexington Avenue when she noticed a flyer that had partially come free from a lamppost. Her own smiling face looked back at her. It was another one of those LOST GIRL flyers. Seeing two of them so close to her apartment was not a good sign.

She reached up to the top of the flyer and ripped it down. Before she stepped off the curb, she crumpled the flyer into a ball and tossed it into a nearby trash can.

That girl might have been lost once upon a time, but not anymore. She had money, a gig, and the man of her dreams. *Nothing* was going to spoil her mood.

LORRAINE

The bitch was leaving.

Lorraine leaned back against the wall of the office, her heart pounding. The entire time Gloria had been at the Opera House—from the moment Gloria shook Spark's hand, right up until the minute her heels clacked up the steps as she departed—Lorraine had been glued to her small window into the barroom. When Gloria had passed on her way to the stage, she had looked directly at Lorraine, almost as if she could see her. She couldn't, of course—it was a two-way mirror. Lorraine could see out, but Gloria couldn't see in. That was the whole point.

Those eyes, though.

Gloria's bright green eyes had unintentionally gazed into hers, and for a moment Lorraine had missed her former best friend. Gloria's eyes were so shockingly familiar—the only familiar thing in New York, certainly—that it made Raine's insides ache.

They'd had so many wonderful times together—getting Glo's bob, passing notes in class about cute boys and haggy girls, going to the movies on the weekends and dreaming about what they wanted to be when they grew up. No other person filled that hole in Lorraine's life. The memories were still sharp.

But even sharper—sharp enough to draw blood—were the memories of how Gloria had shunned Lorraine. Suddenly she'd been too good for Lorraine. So Lorraine had been chucked out into the cold by her best friend while Gloria partied with that two-faced wench Clara, Bastian, Marcus . . . everyone, really. And after everything Lorraine had done for her!

She'd obsessed so much about getting back at Gloria that it had become an elaborate fantasy—never to come true.

But now it had.

That had been the *real* Gloria out there. A too-skinny poor girl in last year's dress, singing her heart out to an empty club. Or trying to, anyway. Much as Lorraine hated Gloria, she couldn't help getting miffed at Felix's erratic playing. Gloria's face when she asked to start over was one of the most pathetic sights Lorraine had ever seen. It should have been hilarious to finally see Gloria fall flat on her face. But it wasn't even amusing.

No, Lorraine couldn't go soft because of some cherished memories.

She was a bitch. Gloria was a selfish bitch.

And that was the whole reason Lorraine was here, working for Carlito. *You reap what you sow,* Lorraine reminded herself, running her fingers through her hair and blotting at her forehead with a napkin. She needed a stiff drink, but she was working.

No fair.

At least Spark had done a decent job with the script Raine had prepared for him. No major mistakes. Gloria didn't seem to suspect a thing.

At that exact moment, Spark's head poked through the doorway.

"What?" Lorraine asked, her voice sharp as he pulled the door shut.

"I did it like you told me, boss. Even gave her the money."

"The advance," Lorraine replied. Carlito thought offering an advance to Gloria would give them a little extra insurance—no way a desperate girl would pass up free money. "It was for food," she said. "I know skinny is the fashion right now, but no one's gonna wanna watch a rail shake it on the stage."

"Just seems weird to pay her when she ain't done any work yet." Spark sat down in a chair and loosened his yellow bow tie.

Lorraine nodded. "What's weird is you," she replied in a monotone. "I'm surprised she didn't take one look at your mug and go running."

"Ha! I was nervous for a little bit there. That girl seems like a sharp tack." He leaned his bony elbow on the arm of his chair. "Those certainly were some screwy questions. What did they mean?"

She scowled at him. "None of your beeswax. Go polish something."

Lorraine leaned back in her chair. She *should* have been ecstatic. Wasn't her plan—okay, well, Carlito's plan—coming together exactly the way she'd wanted?

"Someone's gotta get the club ready to open, anyway." Spark walked out, whistling "Downhearted Blues."

Lorraine pulled out a pad of blank telegram forms. She uncapped a pen and sat with it poised over the paper. She thought for a moment, then wrote:

GLORIA HERE. STOP.
WHAT NEXT?

She frowned, ripping the form into pieces and tossing them away. Carlito had instructed her never to mention Gloria by name, in case the telegram was intercepted. She needed some kind of code. That was how the Mob normally did it, right?

She started writing on a new form.

THE BIRD IS IN THE CAGE. STOP.

Lorraine tore that sheet up, too. Who knew whether Carlito remembered their last conversation at the Green Mill as well as she did? She sighed and started on yet another fresh form.

I GOT IT SORT OF. STOP.

Good enough. She reached for a manila folder and slipped the form inside.

Out in the barroom, Spark was polishing the black sconces on the walls. Lorraine walked up to him and bopped him on the head with the folder. "Make sure someone takes this over to Western Union right now."

Spark nodded, and then he was gone.

Lorraine rubbed her temples as she tried to remember everything she needed to do before the club opened for the night. But she couldn't stop thinking about Gloria. She'd seemed so sad, so pitiful. Whatever else she could say about Gloria Carmody, Lorraine couldn't deny that the girl had always had charisma and a sense of fun—something that had been sorely lacking in the second semester of Lorraine's senior year at Laurelton Girls' Prep.

Without Gloria around, Lorraine's classmates had stopped speaking to her. The photos from Gloria's engagement party in all the newspapers only confirmed what her classmates had always thought: Lorraine was a drunken quiff. And when Lorraine did receive notes at school, they said things along the lines of *No one cares what you look like, Lorraine, so why do you still bother with ten pounds of war paint? Tramp.*

"'Scuse me, Raine, coming through," called a busboy wearing the customary white shirt and black pants. He was carrying two trays full of highball glasses. She realized she was standing right in front of the door to the kitchen.

She jumped out of his way and straight into Ruby, the new waitress. "My foot!" the brunette yelled, hopping up and down on one high-heeled shoe.

"Sorry," Lorraine mumbled. She noticed Rob across the room near the steps, lugging his bass case toward the stage.

There—getting the band set up! She knew *that* was on her to-do list.

She walked over and lifted one end of Rob's bass. "Here you go," she said.

Before they'd taken two steps, though, she became lost in her thoughts: What were Gloria and Jerome living on? Gloria had looked so excited when she got the job. As if she were thinking, *Hooray, I finally have enough money to buy a can of tuna!* Even after months of practically living on the street, Gloria hadn't lost that dippy charm she had. Always so hopeful. Always so naïve.

That was when Lorraine forgot where she was going. She banged the end of the bass against a chair, then dropped it. The strings thrummed in deep alarm.

Rob stopped in his tracks. "Dammit, Lorraine! What the hell are you doing?"

"Don't you dare swear at me!" Lorraine yelled back. People were staring. She needed to pull herself together. This was only the first time she'd clapped eyes on Gloria since she'd arrived in New York. She was going to have to see that perfect face of Gloria's plenty more times before this mission was over.

"I'm gonna go see how Vinny's doing," Lorraine announced. She cringed at the whispers filling the room as she climbed the steps.

Outside in the alley, Vinny was alone, presiding over a line of women and a few young men. A small table with a cash box, where he would place each guest's $2.50 cover charge, stood next to him.

It was a sweltering night. A few of the bobbed, fringe-covered young women waved feathered fans in front of their perfectly made-up faces. Lorraine didn't even look at the men—*that* was how distracted she was.

"Hi, Rainy Day," Vinny said as Lorraine lit her cigarette. "What brings you out here?"

"Just making sure everything is copacetic. What's the password tonight? Spifflicated?"

Lorraine gasped as she noticed the smug grins that suddenly adorned many of the flappers' faces. She thought she had been whispering, but apparently that hadn't been the case.

Vinny groaned. "Not anymore, it's not. You think you can watch the door for a minute? I've got to let 'em all know we're changing it."

Vinny ducked inside.

"You gonna let us in?" a girl with black hair asked with a smile. "We know the password."

"Shut up," Lorraine snapped.

"Or what?" the girl asked in an annoying tone.

"I'm not even going to deign to give you an answer," Lorraine said, taking a drag of her cigarette and staring the girl down. "I eat girls like you for dinner. No, for breakfast! I could skin you and wear you as my fall coat!"

The girl looked shocked and stepped away, turning and whispering to one of her friends.

"Come back here!" Lorraine shouted. The rest of the line was watching, but what did she care? "Open up your purse."

The black-haired girl raised one thin eyebrow and was about to protest, but then her friend—another girl around the same age, maybe seventeen or eighteen—pinched her and the girl opened the clasp of her purse.

"That's more like it," Raine said, spotting exactly what she was looking for. A flask. It shone as brightly as the dozens of pairs of earrings the flappers were wearing, brighter than all their necklaces and bracelets combined. She pawed it out and took a swig.

"Hey, that's my—"

"Your mouth is as big as the house I grew up in!" Lorraine

said, swallowing the cheap vodka and burping. "And I grew up in a mansion. Here." She passed the flask back to the girl. "Thanks."

"You going to let us in now?" the girl asked, hopeful.

"Nah," Lorraine said. "We don't allow outside hooch in our joint. Against house rules."

Vinny returned and gave Lorraine's hand a much-appreciated squeeze before she went back inside. She took out a cigarette and lit up as she walked downstairs.

Lorraine was glad to see that everyone was too busy to pay attention to her and her screwups. The band launched into a number, and people began filing downstairs behind her. She watched a group of girls dance the Breakaway together. They were a pretty bunch—a blonde, a redhead, and a brunette, all in dresses with exquisite, Egyptian-looking patterns. Their laughter mingled with the band's upbeat piano and saxophone. Had she, Gloria, and Clara ever looked like that?

Clara. She sighed. Thinking of Clara also meant thinking of Marcus, and Lorraine tried to think of him as little as possible. Where was he now? Already in Manhattan? Lorraine knew now that she had been wrong to fall for an idiot like him in the first place. If she saw his swoony blue eyes at school in the fall, she had no idea what she'd do. Vomit? Keel over? Slap him?

Cecil walked over and gave Lorraine a glass of ice water. She gratefully pressed the cool glass against her cheek.

"The boss wants you to come talk to him at the bar," he said.

Lorraine swallowed as she followed Cecil. A few days after she'd started working at the Opera House, he'd told her a story about a waiter who'd mixed up orders a few years back. The boy had lost a hand, Cecil had said. He wouldn't tell her precisely how.

Lorraine slid onto a stool next to Puccini. When he turned to her, his cheeks were rounded into a jolly smile.

At first glance, Puccini looked almost as friendly as Vinny did when he wasn't performing his bouncer duties. Puccini was a short, overweight man wearing a fedora and an easy smile. But unlike Vinny, no matter what expression was on Puccini's face, his eyes remained empty black holes.

Puccini took off his hat and laid it on the bar, then pulled a white handkerchief from his pocket and dabbed at his sweaty face and neck. His thin mustache left plenty of room on his face for his wide, creepy smile.

He pointed toward Lorraine's water glass. "I could use something like that myself," he said. His voice was oddly pleasant—almost musical. "Vodka on the rocks, and another for the lady."

Puccini was the last man in the world Lorraine wanted to drink with, but she didn't dare say so. She held her glass of vodka to his. "What are we toasting?"

"Our new songbird," he said as their glasses clinked. "Spark told me you hired a real canary today." He drank the vodka down in one gulp. "Can't wait to hear her sing. You know, that's why they call me Puccini—I love singing so much."

Lorraine blinked. "Oh, I just thought that was your name."

He raised his bushy eyebrows. "Giacomo Puccini is one of the greatest artists who ever lived. You've really never heard of him?"

She shook her head, setting her mostly full glass back on the bar.

"We're gonna have to teach you some culture, young lady," he said. "What about Carlito? You hear anything about him lately? 'Cause I need to have a talk with him." Puccini gripped her wrist tightly. "I might have to let him know that his little recruit is screwing with my kitchen, busting up my band's expensive instruments, and giving away my passwords. Is that what you want?"

Getting in trouble with Puccini—no, no, no, Lorraine did not want that. Puccini had only hired someone as young as Lorraine because he was an old friend of Ernesto Macharelli, Carlito's father and the right-hand man to Al Capone. Puccini did *not* know about Carlito and Lorraine's plan regarding Gloria and Jerome. It was Lorraine's job to make sure things stayed that way. If Puccini found out about Tony's murder, it would get back to Ernesto. And Carlito had made it clear to Lorraine that he wanted to keep his slipup from his father most of all.

Lorraine swallowed hard. "No, Puccini. It's not."

He gave that a moment to sink in, then showed off those yellowish teeth once again in what was almost a smile. "How about you take the night off, doll—clear your head a little?" He turned away, making it clear that Lorraine didn't have a choice in the matter.

◆ ◆ ◆

It was only once she was a few blocks away that Lorraine released the breath she had been holding. She stopped walking for a minute, ignoring the annoyed huffs of anyone who had to move around her. She had messed things up today, all because of Gloria. How typical.

Puccini could have done much worse. As long as she cleaned up her act, he wouldn't punish her or tell Carlito about her mistakes.

And a night off wasn't exactly the worst punishment.

Once she reached Broadway, the sidewalk became crowded. Groups of young people waited for tables at *chic* cafés, while others puffed on cigarettes and talked loudly. In front of her was a group of men who couldn't stop talking about an upcoming game at the brand-new Yankee Stadium. Outside Webster Hall, women in gowns of every imaginable color and men in tuxedos stood around waiting for some sort of show. Everybody looked happy and fabulous and Lorraine hated them all.

Inside her fourth-floor apartment, she dumped her bag, shucked off her heels, and headed straight to her bedroom.

She dropped her black dress to the floor, pulled on a short white nightgown, brushed her teeth, and washed off her makeup.

And then, not five minutes after arriving home, Lorraine crawled into her silver-framed bed. She pulled the silky bedspread over herself. The sun had barely even set, but she was ready for this day to be over.

As she reached for the lamp, her eyes caught on a flyer hanging on her wall.

Unlike the Gloria who'd come into the club desperate for a job, or the Gloria who had fled Chicago with her boyfriend the piano-playing killer, the Gloria on this flyer was a girl Lorraine *knew*.

She switched off the lamp, dropping the room into shadow.

But she could still see the flyer. A blinking light illuminated the words LOST GIRL. The light blinked again, and Gloria's bright eyes glared at Lorraine in accusation.

Lorraine rolled away, buried her head in her pillow, and released the racking sobs that had been mounting in her chest all day. But the tears weren't just about today. They were about *everything*. She wished she could climb into that flyer so that she and Gloria could be the good girls they'd once been. Back before Lorraine had any idea what it was like to have a thug threaten her, back when she still thought she and Gloria would be friends their entire lives.

But her tears stopped suddenly when there was a loud, menacing knock at her door.

CLARA

Clara was nervous.

She took a sip of her coffee and frowned. This shop wasn't the classiest of joints. A single old man was working behind a smudged counter. She couldn't fault her old roommates for choosing a cheap place, but this one was just a dump.

Leelee and Coco had been her very best friends. It was living with the girls in their tiny apartment on Bank Street that had taught Clara how to really let out her wild side. The two of them knew Clara better than anyone did, even Marcus.

So why was she so worried?

Clara had run into them a few days earlier. She'd been leaving the Brooklyn Museum, about to take a stroll in Prospect Park, when she'd heard two female voices call her name.

Clara froze—she'd recognize those voices anywhere—and plastered a smile on her face. Leelee and Coco looked as fashionable as ever: Leelee in a tight pink sailor dress and Coco in an embroidered white dress with a floral design picked out in lace. Unlike Clara's, her roommates' dark bobs were perfectly maintained. Leelee had a doll-like face and wide blue eyes, while Coco was all sharp angles and mystique.

"Darling!" the girls squealed simultaneously, kissing her on both cheeks.

Clara hugged them back, shocked but genuinely glad to see them.

Leelee giggled. "Clara Knowles! What are you doing kicking around here? After the wardens dragged you off, we thought they threw away the key."

Clara's roommates always referred to Clara's parents as prison wardens. Though maybe they were talking about the time she'd actually been in jail.

Clara thought it best to turn the tables. "Whatever brings you to Brooklyn?"

Leelee shrugged. "Someone said this museum was nice. But it's just like any other museum—lots of old things that we're supposed to be impressed by."

Coco asked, "But why are *you* here?"

Clara smiled. "It's kind of a long story. . . ."

Coco put a hand on Clara's arm. "Of course it is, sweetheart. We're just on our way to meet Beverly and Wendy at the Fat Black Cat. Come along and you can tell us all about it over a drink!"

Leelee giggled again, even though nothing was funny. "It'll be just like old times! We'll break out the champagne!"

Clara remembered the Fat Black Cat well: its beat-up booths and roaring band, all buried under a constant cloud of smoke. She'd even met Harris there once or twice. The smallest part of her was curious to see whether the place had changed since she'd been gone . . . but the new Clara didn't spend her afternoons in speakeasies.

"Sorry, girls, I can't. I actually have an important meeting to get to."

Her ex-roommates narrowed their eyes. What could be more important than a good time with booze and old girl-friends?

"It can't be *that* important," Coco said.

Leelee giggled. "Important!" she repeated.

But Clara stuck to her guns. "I really can't!"

Coco gave an elegant shrug. "All right. But we absolutely *must* get together soon. How about Thursday?" She grinned, catching Leelee's eye. "There's the sweetest coffee shop that just opened up on MacDougal called the Smoking Kettle. . . ."

◆ ◆ ◆

The Smoking Kettle was a fitting name for the place, Clara discovered, since the coffee tasted as if someone had left it on the burner until they damn near burned the house down.

Bells on the door chimed as Coco and Leelee breezed in.

They took off their hats and smoothed down their bobs in easy, identical movements. Leelee wore a two-tone dress in brown and red with a large bow on the shoulder. Coco was dressed more simply in a lemon day dress with orange satin details at the waist. Clara's short-sleeved floral dress was positively drab by comparison.

Leelee and Coco both bent to kiss her on each cheek. Leelee gave a happy sigh. "Oh, Clara, I'm just so nostalgic right now! It makes me want to cry, boo-hoo. We've missed you so much."

Coco nodded. "We truly have."

"I've missed you too," Clara said, and realized she meant it.

The girls were still standing, so Clara pointed to the two empty chairs. "Want to sit down and order some coffee?"

Her friends exchanged a cryptic look. "Oh God no," Coco said, adjusting her purse strap, "the coffee here is *terrible*."

"We thought we'd try the back room," Leelee said. "It's more private." The pains Leelee was taking not to giggle were obvious. "*Way* more private."

Before Clara knew what was happening, Leelee and Coco had each grabbed one of her hands and pulled her to her feet, dragging her down the narrow hallway toward the men's and ladies' rooms. Leelee pushed open a door marked EMPLOYEES ONLY and led the way through a tiny space crowded with a large sink and racks of dirty mugs, plates, and silverware.

A black man in work clothes looked up from the dishes he was washing. "Now, where are you ladies off to?"

"We're going to see my mother at the beach," Coco replied. "I've got to let her know that she left the oven on."

The man nodded and removed a set of keys from his pocket. He unlocked a door beside the sink, and Clara could see that it led to a dark staircase going down.

"Enjoy yourselves," the man said as he closed the door behind them.

Walking down the steps, Clara heard the smooth sound of a saxophone improvising a solo. Light streamed in through a row of narrow windows close to the ceiling, revealing dust and scratches on the dark hardwood floor. Most of the guests at this hour were businessmen in suits, though there was one group of girls reclining in a booth and sipping gin. There was no stage—the bass player and the saxophone player just set up next to a piano in the corner.

"This is a speakeasy?" Clara asked, though it obviously was.

The very kind of place she'd sworn to abstain from.

Coco laughed. "As if you don't know a speakeasy when you see one."

"Or do you only recognize it from the bottom of the ladies' room floor?" Leelee said, nudging Clara with an elbow to the ribs.

Leelee wasn't trying to be rude. It was true—the three of them had spent practically as much time puking up all the gin they'd guzzled as they had drinking it in the first place. But how could Clara explain to Coco and Leelee that she wasn't that girl anymore?

Leelee ran an open tube of red lipstick over her rosebud lips. "It's called the Pink Potato."

Clara stopped in her tracks. "Why didn't you tell me where we were going?"

Coco pulled her by the arm. "We wanted it to be a surprise, Clarabella! You used to love surprises."

"I used to love a lot of things that I don't like anymore," Clara replied, putting her wide-brimmed hat back on her head. "I should go. I can't spend my time in places like this anymore. It reminds me too much of—"

Leelee put her hand to her mouth. "Of that pig Harris, of course! I'm so sorry, we weren't even thinking."

Coco reached over and grabbed the hat off Clara's head. "*Please* don't leave," she said. "I'll simply *die* if I have to go any longer without hearing what you've been up to."

Clara exhaled. She couldn't have expected Leelee and Coco to know not to bring her here. And she couldn't just abandon her friends because she was feeling jittery.

"All right," she said, taking her hat back from Coco. "One drink."

Leelee and Coco clapped happily and slid into a booth. The waiter looked surprised when Clara only ordered water, but Leelee and Coco were polite enough not to comment.

Once the girls had their drinks, Coco leaned forward. "So what happened between you and Harris? Everyone knows he went to Chicago to bring you back."

"It was creepy," Clara said. She told them the whole sordid tale—how Harris had sent her cryptic notes, how he'd shown up at her cousin's engagement party. But though Leelee and Coco gasped and touched her hand in sympathy at all the right points, Clara noticed their eyes wandering over to two handsome men at the bar. *Nothing changes,* Clara thought.

When the waiter returned, the girls laughed and ordered more drinks.

"We're going to get sloppy!" Leelee announced.

"It's the middle of the afternoon," Clara said.

"Down here it's *always* midnight," Coco said.

Their second round arrived, and Clara began wishing she'd left when she had the chance.

"So," Leelee said, tracing her fingertip along the top of her glass, "was it tough seeing Harris again? Scummy or no, he *is* a sheik."

"It wasn't as bad as I expected. You see"—Clara couldn't stop her shy smile—"I've met someone else."

"Oh, I almost forgot!" Leelee squealed. "I met someone, too. I went out on the sweetest little yacht the other day. . . ."

After Leelee's ten-minute story about dancing with a Valentino look-alike at a party and how he said *she* looked like the silent film star Louise Brooks, the conversation veered back to Marcus. Clara's old friends were full of questions—about what Marcus looked like, what his father did for a living, how much he was worth. Leelee and Coco squealed at the Cartier bracelet on Clara's wrist but were far less interested in the story behind it.

"What about the deb cousin?" Coco asked. "Did she wear

those dresses with the high collars? Did she convince you to join her weekly prayer circle?"

Clara gave an uneasy smile. Clara had thought Gloria was a complete square at first, too, but she'd been wrong. Gloria had a shocking amount of moxie. Much more than it took these two to get drunk every night and allow rich men to take them to parties and the theater. Gloria would never fit into the tiny box Coco and Leelee were trying to put her in. So why try explaining?

"Well, her room looked like someone poured a bottle of Pepto-Bismol all over it," Clara said. "Oh, and her best friend was a real wet blanket. I think raccoons have a better grasp on how to use eyeliner. . . ."

From that moment, Old Clara was back—or some shadow version of her, anyway. Clara played the role Leelee and Coco wanted her to play, feeding them snippy answers to their questions, taking shots at every single debutante who had befriended her in Chicago. No one escaped the barb of her wit, and soon her friends were red-faced with laughter. Poor Leelee could barely breathe.

Clara gave the girls a smile, but inside she felt emptier than her silver flask.

Once Leelee had finally caught her breath, she stood up. "Well, I'm off to the ladies' before I wet myself."

"I'll join you," Coco said, scooting out of the booth. "And when we get back, we want to hear more about this absurd deb ball!"

Clara slouched down in the booth while they were gone. She couldn't wait to get out of there and go to meet Marcus for dinner.

All through her time in Chicago, she had missed her wild New York life. But now she couldn't understand why. If this meeting with Leelee and Coco had shown her anything, it was how grateful she should be that she'd found Marcus. She had received a chance at a *real* relationship, rather than one based on booze and pointless yarns.

Marcus loved her. He wanted to be with her—in fact, he wanted to be with her so badly he'd even had his parents get her accepted into college. He wanted her to live near him instead of so far away. If anything bad could be said about Marcus, it was that he loved her *too* much. But that wasn't bad. It was good. It was everything she'd ever wanted.

So why hadn't she jumped at his offer?

Clara noticed Leelee and Coco standing next to a man sitting on one of the wooden stools. Had they even gone to the ladies' room?

And then she recognized the young man.

That slicked-back brown hair and oh so *au courant* designer suit, that insouciant slouch and tipped-back hat—it could be none other than Philip Helmsworth. Back in the old days, he had come out on the town with Clara, her roommates, and Harris Brown. Harris's friends were no better than he was—the fact that Philip was married hadn't stopped him from sleeping with Coco on more than one occasion.

Clara couldn't believe that her friends were flirting with the pal of the man who had broken her heart. The man Clara had *just finished* telling horror stories about. She gathered her things, stood up, and headed for the stairs.

A strong hand caught her arm. "Where are you rushing off to?"

Clara turned and looked up into the striking face of a man in his early twenties. He had wavy dark brown hair and vibrant green eyes. His nose was perfectly shaped, perfectly straight, his cheeks dusted with stubble, his chin strong and square. He wore a sharply cut gray suit and a red silk tie. He was some kind of handsome—if a girl was looking to find a handsome boy. Which she wasn't.

"I don't see how that is any of your business," Clara said.

His grin showed off a set of gleaming, straight teeth. "I *knew* it was you."

"You've mistaken me for someone else."

"No, it's you." He tapped the brim of her hat. "It was hard to tell with this enormous horrid thing. Yours is the kind of face that should never be hidden under a big hat. If that's what this is."

Clara stared at him, confused. "Have we met?"

"Unfortunately not," he replied. He extended his hand. "I'm Parker Richards."

"Hello, Parker Richards. Do you want to tell me how you know me?"

He dragged a stool away from the bar and sat. "You're

Clara Knowles. Biggest cheese of the New York City flappers. Queen Sheba of the Flapper Scene. Sultana of the Sweet and Vicious. Everyone knows who you are."

Clara blushed. She thought she had spent long enough away that her reputation would have all but dissolved by now. It was distressing (and she had to admit it: a little flattering) to learn that it hadn't. Good-looking men like this one still knew who she was.

"Not anymore, I'm not," she replied. "That part of my life is over."

"Is it?" He pulled out the stool next to him. "How about you park your chassis, chat with me a spell?"

The old Clara would have hopped right onto the seat, if not into the man's lap. "No, I really have to be going—"

"Just for a minute," Parker said with another self-assured smile. "I have a proposition for you."

"I'll bet you do." An afternoon in a speakeasy plus a man offering a "proposition" equaled trouble.

"No, nothing like that," Parker said. "I'm one of the good guys. Promise. I have a job opportunity that I'd like to run by you."

Clara's ears perked up—he wanted to offer her a *job?* Doing what? Against her better judgment, she took a seat.

"I just got a gig editing *Manhattanite* magazine," he said.

"Never heard of it," Clara said.

He chuckled. "You will. Our debut issue just came out."

"How convenient," she said. Despite herself, she was

impressed. How did someone so young become an editor of a magazine?

"You're a sharp one, just like people say. Kind of like the *Manhattanite* itself. See, I don't want this magazine to be the same society-worshipping drivel you see everywhere else. This magazine is going to be innovative. Smart. Witty. We're going to turn everything on its head. While every other writer gushes about Barbara Stanwyck's newest headband, my magazine's going to be digging deeper. One angle I have in mind is an exposé on the flapper style.

"What leads these women to live and die by makeup and accessories? What separates the *real* flappers"—he glanced at Clara—"from the shallow followers?" He cut his eyes sidelong down the bar; it took Clara a moment to realize he was looking at Coco and Leelee.

"We need someone who already knows the underbelly of the flapper world to write smart about it. Someone like you."

Clara laughed. She couldn't help it. He wanted her to write an article?

Sure, she had always loved reading. She consumed books the way other people did water. Sherwood Anderson or F. Scott Fitzgerald, Edna Ferber or Pearl S. Buck, it rarely mattered what the book was about—if it was bound between covers, it would find its way into her hands. And yes, she'd thought about writing for a magazine, but thinking and doing were two very different things. What if she was terrible at it?

She shook her head. "Thanks, but I'm not a writer."

Parker chuckled and leaned in closer. "Just because you haven't written anything doesn't mean you're not a writer. I used to hear about you from my friends at Columbia. They always talked about your stories—all your wild escapades. You were always so cuttingly witty, the life of the party. All I'm asking you to do is write that stuff down so people can read it. And you can get paid for it."

"I already told you—I'm done with that life," Clara said.

"But that's why you're perfect for this!" he replied. "We don't want someone who's dazzled by the glitz and glamour. We want someone who's seen the dark side and has the cleverness to tell our readers all about it. You'll go to the parties, sure, but you'll be there as a reporter, ready to jot down every biting detail once you get home."

She felt a slight smile cross her lips. "You think I'd betray my friends so easily? I think you're underestimating my integrity, Mr. Richards."

"And I think you're underestimating your own talent," he shot back. He slid a glossy magazine out of his briefcase. *The Manhattanite* was written in an elegant script at the top. On the cover, a beautiful model with a dark bob and a short sheath dress shot a come-hither glance over her shoulder. Her smile was close-lipped and mischievous.

Parker tucked a business card into the magazine and handed it to Clara. "Give this a read and get back to me." He put on his gray derby and stepped close, whispering into her ear, "I bet you'll be a better writer than anyone in there."

Clara nodded, a little shaken by his nearness. "I'll think about it."

He tipped his hat in her direction. And he was gone.

It was an impossible proposition. This gig would be the exact opposite of what she'd promised herself she would do. It would force her to submerge herself in the very parties and people she'd sworn to leave behind.

There was no way she could do it. And yet . . .

Writing for the magazine, Clara wouldn't just be the ex-flapper, or the fake country belle, or Marcus Eastman's girl-friend. She would be a *writer*. A dream she'd never thought would actually come true.

"Excuse me," she called to the bartender. "Could I have a whiskey on the rocks?"

She shouldn't be drinking, but if she was going to settle back into the late-night world of flappers and speakeasies— a sleek machine that ran on gin and vodka—then she was going to need some practice.

VERA

Vera stood near the clock in Grand Central Station and waited.

It had been nearly a week since she'd followed Gloria from the post office and intervened between her and the mysterious Sunglasses Woman. She'd missed a golden opportunity to follow Gloria. She'd lost her best chance of finding out where Jerome was living. Of warning him. Of saving him.

She'd mailed the note to Jerome, and here she was—waiting—but he'd yet to show up. Had he not received the note, or did he not want to see her?

She snapped out of her reverie when Evan stepped up beside her. "Vera! You'll never guess what happened—I landed a gig!" He let out a happy laugh. "A buddy back in Chicago told me to try the old Club De Luxe on a Hundred and Forty-Second. They've been searching nonstop for new talent since they relaunched as the Cotton Club last year. It's the real McCoy, with cats like Duke Ellington and Bessie Smith playing every weekend. I auditioned and a guy called Big Frenchy hired me on the spot."

Evan pulled some folded bills out of his pocket. It was more than what they'd brought with them. "He even gave me an advance so we can get rooms for each of us in a boardinghouse," he said. "Isn't that great?"

"Of course it is," Vera said. After a week of sleeping on the couches of friends-of-friends-of-friends, her very own room sounded like heaven. "A club like that—that will be so amazing for your career."

Evan could clearly tell something was wrong. "No sign of Jerome? There's time. Think about it—we've barely been here a week and you've already seen Gloria. Jerome can't be far away. You've got to relax." Evan thought for a moment, then snapped his fingers. "I've got it. We'll walk over to Central Park. Get your mind off things."

"You know where that is?" Vera asked.

"Sure—it's in the name. It's gotta be central, don't it?"

◆ ◆ ◆

Vera didn't know what to make of what she was feeling.

They walked hand in hand, and with every passing second, pleasant shocks ran through her fingers and up her arm.

Even if Evan just thought he was being a good friend, it was nice to pretend that he might be something more.

As they walked, they passed a few families, mostly white. Everyone was in a cheerful mood, and one little girl with blond pigtails hopped up and down as she asked if she could feed the ducks. To everyone else in Manhattan, Vera supposed, it was just a beautiful summer afternoon. Right before they reached the park, Evan stopped outside a grocery store.

"I need to pop in here for a second," he said. He came out fifteen minutes later with a large bag.

Vera looked at the sack. "So what'd you get?"

"Just some odds and ends," he said with a smile.

They'd walked only a little farther when he stopped outside another market. He emerged with another, smaller sack and again refused to tell her what he'd bought.

Across the street from the park, he irritatingly ducked into yet another store. When he walked out with yet another sack, Vera said, "Okay, it's not funny anymore. What have you got in the sacks?"

"Stuff," he said. "Dunno when you became so nosy."

Vera rolled her eyes and crossed the street with him, and they entered the park.

Someone had taken a vast slice of everything Vera loved about the outdoors and dropped it smack in the middle of this hard, gray metropolis. Rolling oceans of green grass stretched as far as she could see, and everywhere she looked was some new lovely thing—wide pools of water, towering trees full of chirping birds, wooden gazebos laced with wisteria vines—the park seemed to go on and on. "It's so beautiful," she said quietly.

"That it is," Evan agreed.

A group of teenagers on shining bicycles raced past, and Evan and Vera followed them deeper into the park. People seemed to be everywhere: sitting on benches or lying on blankets or walking hand in hand. Some young men were tossing a football back and forth in a broad, grassy field.

Evan stopped beside a large cypress tree and set the sacks on the ground. "See, now, I think this is a fine spot for a picnic." From one sack he pulled a checkered blanket and spread it on the grass, and started laying out the food he'd procured: a loaf of bread, jars of peanut butter and strawberry jelly, a tin of cookies. The last sack contained a bottle of soda water and some cheap silverware and cups.

"I know it's sandwiches again, but I'm hoping the combination of the natural atmosphere and the extreme adorableness of the gesture will—"

Vera cut him off by enveloping him in a hug. She squeezed him so tight he coughed.

"It's not *that* nice a picnic!"

"This is amazing, thank you," she said softly into his ear. She'd had a few beaux since she started working at the Green Mill, but no boy had ever done anything like this for her. "Though it makes it slightly less adorable when you point out its adorableness before I do."

Evan laughed and straightened his bow tie. The two of

them sat down and began making their late lunch or very early dinner.

Once they were both munching on peanut butter and jelly sandwiches, Vera leaned back and grinned. "So, Evan, is this how you impress all your girls? By showing them your master-chef sandwich-making skills?"

Evan wiped the peanut butter off his hands with a napkin. "Who are these girls you're talkin' about? Not that I'd mind having so many that you had to refer to them as *all* my girls."

She smirked. "Really, though. You must've had girlfriends at some point." Back before she'd dropped out of school, she'd known plenty of good-looking boys. Girls followed them around and drew hearts around their initials in school-books. And those boys hadn't been anywhere near as talented or handsome as Evan.

He shook his head. "Not really. I liked a dame or two back in my time, but I was always more focused on my music."

"You and Jerome both," Vera said. She took a sip of soda water. "He was always raising hell with my parents, telling them he wanted to be like Jelly Roll Morton rather than work in a grocery store like our daddy."

"Yeah, my mom wasn't too enthusiastic, either, after Dad passed on. I always felt kinda sorry for my brother, Rodney. There he was, going to school and getting good grades, and there I was, sneaking out at night to play gigs and getting all the attention." Evan peered at her. "Did you ever feel like that with Jerome?"

Had she?

Her brother had always been the star—that much was clear. But Vera had never resented him for it. She loved him. But maybe there *was* a tiny bit of resentment buried somewhere deep underneath her skin. Was that what had led her to betray Jerome and Gloria?

"Jerome was a piano prodigy," she finally said. "He'll always be the one in the spotlight. Even now. I'm putting my entire life on hold for my big brother." She frowned as she realized how awful that sounded. "Ugh, I'm a terrible person."

Evan reached over to catch her hand in his. "No, you're not. What you're doing is pretty damn selfless, if you ask me."

Vera looked down at Evan's fingers entwined with hers. As they sat in this beautiful park with the wind blowing through the tree branches overhead, his hand felt . . . alive. Vera rubbed her thumb in small circles on his palm. "So, you said you haven't been out with too many girls. Would you consider *this* a date?"

In the slightly confusing silence that followed, she felt her heart beating just a little bit faster than it had all day.

"No, I wouldn't." Evan laughed as her shoulders slumped. "But I wouldn't say it's *not* a date, either."

She didn't know what to say to that. "Well, it's the best not-a-date I've ever been on."

Evan took a bite of his sandwich. "Me too, Miss Johnson. Me too."

GLORIA

St. Louis woman with her diamond rings
Pulls that man round by her apron strings.
T'weren't for powder and for store-bought hair,
The man I love wouldn't go nowhere.

Gloria blinked in surprise when Jerome stopped playing. "What's wrong?" she asked.

Sheet music marked up with notes in both Gloria's and Jerome's handwriting was strewn all over the piano and kitchen table. They'd spent the morning trying to figure out what she would sing for her debut at the Opera House. "St. Louis Blues" was one of her first choices.

"Don't be afraid to let yourself *go*," Jerome said. "This whole song is a buildup of emotion. You start out just moaning about being sad, but by verse three, you're finally able to belt out everything you feel. Understand?"

Gloria nodded. Practicing with Jerome had come a long way since the time when he'd explained to her how to breathe with her diaphragm in the dingy basement piano room at the Green Mill. These days he was teaching her how to maintain volume and control her phrasing. And he was teaching her about nuance, about interpretation: how to convince the audience to feel the songs as though she were singing just for them.

There was still so much to learn. How could she ever hope to make it as a professional singer? But then Jerome would stop, take her in his lithe piano player's arms, and whisper that anybody who didn't think they could always learn something new was just silly—everyone could get better and better.

"Even you?" Gloria would ask, resting her head on his shoulder.

"Especially me," Jerome would say.

Now he began again to play the short, woeful introduction. "Let's start from the top."

Gloria straightened up, breathed deeply, and began to sing:

> *I hate to see the evening sun go down.*
> *I hate to see the evening sun go down.*
> *'Cause my baby, he done left this town.*

Jerome banged the keys hard and stopped playing. "You need to get out of your head." He pointed to the area a few inches south of his throat. "*This* is where the song needs to come from. Let's try again."

She got only a little further before Jerome slammed the keys again. "You're using too much vibrato," he said, sounding annoyed. He rubbed his temples with his fingers. "You're not singing in a damn school recital."

She narrowed her eyes. "Marion Harris uses plenty of vibrato when she sings it."

He gave a mean laugh. "Just 'cause you got yourself a gig doesn't make you Marion Harris, darlin'." He shuffled through the pages of music strewn on top of the piano, then handed a few to her. "This might be more your speed."

Gloria read the title: "Second Hand Rose." Fanny Brice had sung it in the Ziegfeld Follies and it had been a huge hit. Gloria hated the song. It was a cutesy tune, annoying, whiny—and about as sexy as her mother in her flannel nightgown. And singing it required hardly any real skill. She wanted songs that would show her off, that would make people at the Opera House take her seriously. She'd thought Jerome wanted that, too.

"I think 'Second Hand Rose' is a little boring," she replied in a measured tone.

Jerome looked away. "If you don't want boring, then stop singing like that."

Gloria slapped the sheet music down. "Okay, that's it! What is the matter with you?" Jerome had always been a strict but straightforward coach, never snide. "This can't just be about my singing."

Jerome stared ahead in silence for a moment, then turned

to look at her. "Aw, honey," he said, reaching up to stroke her cheek.

But Gloria ducked away. "Seriously. What's wrong?"

He moved over to one side of the bench, patting the spot next to him. Gloria sat.

Gone was Jerome's scowl—now he just looked sad and tired. "Glo," he began, "you know I'm proud of you for getting this gig and all. I really am. But it hurts, having you pay the bills, having you support me like this."

"Because you think *you* should be supporting *me*," Gloria replied. "How many times do I have to tell you? That doesn't matter to me."

"Well, it matters to *me*," he said quietly. "How do you think it feels, you bringing home cash when all I do is sit around all day and nick some food when I can?"

Gloria clasped his hand in hers. "You'll find something soon," she said. "Me making the money, that's just temporary."

"Even if I do, it'll be a long time before I'll be able to afford to marry you."

Marriage.

Jerome had told her before they ran away from Chicago that he wanted to marry her, but they hadn't discussed it since. They had enough problems to deal with in the present—the future could wait. "So? It's not like we're in any rush."

Jerome chuckled, but there was a hollow note to his laugh. "I don't know why I'm even worrying whether or not we could ever afford to get married. Who would marry us, Gloria? They'd chase us down with torches and pitchforks first."

He touched a black key on the piano, the sound ringing through the heavy silence in the apartment. "I'm this." Then he moved his finger a little to the right and played a white key. "And you're this. Nobody minds seeing all this black and white together on a keyboard, but that's not how it is out in the world."

This wasn't exactly news. Gloria forced a smile. "What good is marriage, anyway? What does it mean to anyone?"

"It means not living in sin, Gloria."

"My father left his marriage the minute he found a younger woman he liked better. Harris Brown was going to marry some girl, but that didn't stop him from carrying on with Clara and almost ruining her life. All that pressure to get married had *me* ready to shackle myself to Bastian!" She took both of Jerome's hands in hers. "Marriage doesn't prove anything. It's love that counts, and we've got more than enough of that."

Jerome looked down at their intertwined hands. "Well, I love you, but I'd also love to marry you. If that makes me a fool, then so be it."

"Jerome . . ." Gloria trailed off, unsure of what to say.

She moved closer and kissed him on the lips. His arms wound themselves around her, and he kissed her back. Hard. As he wove his fingers through her hair, a single tear rolled down her cheek. She hoped he wouldn't notice.

The truth of it was, she didn't think Jerome was a fool at

all. She wanted to marry him, too. She wanted a house and children with him. Their strange living arrangements were all right for right now, but a year from now, would she still be stuck climbing through a fence to get to her apartment? In three years? A decade? Would their love *ever* be acceptable?

Jerome leaned his forehead against Gloria's. Then he stood abruptly and shuffled the sheet music into a tidy stack. He slid the pages into his worn-out brown briefcase.

Gloria watched, confused. "What are you doing?"

Jerome took his straw hat off a hook on the wall. "I need to take a walk, get some fresh air." He gave her a quick kiss on the forehead. "Sorry for being a jerk before."

Without looking back, he walked out and shut the door.

This was the closest she and Jerome had come to having a fight since they'd arrived in New York. They'd been so focused on trying to survive each day, they hadn't had time to argue about the future. But he was right: What could they do when no one out in the world would ever accept them as a couple?

What would happen if Gloria called the whole thing off—if she crawled back to her mother in Chicago?

Beatrice Carmody would be angry, but Gloria knew she would be happy to see her daughter. Her mother was probably the one behind all those LOST GIRL flyers, after all. Her mother would hug her and scold her and hug her some more. Then Claudine would make Gloria hot tea with lemon, Gloria would take a bath with lavender bath salts, and she would sink into her pink bed and sleep for days. She would miss Jerome, of course, but he would understand. They would be better off—free to find people of their own races to love.

No! She could never just abandon Jerome like that. And even if she could, Jerome wasn't the only reason she couldn't return to Chicago. There was a darker reason, and that reason had had a name—until Gloria had snuffed out his life: Tony.

On the few occasions when she allowed herself to remember the cherry-red blood flowing from his body, smoke rising from the hot pistol at her feet into the winter air, she also remembered that she could never go back to her old life. That life had died with Tony in the pearl-white snow.

She sat down at the kitchen table and shuffled through the newspapers piled there, her fingers pausing on a recent Chicago *Tribune*. Back when they'd had money, she had extravagantly bought a year's subscription by mail. It helped the homesickness to know what all her old socialite friends were up to in her absence.

She started in the society pages. Witless Ginnie Bitman was engaged to Wallace Worthington II. Boring. Then a familiar image caught her eye: a small photograph of Bastian, standing in a light-colored suit against a dark background. His hair was slicked back and his mustache was perfectly trimmed. Gloria had almost forgotten how handsome he was.

She let out a gasp at the headline next to the photo:

KILLER OF ARISTOCRAT
STILL ON THE LOOSE

The search for the murderer of Sebastian Grey III, 23, continues. The deceased was a banker and a well-loved stalwart on the Chicago social scene. Grey's body was found on a dock at the Chicago Harbor early Sunday morning. Police have no leads as of yet, but friends remain hopeful.

Gloria took several deep breaths. Bastian had been *murdered*?

She had grown to hate Bastian while he was still alive. He'd never loved her—he had only wanted to marry her for her father's steel fortune. And Bastian had been behind Carlito's attempt on Jerome's life. Bastian was the reason everything had gone so wrong. The reason Gloria could never go home again.

Staring at Bastian's photograph, the man she'd once thought she loved—who *looked* the part of a proper husband, crisp and dapper and handsome and *white,* who impressed her parents and knew the right things to say at parties, who'd gone to college and liked holding her hand when they took walks in the park but hadn't ever really loved her—Gloria wondered what would have happened if she'd never decided to run away with Jerome. If she had walked away from the Green Mill and everything that went with it to marry Bastian.

If she had, Tony would still be alive. Jerome would be still playing at the Green Mill. Gloria would have been away from all that, living in a beautiful house with Bastian and all the money either of them could ask for. They wouldn't have been happy, but at least they'd have been on the right side of the law. And alive.

If Bastian had been killed, it was because of the people he ran with. The people who were hunting Gloria and Jerome. And if they had come for Bastian, they might come for her. For heaven's sake, what was she doing here in this apartment, a sitting duck? She was just a schoolgirl, after all— lost and confused and scared and barely eighteen.

For the first time in a long while, Gloria wished she still had Bastian's pistol.

She was going to need a gun.

LORRAINE

It had been a Bad Night.

Lorraine hadn't slept very well or for very long and was planning to stop by Julia's Café and have a long, lazy breakfast before she went to work. After the day she'd had yesterday, she was pretty sure she'd earned it. Besides, she needed to catch up on her *Vogue*.

She started when she heard a light tapping on the door.

Another knock? Another mystery caller? Lorraine ran her hand over her bob and straightened the sailor collar on her burgundy day dress. It was always necessary to look good—one never knew when a gorgeous young man might come tip-tapping on one's apartment door.

Lorraine smiled and opened the door. "Hello there," she said. "What brings you back so soon?"

The young man's chestnut-brown eyes glittered at her

from under his dark hair. "I just wanted to apologize for disturbing you last night. It was awfully late to come asking a stranger for a screwdriver. But that leaky sink would've kept me up all night."

"Don't be silly," Lorraine said quickly. "I was happy to help! No one likes a drip."

He'd been the only bright spot last night. Allowing her new neighbor to think he'd woken her was a far better excuse for her disheveled appearance than admitting that she'd been crying her eyes out.

"So you need a screwdriver?" she'd asked, wondering if she had any orange juice and vodka and whether suggesting a drink to this tall, dark stranger would look desperate or oh so cosmopolitan. "That's made with . . . ?"

"It's a tool with a flat blade used for tightening screws," he'd said with a dazzling smile. "I've got to fix up the tap before it washes everything in my apartment into the street."

"Right!" she said. "Daddy sent me a tool kit when I moved here. Now to find it."

The young man's friendly manner and easy smile were just what Lorraine needed. They'd only spoken for a minute or two before she found the tool kit beneath a teetering pile of hatboxes she'd built into a pyramid in the hall closet. She handed over the screwdriver and said, "Any time you need anything, just say the word."

"Thanks," he said. And then he paused. "What word should I say, exactly?"

She thought hard. "I don't know."

And then she'd shut the door in his face. Without even getting his name. So clumsy! But it didn't matter: She knew he would be coming back for more.

Besides being in his early twenties, he was absolutely *gorgeous*. With his tanned skin and chiseled features, he was the opposite of a soft, boring prep-school boy like Marcus Eastman. Lorraine had wanted to jump into his arms the moment she saw him. She hadn't, though. Restraint was key. Anyhow, there was always time for a quality smooch session once the important questions had been asked, such as "What's your name?" And "Do you drink?"

And here it was the next morning, and he was back. Thank *God* she'd had the wherewithal to put on a decent outfit and some makeup. "Would you like to come in?"

He nodded and followed her inside. He removed his newsboy cap and held it in his hands. In his gray vest and plain white shirt, he looked simple yet elegant. He had taste, and that was important. Sort of.

"I'm Hank," he said, breaking the silence.

"That's so . . . masculine," Lorraine said, fanning herself with her hand.

He chuckled. "Well, Henry, really, but everyone calls me Hank."

"Who's everyone? Your dozens of girlfriends?"

"Naw," he said, shaking his head. "I'm single. I guess just my friends. My mom. You know—the important people."

The awkward silence began to take root again.

"And *you're* Lorraine," he continued.

Had she told him her name? She didn't remember that, though she might have talked about herself in the third person—she was doing that way too much lately. "Lorraine would never stand for that!" and "Lorraine will have something to say about that!" and so on—Spark was always making fun of her for it.

"Would you like some . . . coffee or something?" she asked, hoping she *had* coffee.

"That would be great, actually," he said, and sat down on the sofa.

There was a bag of ground coffee in the icebox. As she spooned it into the percolator and put it on the stove, she hoped the resulting brew would turn out all right.

"Be right back!" she called, scurrying to her bedroom to check her appearance in the full-length mirror. She freshened up her mascara. She bit her lips and pinched her cheeks for added color. There, that was perfect. She looked good. Ish. Good-ish. It was morning, after all.

A few minutes later, she rejoined Hank with two cups of hot coffee.

She sat next to him on the sofa, though not *too* close. She didn't want him to think she was too much of a roundheel. "So, Hank, what do you do when you're not fixing leaky faucets?"

Hank took a sip, then set the cup on the coffee table. "Nothing as of yet. I just moved here from Los Angeles."

Lorraine set her cup down, too. The coffee didn't taste so

great. "Oh, California! I've always wanted to visit. Ever meet any movie stars?"

"I thought I saw Norma Talmadge in a coffee shop once."

"*Smilin' Through* is my favorite movie!" Lorraine exclaimed. She'd seen the film the year before with Gloria, and it had had her in tears by the end. "It's *so* romantic." She touched his arm lightly. "So what did you do for a living out there in Los Angeles?"

Hank stirred his coffee. "Oh, you know, a little of this, a little of that." He met her eyes. "What do *you* do, Lorraine?"

Lorraine wasn't allowed to talk about her job at the Opera House, of course. Puccini and Carlito insisted she be "discreet." But what was discreet for a nun, say, was different for a flapper—how discreet did she need to be, really? Hank was being so evasive, she had to wonder whether he did something similar for a living. She made a quick decision.

She leaned back against the purple sofa cushion. "Tell you what. I'll tell you about my job if you tell me about yours."

Hank gave her an apprehensive look. "All right. I'm outta work now, but the truth is . . . I'm a bartender. That's not news I really like to broadcast."

"I can get you a job!" Lorraine said with a little clap of her hands. She could help this beautiful man *and* have an excuse to spend tons of time with him. It was just too exciting. "I work at this swanky new joint called the Opera House, and we just fired—misplaced—lost our bartender."

Hank cocked his head in surprise. "Well, now. There's some good timing."

Suddenly Lorraine remembered she'd sworn off bartenders. *Oh well.* What fun were rules if she didn't give herself permission to break them every once in a while?

Note to self, Lorraine thought. *Get rid of current bartender. Pronto.*

◆ ◆ ◆

Lorraine took a deep breath as she stepped down the spiral staircase. She'd never fired anyone before. But it couldn't be too hard. It was good luck that Cecil wasn't working tonight. She wasn't sure she had the heart to kick him out to make room for Hank.

Instead, the bartender who greeted her when she got downstairs was Roderick, an older man with frizzy gray hair and fuzzy gray eyes. He was actually pretty good at his job, but . . .

"How's it going, Raine?" Roderick asked as Lorraine approached. "Fancy a drop?"

She shook her head. "It's not going too well, Rod. I'm sorry, but we've got to let you go."

"Excuse me?"

It was a bit much to hope he would just accept what she said and walk out the door. "Rod, you heard me. I don't want to get into all the messy details. Now scram."

Rod set the bottles down and walked out from behind the bar. He pointed at Lorraine, his finger only inches from her face. "Now, you listen here, missy. What kind of authority have you got to fire me without even tellin' me why?"

"You broke that bottle of gin last week." Lorraine took a step back.

"No, *customers* broke that bottle and I gashed my arm on broken glass cleaning up after them."

"That was clumsy of you. We can't have you bleeding all over our customers."

"I got shoved by that crowd of drunks!"

"And you complain too much."

He raised his bushy eyebrows. "I'm complaining because you're firing me for no damn reason! I got a wife to support, and—"

"Okay, *fine*. You can stay and push a broom around or something. And be careful with broken glass. Use a dustpan."

"Is this a joke?" Rod looked around as though there might be someone else running the show. Lorraine hated it when her employees did that.

"Push a broom? I'm an old man, Raine. That ain't my job. And the tips! I *live* off those tips!"

She shrugged. "Not anymore, you don't. It's either Broom Boy or no job at all—your pick."

He met her gaze stubbornly for a few moments, then scowled and walked in the direction of the broom closet. She leaned her hand against the bar and exhaled. There, that hadn't been so terrible, had it?

Then she noticed Jimmy walking toward her.

He wiped off his brow the sweat caused by whatever work he'd been doing upstairs. "Hi there, Lorraine." He noticed Rod sweeping the floor and muttering under his breath. "What's Rod doing with that broom?"

"Not your problem," Lorraine replied. "What's up?"

Jimmy handed her a small white envelope. "This came in from Western Union earlier."

Lorraine felt a nervous flutter in her stomach. Only one person sent her telegrams. "Thanks, Jimmy."

She ripped open the envelope.

ABOUT TIME YOU FOUND BIRD. STOP.
JOB ONLY HALF DONE. STOP. NOW YOU
NEED TO FIND BIRD'S MATE. STOP. GET
HIM AND YOU GET YOUR REWARD. STOP.

She read the telegram a few times, then folded it and slipped it into her purse. The odds of Jerome's falling for an oddly specific ad in the paper were slim. WANTED: BLACK MALE PIANIST TO PERFORM WITH REDHEADED FEMALE SINGER WITH WHOM HE IS ALSO LIVING IN SIN. No way.

But once Lorraine reeled Jerome in, she'd be done. She'd have her revenge on Gloria and then she'd prance off to school, a little extra spending money in her clutch to burn on nights out with her Barnard classmates.

She looked up as Spark walked into the barroom. He wore his customary straw boater, suspenders, and a purple and green polka-dotted bow tie. You could say this for the man's taste: It was entirely his own.

He grinned at Lorraine. "I see you noticed the new mirror."

"What mirror?"

Spark gestured toward a new mirror behind the bar. It took up the entire area between the shelves of bottles, and THE OPERA HOUSE was written in cursive across it. "That way there's no more confusion about the new name. Looks nice, right?"

Lorraine glanced at it again. She almost didn't recognize the girl staring back at her. Sure, the girl in the mirror had the same dark bob, the same milky complexion, smooth cheeks, and made-up lips as she did, but this girl's eyes looked scared and weary. She was a bit too thin, too jittery, and there was something about her . . . something like guilt. That girl in the mirror wasn't a person who would fire an old man to spend time with a cute new guy, who would betray her (former) friends to a bunch of mobsters.

Lorraine blinked. The girl in the mirror was still there.

But then she turned around, focusing her gaze elsewhere—on the crimson mural, on the hardwood dance floor—and thankfully, the girl in the mirror was gone.

◆ ◆ ◆

Finally Lorraine was alone in the back office. She had only just begun to experiment with her new set of false eyelashes when someone knocked on the door. She groaned and put the eyelashes aside.

It was the new waitress, Ruby, holding a layout for a glossy poster.

"Sorry to bother you, Raine," Ruby said, "but Puccini's son brought this mockup from the printer and said it needs to be approved as quickly as possible."

Lorraine took the poster. It showed a beautiful redheaded woman in a red dress singing on a stage under the white cone of a spotlight.

It read:

10:00 P.M.

JULY 12TH

A beautiful songbird debuts:

Zuleika Rose

GIRLS! DANCING! MORE GIRLS! MORE DANCING!

Catch Spark for the Locale and Password

Lorraine handed the poster back to Ruby. "This looks fine—consider my approval given. Oh, and Ruby? Send in Spark, would you?"

A few minutes later, Spark walked in. "You asked to see me?"

"Mmm-hmm." Lorraine removed a tube of lipstick and a compact from her purse and touched herself up in the mirror. "We need a new piano player."

Spark sat across from her, frowning. "What's wrong with the one we've already got?"

"You saw how he played during that girl's audition."

"Yeah, but Felix . . . he's a good kid."

"And the man smiles too much. And he has too many teeth, I think. It's unnatural."

Spark stared at her in silence for a few seconds, then burst out laughing.

"And that goes for you, too," she snapped, slapping her hand against the desktop. "Why the smiles all the time? What is everyone so damn happy about?"

"All right, Raine, Felix is gone." Spark pulled a pad and pencil off the desk. "How do you want the ad for a new one to read?"

"We want somebody with experience, of course, and handsome. Young, nineteen or twenty. Dark hair, big brown eyes, and he shouldn't be too tall. Five-ten or five-eleven should do it," Lorraine said, thinking of Jerome. "Oh, and he needs to be black."

Spark looked up from his pad. "With a white band?"

"Yeah. People like seeing blacks and whites onstage together."

Spark blinked slowly. "Which people?"

"Shut it," Lorraine replied. "What about that joint uptown, the Cotton Club? It's all the way up in Harlem, and our customers are flocking up there in droves. We need a little of that jumpin' jive down here. A black pianist with a white singer will give us a line around the block, trust me."

Spark shrugged. "If you say so. I'll put the ad in the paper tomorrow. Does it need to be so specific?"

Lorraine put her hand up to stop him as he started to stand. "Actually, an ad might not be necessary. How about you ask that new singer we hired—what's her name? I'm sure she knows tons of musicians."

"Black ones?"

"She *does* live awfully close to Harlem."

Spark stood up and stretched. "I'll ask her. Any other requests, my liege?"

"My *lady,* you mean." She drummed her fingers on the desk. "I put Rod on cleaning duty."

"Yeah, I noticed him yelling at the mop." Spark paused, seeming to wonder whether he should ask the next question. "So who's gonna be tending bar tonight?"

"A man named Hank is coming in for an interview in about twenty minutes. And you're going to hire him."

It was only after Spark had left that Lorraine allowed herself to grin.

Being powerful felt good.

CLARA

Clara waited as patiently as she could outside Parker Richards's office—which wasn't quite as glamorous as she had expected.

In her mind's eye, the place had been a series of glass-walled private offices with a secretary stationed at a desk in front of each door, typing. Clara loved the noise of a type-writer. It sounded to her like hard work, and joy, and a little bit of magic.

But it wasn't like that at all. When she'd dropped off her first article a few days earlier, she'd gotten an eyeful. Instead of a line of smartly dressed secretaries and glass doors, Clara saw only two older women at the front of the office, garbed in drab dresses. Most of the writers worked in a bull pen, and there were only a few offices at the back of the common area. Worse, nearly all the men in the office were bald, bespectacled, a tad overweight, or all three. *You don't have to look good to write well,* she told herself.

"Clara?"

Parker gestured for her to come inside his office. Clara followed him and perched on the edge of the cushioned chair across from his desk. Now, *this* was more like it.

Parker's office was stylish and professional—with floor-to-ceiling windows, and framed articles and magazine covers on the ivory walls. The oak desk was flanked by matching bookcases, filled with newspapers, issues of *Vogue* and *Vanity Fair,* and books. Behind Parker's leather office chair, Clara could see a gorgeous view of midtown Manhattan.

Parker didn't look too bad himself. He was casually devastating in a dark green blazer that brought out his eyes, and a white dress shirt, his wavy hair slicked back and fixed with a bit of pomade. She immediately thought of Marcus and felt slightly guilty that she'd been admiring Parker, but there was nothing wrong with looking, was there?

And there was something unique about Parker. More than his good looks, it was his *energy* that made him attractive. Intelligence shone like a light behind his eyes, and his presence, or charisma, or whatever it was that he radiated, made the spacious office seem too small to contain him. She waited for the smile that would finish off the effect.

It didn't come.

Though Parker undoubtedly looked good, Clara's editor did not look happy. He held up Clara's first column. The pages were so marked up with red ink, she wondered if anyone would even be able to read the words she'd typed.

"You want to tell me what you were thinking?" Parker asked. "Because this flat tire of a story could have been written by any of the stiffs in the city morgue."

Flat tire of a story? She'd obsessed for hours over her column—over the metaphors she chose, over the way she described the dresses, over her clever jokes.

It was about an evening she'd spent at the Spotted Hen. She'd never been to this particular speakeasy in her flapper days, but she'd needed to go to a bar where no one would recognize her. There she'd been free to sit on a wooden stool at the bar with her seltzer and observe the drunken antics all around her—the slurry shenanigans of the flappers and their beaux.

She'd written a fine portrait of three rookie flappers trying to dance the latest dances, and how awkward they'd looked. And she'd made what she thought were some very witty comments about two men who had argued with the dealer during a game of poker, eventually revealing that they didn't understand how to play the game at all.

"What's so wrong with it?" Clara asked, a defensive edge in her voice.

"What *isn't* wrong with it would be the better question." Parker tossed the article into his wastebasket. "*Manhattanite* readers want to read about the swanky palaces they *wish* they could go to but can't—not the two-bit gin joints that any dumb Dora can waltz right into. You're supposed to have the inside track."

Worse than having her writing torn apart was the realization that Parker wanted the old, wild child Clara.

"Listen, you *are* an excellent writer—I was completely right about that," Parker said in a softer tone. "But you can't watch the party from the shadows. You need to get into the thick of it! You have to hobnob with the best and the brightest, the drunk and the dumbest. You have to dance in the middle of the flapper-packed dance floor and lead all those dizzy girls in a toast with *your* flute of champagne." He shook his head. "If I just wanted someone to sit on the sidelines and take notes, I would've saved myself some trouble and hired my mother. And she's dead."

"And what if I can't do what you're asking?"

Parker huffed. "If you can't give me that insider scoop on the scene, then I'll need to find someone else. It would be a shame, though. I thought it was fate, you know, when I saw you at the Pink Potato. The kind of mischief you used to get up to . . ." He grinned at a memory, and for a brief, burning moment Clara was reminded of just how dynamic and handsome he was. "I remember you once convinced a party at the Ritz to steal a bunch of mattresses and—"

"Ride them down the grand staircase!" she finished for him, laughing despite herself.

He laughed, too. "How did you manage to get away with that?"

"Bellboys can be *very* agreeable if you treat them kindly," she replied, comically fluttering her lashes a few times. "And if you're a girl."

"That's where I always fouled up."

"We only got through a few runs before they kicked us out. They never did get those silk sheets back, though. My friends and I wore those as dresses for the rest of the evening."

Parker stood up. "See, *that's* what I'm talking about." He stepped around the desk so he was standing directly in front of her. "There's a big to-do going on at the Plaza tonight. It's Maxie Gabel's eighteenth birthday party. You come out of there with a story like the one you just told me, and we'll be in business."

"Really?" Clara was excited that Parker was giving her a second chance, but part of her was filled with dread. It was one thing to write about *other* people having a grand time and getting sloppy, but it was another thing entirely to join in and lead the charge.

But she wouldn't really be joining. She would be *pretending* until she could go home and write about it.

Perhaps she could do both: be a reporter and be the girl she wanted to be—for Marcus, and for herself.

"Will you be going to this party?"

Parker laughed. "Are you kidding? They'd never invite me—I'm a journalist. This party's meant for beautiful flappers like yourself, so be sure to wear your glad rags."

"So, are you excited about seeing *Try It with Alice*?" Marcus asked over the phone. "Paul said he practically died laughing when he saw it. And you know Paul—he's only ever laughed twice before in his life, and both of those times were just so he could fit in."

Clara gasped. She'd completely forgotten: she and Marcus were supposed to see a Broadway show that evening!

After leaving Parker's office, she'd dropped by Leelee and Coco's. Getting into a party without an invitation had never been a problem before. But now Clara couldn't count on her reputation to open doors, while Leelee and Coco's should be more than enough to get them all in.

And then she'd stopped in at a barbershop to have her hair transformed back into its old bob. She walked out and relished the feel of the summer breeze on her neck. She barely had enough time to purchase a shimmering Chanel masterpiece overflowing with gorgeous beadwork before rushing home to get ready. She'd used most of the cash she had to buy the dress, but as long as she kept the tags on, she could return it the next day.

She sighed and sat down on the bed, holding the black telephone receiver to her mouth. "Marcus, I'm sorry, but I think I have to cancel."

"What?" he said. "It sounded like you just said 'cancel,' but that can't be."

Clara had resisted the telephone that Marcus had insisted she let him install in her apartment. He wanted an easy way to talk to her when she was "all the way out in Siberia." But right now she was thankful: Marcus couldn't see her half-made-up face and her apartment strewn with shoes, stockings, and headbands. She was lying to him. Just as she had when they'd first met. Only, now she felt terrible about it.

"I'm so sorry, Marcus, I should've called earlier, but I've just felt so awful. I've had this—*cough, cough*—horrible cough since the afternoon. I think I may even have a fever."

"Oh, darling," Marcus replied, all annoyance gone. "I guess I'll try to get tickets for another night. How about I bring you some chicken soup?"

"No, no, you don't have to brave that subway ride for my sake," she said quickly. "I think I just need to get some rest."

Marcus was silent for a moment. "Are you sure? I really don't mind. You know I'm kidding around when I whine about trekking out there to visit you."

Clara checked the clock. She still had to finish getting ready, spend an hour on the subway, and meet up with Leelee and Coco. "I'm honestly falling asleep over here. Go out and enjoy the night with your friends."

"Paul did say Charles Drakeman just got into town," Marcus said hesitantly. "They're going to play pool. And not the billiards sort, apparently, but something to do with big blue pools of chlorinated water and bathing beauties in floats. It sounds stupid and decadent."

"Yes, do that!" Clara said with too much enthusiasm. She tried to cover with another cough. "I mean, that sounds like fun."

"It won't be fun without you." Marcus exhaled. "All right, I will play pool. Rest well, and we can meet up for lunch tomorrow if you're better by then. I love you."

"I love you, too."

Clara hung up. She'd done the right thing. Marcus wouldn't understand what she was doing for the *Manhattanite*—he'd worry that she would fall back into her old ways.

But Clara *would* keep hold of her new values, and she *would* go to this party purely to work. She would prove to Parker and to everyone else that she wasn't a stylish but brainless floozy. She would prove that she could be something on her own.

◆ ◆ ◆

Clara twirled her martini glass and watched the olive spin around.

When they'd reached the Pulitzer Fountain and seen the crowd of photographers and reporters swarming around the Plaza's entrance, the party had looked promising. And once they'd pushed through the people and gotten inside, it had looked more promising still: The ballroom upstairs had recently been renovated, and even Coco had to admit it was beautiful. The city at night was visible through the grand arched windows, and delicate chandeliers bright with light hung from the coffered ceilings.

At the far end of the room, across the vast polished parquet floor, Clara saw Joseph C. Smith's band on a bandstand, and a bar discreetly tucked into the corner behind an explosion of palm fronds. That was where the partygoers were thickest, where the guests could drink booze served by waiters in tuxedos. Maybe it was just the blaze of the chandeliers overhead, or the soft jazz that pulsed in the room, or the two drinks she'd already had, but from this distance, for a brief moment, it seemed to Clara that all the young men here were terribly handsome and the women were elegant goddesses in sequins and gold lamé.

The illusion was quickly dispelled.

While these girls looked like flappers, they certainly didn't act like them. Where were the wild toasts and vamps dancing on tables? Could the New York social scene have changed so much in her absence?

"To think we all got so dolled up for such a yawn of a party," Clara said. But her old roommates *did* look fantastic. Leelee's feathered headband coordinated beautifully with her sheer, netted dress. Coco was a shock of silver fringe, and a glittering headdress covered most of her dark bob, accentuating her sharp features.

"Oh no, darling," Leelee said with a hand on Clara's arm, "if anyone is a waste of beauty tonight, it's you. You should move back in with us only so I can steal that dress from your closet."

Clara looked down to admire her bronze Chanel. The two tiers of delicately beaded cotton tulle fell gracefully just past her knees. It was a perfect match for her bronze headdress, a complicated number inlaid with pearls, with even more pearls hung off the sides in elegant loops.

"What do you girls say to cutting a rug?" she asked. Teddy Brown was up on the stage playing his heart out on xylophone with Smith's band, but no one even seemed to notice. "We need to show these kids how to appreciate good jazz."

"We probably need to show them how to dance, too." Coco lifted her shoulders, then dropped them. "I doubt these palookas know anything other than the foxtrot."

Clara clung to the golden banister as she and the girls made their way down the steps. She was a little tipsier than she'd thought. She, Coco, and Leelee wandered through the crowd, searching for suitable partners. Clara stopped and tapped the shoulder of a blond boy with pretty brown eyes.

He turned to her and raised his eyebrows. "Well, hello there," he said with a grin. "What's your name?"

"My name's not important, sweetheart." She said a silent apology to Marcus. "What's important is that hardly anyone is on that dance floor. It's practically scandalous."

"We can't have that, can we?"

"Absolutely not!"

He took her hand and led her out onto the floor.

Clara allowed herself a moment to savor the Charleston. Her body found the rhythm, and before she knew it she was bobbing and swaying to the song, forgetting herself and her worries—Marcus, her uncertain future—and just glorying in the dance. It was impossible not to be happy when she was dancing. And everyone could see it: People turned to watch as she and her girlfriends allowed the jazz to seep into their bones.

Sadly, after a few minutes, the boy's eyes widened and his hand flew to his mouth. He made it to an empty champagne bucket just in time and was loudly and violently sick.

"This shindig is all wet," Leelee said.

Clara sighed. "This is a bust. Let's skedaddle."

A clock began to chime as they made their way to the exit. So Clara wasn't a journalist. She still had a wonderful boyfriend who loved her, and a prestigious education waiting for her—

"Everyone pipe down!" a man yelled. Instantly everyone in the room held still, fixed by the voice. It was what they'd been waiting for: someone to command them.

Clara looked up and saw a young man at the top of the staircase, addressing the entire room. He was tall, sharply attired, and handsome, with dark hair slicked away from his face. "As you all know, our good friend Maxie is now a man." At this, the teenage crowd exploded into applause, and a few whistled.

"But wait!" the boy said. "If you know Maxie anywhere near as well as I do, you know he has spent his first eighteen years indulging in some very *questionable* behavior." Several guests laughed. "And I don't think the sophisticated ladies at Yale will be impressed. So we have decided that Maxie needs to wash away his sins in the pond in Central Park. A baptism into his new life, as it were. And I invite all of you to witness the ceremony!"

The young man stepped aside, and Clara could finally see what had been going on: The group of teenagers was working to pull a white dress shirt off a young man with dirty-blond hair. They succeeded, leaving him in only his undershirt and trousers.

This had to be Maxie Gabel, the birthday boy. Maxie was obviously drunk but was trying his hardest to escape his friends' clutches. Once he'd lost his pants as well, he managed to slip away from the group and bounded down the staircase.

"Get him!" Maxie's friend yelled, running after the guest of honor.

The crowd roared in excitement and turned as one to chase Maxie and his friends out of the ballroom. Scores of sparkling teenagers tumbled down the stairs and through the hotel's restaurant.

"Stop that man!" they yelled, laughing hysterically as they bumped and sprawled across the late-night diners' tables and knocked into waiters carrying trays of food. Then they were out the other side, through the lobby, and into the summer night.

Clara was exhilarated by the chase. As they moved through the Central Park trees, the party guests fanned out and cornered Maxie along the shore of the pond. He stood ankle-deep in water, panting and looking desperate, staring daggers at the boy who'd made the speech on the staircase. "Arthur, please don't make me do this," he said.

"I'd really rather not, dear friend. But you are a dirty, dirty boy. And this is for your own good."

Maxie glanced at the boys on either side of him, who stood ready to push him into the pond.

"The cleansing will work far better if you submit to it willingly!"

Then Maxie gave a defeated shrug. "Oh, may as well!" With that, he stripped off most of the rest of his clothing and belly flopped into the water.

"Attaboy!" Arthur exclaimed. The partygoers cheered.

Maxie disappeared under the water and resurfaced some distance out. "You all should join me—the water's fine!"

Clara had no idea where Coco and Leelee had gone off to. She glanced around at the smiling faces—there was the mayor's son, making out with a girl she recognized as the daughter of Terri Pottington, a famous New York socialite, and there was Frankie Marlborough, heir to the cigarette throne, puking in a bush. She made a few quick mental notes for the column she was going to write as soon as she got home.

"That's the spirit!" the boy called Arthur said, and he charged into the water with his tux still on.

The other boys who'd chased Maxie jumped in as well. The sound of splashing water and laughter filled the warm summer air. After a moment of hesitation, during which they were probably worrying about ruining their dresses, the girls followed in a shrieking, giggling tide, flashes of red and green and yellow disappearing into the ink-black water, illuminated only by the amber light of a handful of streetlamps.

Clara stared down at her own dress—her beautiful, *expensive* Chanel work of art. But she knew that what she would get by diving into the pond would be worth much more than any old dress. She'd have to ask Parker for an advance on her next paycheck—there'd be no returning this dress once it got soaked.

She kicked off her shoes and jumped in, gasping at the cold. She wiggled her arms and legs, trying to warm herself up, and splashed over to Arthur, nudging his arm. "That was quite a speech," she said.

"Why, thank you," Arthur said. He was even handsomer up close, but in a more imperfect way than she'd thought from a distance. His wet brown hair looked almost black in the darkness and stuck out in every possible direction, the pomade that had been taming it washed away. His large hazel eyes crinkled when he showed off his slightly crooked but adorable grin. "Do I know you?"

Clara shrugged, using a wet hand to remove her ruined

headdress. "I don't know. You'll definitely know me if you introduce yourself."

He stuck out his hand. "I'm Arthur Spence."

"Spence . . . as in Julia Spence?"

"She's my older sister. " He gave a full-throated laugh. "Oh, you're Clara Knowles! Julia *adores* you."

"And I adore her!" With her flaming red hair and practically violet eyes, Julia would have put every would-be flapper at this party to shame.

"Arthur, my head's starting to hurt," Maxie called from the other side of the pond.

"Oh no!" Arthur said. "Well, I know a remedy for that. It starts with a *g* and ends with *in*." He raised a finger into the air. "Back to the Plaza, everyone!" As he waded out of the water, he extended his hand toward Clara. "Come along now, Clara Knowles, you've got to tell me everything you've been up to so I can report back to my sister. She'll never believe I ran into the Queen of Sheba herself."

Clara took his hand and enjoyed the warmth of the evening air. "Pos-i-lute-ly." She stepped into her shoes, felt mud squish against the toe straps. "You seem like exactly the sort of depraved fellow a girl should know."

As she mingled with Arthur, Maxie, and their friends, she mentally filed away a dozen new leads for articles. The Cotton Club was up in Harlem, and a new Greenwich Village speakeasy called the Opera House had just opened.

When Clara at last stumbled into her Brooklyn apartment, it was already getting light outside. But rather than sleep, she sat down in her desk chair without even taking off her wrinkled dress and stockings. She rolled a piece of paper into her Royal 10 typewriter and began to write:

```
GLITTERING FOOLS: WET & WILD
Maxie Gabel may have started Friday evening as a
meek young schoolboy, but at the stroke of midnight,
he arose from the waters of the Central Park pond a
new man.
```

She typed furiously through the early morning until the column was finished. As she read through the pages, a smile spread across her face. She didn't need Parker's stamp of approval or anyone else's. She knew this column was good.

After a load of mistakes and self-doubt, Clara had finally figured out who she really was.

She was a writer.

PART TWO

FOOL'S GOLD

◆ ◆ ◆ ◆

Nobody has ever measured, not even poets,
how much the heart can hold.

—Zelda Fitzgerald

VERA

Vera studied her reflection in the mirror.

After two weeks of running all over the city looking for Jerome, she was exhausted. She'd checked practically every club in Harlem that had a piano. A few musicians had heard of her brother, but none could give her any help in locating him. And she'd waited under the clock in Grand Central, but if he had picked up the note she'd mailed, he never showed up.

Now she was back at the Harlem boardinghouse where she and Evan were staying. Her room offered only the absolute basics—a cotlike bed, a dresser, and a flimsy table with a mirror hanging over it. But it was cheap, there were regular meals, and the room was right below Evan's.

The boardinghouse was only a few blocks away from the Cotton Club. It hadn't been all that long since gangsters had seized the Club De Luxe and transformed it into the Cotton Club, but the joint had already built a reputation for staging one of the glitziest revues in town.

Vera was planning to make her first visit to the club that very evening to see Evan play. "Ethel Waters is making her Cotton Club debut," he told her, "and I think you should be there."

"Ethel *Waters*?" Ethel Waters had taken Harlem by storm when she'd come to New York a few years earlier, and she had quickly become one of the most famous blues singers in the country. A poster showing Waters hung on Vera's wall back in Chicago.

"The very one. So gussy yourself up and take a night off," Evan told her.

At least Vera still had the glitzy clothes she'd brought with her from Chicago.

She shimmied into a silver beaded dress and pinned an Egyptian-inspired silver headdress to her hair. She clasped on her T-strap heels, added a spritz of perfume, and was ready at last.

At the foot of the boardinghouse stairs, a few men were shooting the breeze. One hard-boiled character with a scratchy beard whistled as she walked to the door. "Hey, beautiful, you off to the Cotton Club?"

"I am!" she said.

"You better be in the chorus, then, doll face," the man said. "Even a beaut like you won't be able to get in the front door."

"I guess we'll see!" She waved goodbye and set off.

If Vera got her way, a chorus girl was exactly what she would be by the end of the evening. She wasn't an idiot. She knew she wouldn't be able to get in through the front door of a whites-only joint like the Cotton Club. Even the name of the club was racist—it was supposed to bring to mind a cotton plantation. Blacks worked themselves to the bone onstage while the whites lounged in the audience and enjoyed themselves.

A few minutes' walk, and Vera could see the bright lights spelling out COTTON CLUB on the awning above the club's entrance. Cadillacs, Lincolns, and Rolls-Royces were parked out front—fat cars for fat men with fat rolls of dough. Some wore pin-striped suits and fedoras, while others were decked out in tuxedos. The sequined dresses, beaded handbags, and feathered boas on the women were some of the finest Vera had ever seen.

When she reached the edge of the crowd, she turned and made her way down the dark, trash-strewn alley alongside the building. At the back of the Cotton Club, she found another line—one of black singers, chorus girls, musicians, and workers unloading instruments.

Vera slinked through the group and tried to pass two men in tuxedos.

"Hey there," a young man with a mustache called as he lifted a tuba case. "Where do you think you're goin'?"

"Who, me?" Vera asked, making her best doe eyes. "I'm here about a job."

"Oh, really?" Mustache put down the tuba case and

walked over. "Sad to say, we've got more than enough girls right now."

"Are you sure they're the *right* girls, though?" Vera asked slyly.

Mustache chuckled and shook his head. "What's your name, darlin'?"

She extended her hand. "Vera, Vera Johnson."

Another man looked up from the trunk he was unloading. "Oh, don't you worry none about her, Ralph, that's Evan's girl—the one he's always flappin' his gums about."

Evan had called her his girl? "Yep, that's me."

Ralph shook her hand. "Ralph Escudero. Nice to meet you."

The man who'd identified Vera came over. He had darker skin than Ralph and a face that looked as if it never stopped smiling. "I'm Charlie Green. Sorry to cut this short, Vera, but Ralph and me better get onstage or Big Frenchy'll have our heads. Just follow us in. Nobody'll give you any lip."

True to Charlie's word, the bouncer at the door barely gave Vera a second glance. Ralph and Charlie led the way through the winding halls and dim backstage. They passed beautiful women dressed much like Vera—probably other musicians' girlfriends—and she spied the feathered costumes of the chorus girls.

Charlie and Ralph both shook her hand again before strutting onstage. The other men in the orchestra were already there, setting up their instruments. Vera leaned past the edge of the stage curtains and saw Evan looking very dapper in his tux, trumpet at his side. He looked up and caught her eye. She grinned widely, and he grinned back.

Vera looked out at the audience. A few scattered white couples were dancing to the Gramophone record that was playing between sets. The bright lights from the stage glinted off the jewelry the women were wearing—princess-cut diamond necklaces and rich emerald earrings and sapphire brooches as blue as the ocean.

A handsome white man with close-cropped brown hair stepped up to the microphone as the song playing on the Gramophone ended. He raised his hand and the crowd quieted.

"Thank you, ladies and gentlemen, and welcome to the Cotton Club!" The room filled with polite applause. "This next act is one that—and I am not exaggerating—will change your life. You haven't heard jazz until you've heard these cats. Without further ado, I give you Fletcher Henderson and His Orchestra!"

A young black singer with a trimmed beard took the mike as a mustachioed black man with slicked-back hair stood up in front of the orchestra, baton in hand. Then the members of the orchestra raised their instruments and a burst of music came forth.

It made Vera want to dance, to sway her hips in time with the luxurious rhythms, the timpani and the bass and the trumpet, the trill of the flute and the sharp, piercing notes of the clarinet. The singer jumped in from time to time with nonsense words that managed to sound cool and jubilant at the same moment.

Vera swelled with pride when Evan stepped away from the group to play a trumpet solo. He looked good up there— the spotlight making him as shiny and bright as any jewel in the audience. The passion that filled his face—no, his entire body—as he played was remarkable.

This was music as she'd never heard it before. This was what jazz was all about. In the old days, musicians marched to the beat of the same boring old drummer, but no more— these days, every performance of a song was different. Modern songs practically burst at the seams with improvised solos and ad-libbed singing and all the energy and life of being young. There was something mad and wonderful happening to music here in New York City; no one would ever think the same way about it again.

"You can see just as well from over here," a man's gravelly voice called from a row of wooden chairs near the back wall. "No reason a pretty dame like yourself should have to stand all night."

Despite his raspy voice, the man barely looked older than Evan. He lifted a silver bucket next to his seat and spat a brown streak of liquid into it. "Tobacco always helps to settle my nerves before I go onstage."

She took in his tuxedo. "Is your act coming up soon?"

The man chuckled. "My act is actually up there right now. I got food poisonin' last night. Redman convinced Fletcher to be a pal and let me skip the first set so I can rest up a bit."

"Oh, you must be Pops! I'm Vera!" she said, then rushed to add, "Evan's told me all about you."

He reached out to take her hand. "Folks sometimes call me Dippermouth, due to my horrible habits. But I'd be honored if you, Vera, would call me Louis."

According to Evan, Louis Armstrong was the best horn player he'd ever met. Fletcher Henderson had worked hard to recruit him out of Chicago.

Louis pointed at her. "Evan's told me a lot about you. You're a Chicago native, too, ain't that right?"

She nodded. "Born and raised."

"I miss Chicago. With all due respect to Fletcher, Chi-town is where the real happening is. They've got King Oliver, the Wolverines, and the great Jelly Roll Morton."

"Yeah, Morton is my brother Jerome's hero," Vera said wistfully.

"You're not talking about Jerome Johnson?" Louis asked.

"I am. Have you seen him?" she asked, hoping he had a lead.

"I saw him play once at the Green Mill. If anyone were going to give Jelly a run for his money, it would definitely be that kid. He's got music in every inch of his fingers."

"I, uh, haven't seen him in a while," Vera said.

"Jerome Johnson?" called a chorus girl in an elaborate

headdress from a few feet away. "Boy came in here a couple of weeks ago looking for a job. We've already got a pianist, so we all recommended he try Connie's. I heard their player quit to look for something more steady."

Connie's Inn. That was one place Vera hadn't looked yet. "Oh, thank you!" she said. "Any chance a singer named Gloria Rose was with him when he stopped by? Pretty white girl with red hair?"

The chorus girl's eyes widened. "A *white* girl? No, it was just Jerome. Owney would never let a white singer audition. He wants his chocolate on the stage and his milk in the audience."

Glad to have another lead, Vera went back to listening to the music. She heard another trumpet solo, then said goodbye to Louis, rose from her seat, and went back to the wings to get a better look at the band.

After Evan's second solo ended, her eyes strayed to the audience. Smiling face after smiling face, all beaming at Evan and the band. And then she saw a familiar bobbed red head at the front of the crowd: Gloria.

She still looked a bit thin, but much more put together than she had at the post office a week earlier. She was decked out in a breathtaking gold dress that fell in layers of fringe over her body. She looked almost happy.

This was it: Vera's chance to save her brother.

Without a second thought, Vera dashed from the wings and onto the stage. A part of her noticed how every eye in the club turned toward her, but she couldn't stop now. "Gloria!" she shouted.

Gloria's green eyes widened with pure and total shock. But instead of running toward Vera, she darted the other way, into the crowd.

Ever the professional, Fletcher continued to conduct his orchestra without missing a beat.

Vera leaped from the stage and somehow managed to land on her feet, despite the crowd and her heels.

She tried to follow Gloria through the swarms of complaining white people, but she quickly lost sight of the girl. "Gloria!" she yelled again. "Come back!"

Before Vera could call Gloria's name a third time, two muscular white men grabbed her arms and dragged her toward a side exit. "You are in the wrong place to be lookin' like you do," one of them said.

"If you know what's good for you, girlie, you won't set foot in this place ever again. We won't be anywhere near as polite next time," the other bouncer said as he pushed her out the door and slammed it in her face.

Thwarted. Again.

Why had Gloria fled instead of waiting to meet up with her? Vera was here in New York to save her, not to hurt her.

Vera walked out of the alley and stared at the club. She considered waiting out front for Gloria to emerge, but then one of the bouncers stepped outside and stood on the sidewalk with his arms crossed.

So she walked away, defeated. She would explain to Evan later. She just hoped she hadn't cost him his job. And she hadn't even seen Ethel Waters perform.

So far her time in New York had been one failure after another. But how many chances would she get? If she didn't find her brother soon, Carlito—or the killer—most certainly would.

GLORIA

Gloria didn't want to make a scene.

But she was desperate to get away from Vera.

She shoved through the crowd on the dance floor and into the dining area, trying to avoid taking down one of the artificial palm trees that contributed to the club's "jungle" décor.

It was only after she had slipped inside the door to the kitchen that she remembered to breathe.

What if the gangsters who ran the Cotton Club noticed her? What if they had one of those LOST GIRL flyers hung up in their back office? How many redheads turned up in these jazz clubs? Who knew how far Carlito's influence reached?

In the kitchen, some servers called orders through a pass-through window while others fed dirty dishes through another. Others stood at metal tables arranging plates and glasses on serving trays before sweeping through the double doors and back into the bustle of the club proper.

"Uh, ma'am, I don't think you're supposed to be back here," a sweet-looking black man said quietly. Three other black men in servers' tails looked up from the metal prep table, and one rushed over: Jerome.

He tapped the man on the shoulder. "It's all right, boys, Robbie—Gloria's here with me. She took in the show from the floor while I watched from back here." His grin faded as he registered Gloria's distressed expression.

"You should explain things better, Jerome. Before you get us all into trouble," Robbie said. "Now, if you'll excuse me . . ." He lifted his tray high and exited through the double doors.

"Jerome, you'll never guess who's—" Gloria started, but he shushed her.

"This ain't the place for idle chatter, Gloria. People are working here. Come on." Without touching her, Jerome led her into a corner, as far as they could get from the bustling workers.

Since the Harlem nightclub was segregated, they'd split up and come in through different entrances. Gloria had dressed up and sweet-talked her way through the front door; Jerome had put on an old suit of tails and joined his friend Robbie's waitstaff at the back.

Gloria had been surprised when Jerome had proposed

making a visit to the Cotton Club. "It's Ethel Waters's debut there. If you're going to sing jazz in New York City," he'd said, "then you need to see the hottest acts. And Ethel is one of the best."

Gloria had never heard so many top-quality musicians playing together. It made her all the more thankful to be here, in New York, following her dream.

Jerome put a calming hand on her arm. "What's wrong, Glo? You look like you've seen a ghost."

"No, not a ghost—your sister. She's here."

Jerome gaped. He didn't talk about Vera much, but Gloria knew he missed his little sister. "Where?"

"Onstage," Gloria said. "I have no idea why. I got scared and ran and I think she came after me."

Jerome glanced over at Robbie, who'd just returned from the bar. "Is there a way to get backstage without going through the bar?"

Robbie laughed and pointed to a door on the far wall. "Course there is. How do you think we get the hooch to the band?"

Jerome led Gloria through the door. They rushed down a grimy hallway and suddenly found themselves backstage.

For a moment, Gloria let herself take everything in: the men and women busying themselves with their costumes and instruments, pitchers of water and glasses of gin and whiskey strewn everywhere, cables and wires and lights and curtains and ropes, the hardwood floor—everything about it was beautiful. Dirty, sure, and sort of cluttered, but glorious nonetheless.

This was where music was being made. Where stars were being born.

A young black man with wavy hair and a big jaw immediately approached them. Jerome laughed and swept up the man in a hug. "Jimmy Roads—how are you?"

"Good, good, and great. Laverne and Juicy let me know you stopped by a few weeks ago—why didn't you tell me you were in town?" Jimmy took in Jerome's outfit and whistled. "A master like you certainly doesn't need to stoop to a waiter job."

"Naw, this is just for tonight," Jerome replied. "Wanted to see Ethel perform. Gloria, this is Jimmy—we used to play together at the Checkered Lounge before I ended up at the Green Mill."

Gloria smiled, but she was distracted, looking for Vera. "It's nice to meet you, Jimmy. It doesn't look like she's still here, Jerome."

Jimmy whistled low again and said, "You mean that black girl who threw herself into the audience? She was standing right where you're standing now, and then she just hopped off the stage like a crazy bearcat."

"That was my sister," Jerome said.

"Well, your sister got thrown out."

"Damn," Jerome said. He turned and glanced at the stage. "But look!" he said, motioning to Gloria. "Isn't that Evan?"

Gloria put her hand to her chest as she recognized Evan

in the trumpet section. She was surprised she hadn't noticed him before. He was the only member of the band at the Green Mill who'd worked to make her feel welcome. At least until the band found out about her true identity. Then he hadn't been so friendly.

Evan looked over and saw Jerome. Gloria expected him to do something crazy—wasn't he shocked they were there?—but all Evan did was nod.

Gloria and Jerome stepped back into the chaos of musicians milling around backstage. "Didn't it look like he *expected* to see you?" Gloria asked Jerome.

"Yeah. But he's playing—there's not much he can tell us until his set is over." Jerome chuckled. "Only a girl like Vera would be dumb enough—and brave enough—to do what she did. Interrupt a show! Leap into the all-white audience!"

Gloria frowned. What were Vera and Evan doing here? If it had been Evan alone, she might have understood—plenty of musicians moved from Chicago to New York. But there was nothing to bring Vera here. Nothing except Jerome. But why now? And how had Vera and Evan even known where to find them? It was a strict rule between Gloria and Jerome: They didn't let anyone know where they were. But it seemed Jerome had told Vera and Evan all about what he and Gloria had been up to.

A mustachioed white man puffing a cigar came through the door. "This ain't a farmyard. We've got an audience trying to hear the music out there, so all of you shut up."

The clump of musicians and chorus girls stopped talking

and moved back toward the chairs against the backstage wall, leaving Jerome and Gloria standing alone. The man took a long look at Jerome, scratching his chin. Then he pointed. "Hey, I *know* you! You're that punk piano player that Carlito Macharelli is looking for."

The man stepped forward and tried to catch Jerome's collar. But suddenly Jimmy and a slew of other musicians came between them. "Go," Jimmy whispered to Gloria and Jerome, "get outta here. Now."

Jerome grabbed Gloria's hand and pulled her across the backstage area and out a door that opened onto an alleyway—into the darkness, into the night.

◆ ◆ ◆

The subway ride home wasn't long at all, but to Gloria it felt like hours.

Jerome sat a seat away from her and said nothing. She glanced over at him a few times but eventually stared at the floor in angry silence. It wasn't her fault that Vera was in New York and that they'd possibly missed their only chance to talk to her.

But they couldn't have hung around. Any mobsters who laid eyes on them would've sent them right to Carlito.

The silence continued as they walked home. At Park Avenue, Jerome turned the corner on his own, while Gloria had to go through with the usual charade. She went to the base-

ment and shuffled through the boiler room, pulling the stifling coat over her beautiful dress.

The last time she'd worn this dress, she'd been planning to
run away with the love of her life to New York. Now she
was wearing it while sneaking through a broken fence just
to get into her tiny, third-rate apartment. *How quickly life
can change,* she thought. *How easily the dreams of a starry-eyed
girl can turn into a murky sort of reality.*

She climbed up the back stairway of their building and
banged on the door to their apartment.

Jerome opened it quickly, his black jacket already off and
his bow tie loosened. "You want to try to be a little louder?
I don't think the entire building heard you hammering."

Gloria slipped off her monstrosity of a coat and flung her
hat on one of the kitchen chairs. "Don't you lecture me," she
said, taking off her earrings. "*I* wasn't the one who suggested
we go to a club full of Carlito's cronies."

"I didn't *know* the gangsters at the Cotton Club were
friends with Carlito."

"He's Ernesto Macharelli's son—every gangster is 'friends'
with him somehow," Gloria replied.

"Oh, I'm sorry, I forgot you were the expert on the Mob.
Miss Zuleika Rose!" Jerome called out, his forehead creasing
with angry lines. "Gangster Know-It-All! Where'd you find
that out about Carlito's father, anyway—one of your society
columns?"

"Who cares where I got my information?" Gloria said.

Reading the society columns was *exactly* how she'd learned all she knew about Ernesto Macharelli—but she wasn't going to give Jerome the satisfaction of being right. "At least I actually *read* the papers instead of sulking all day."

His nostrils flared. "You think I sit here sulking? You know I'm lying low when I'm not looking for work."

"Right. I've learned a thing or two about lying low these past six months. I've climbed through that ridiculous fence every day while you just waltz right through the front door."

"Oh, *you're* going to preach to *me* about the places I can go and you can't?" Jerome asked, yanking his bow tie off and throwing it on the floor.

"I'm not talking about a nightclub or the movies, Jerome," she replied, stepping out of her heels. "This is our *apartment*. Our home." She clenched her fists, trying to keep her anger in check, but it wasn't really working. "I've given up everything for you! And now I find out that you've been telling your sister and your band and God knows who else about what we've been doing, putting us both in danger."

"I didn't—"

"Don't you think I would've liked to write my mother or father or my friends to let them know I'm alive? But no! You said I couldn't!"

"But you've got it all wrong," he said.

Gloria wasn't listening. She looked at their shabby surroundings in disgust. "You already have all your friends here. All I have is *you,* and this dingy apartment." She banged a fist on the piano, and there was a muddy jangle. "If I'd known you were telling everything to your old band buddies behind my back, I would've at least sent my mother a letter. Or sent Clara a postcard."

Clara. Just saying her name made Gloria feel guilty about ignoring her cousin, who had been so kind to her those last days in Chicago.

Gloria stopped, out of breath, willing herself to calm down. But then she looked up at Jerome—handsome, strong-willed Jerome—and everything, the anger and the frustration and the sadness, came rushing out in a torrent: She complained about the stealing, the constant rejection at auditions, the endless chores she performed to take care of their atrociously tiny home. After so many months of grinning and bearing this sad excuse for a life, she let all her frustration out. She couldn't stop herself. At last she lowered her voice, her throat scratchy and raw. "I killed a man for you, Jerome." She wiped tears from her cheeks. "That's supposed to mean *no secrets* between us. Don't you get it?"

Jerome's eyes were wet and glistening. "For your information, Gloria, I have not been in contact with Vera or my band. I sent Vera a postcard when we first got here so she would have our post office box number in case of an emergency, but that's it. I was as surprised as you were tonight— I've got no idea what she and Evan are doing here."

He cast his gaze around their squalid little home, finally letting his eyes rest on the scarred wooden floor. "As for the other stuff, well, I thought you did all those things—leaving home, sneaking into our apartment every day—because . . . you wanted to."

Then he lifted his head and pierced her with cold, dark eyes. It was strange, Gloria thought, how the same eyes she looked into so lovingly could at times be so hurtful.

"I didn't know you thought you were making some high-and-mighty sacrifice for me," Jerome said. "I don't need your charity, all right? I don't need your accusations. You think I love this life any more than you do?"

Gloria blinked. "Of course I know you don't *love* it, but—"

"But what? You think the poor black boy likes this because he's used to it?"

She paled, suddenly lost for words. "No, Jerome, that's not what I—"

He put his hand up to stop her. "Save it. You are not the only one who had to leave Chicago. You are not the only person all of this happened to. I've been fighting my whole life for what I want. You do it for a few months and think you deserve some kind of medal." He didn't look angry anymore, just hurt. "I thought us being together made all this worth it. I guess you don't feel the same way."

He stalked into the bedroom.

Gloria sat down heavily on one of the kitchen chairs, breathing hard.

Jerome was right—he *had* spent his life fighting. He'd

fought his father's disapproval of his career choice, fought to stay alive among the gangsters who ran the clubs. Fought through the grief at the death of his mother—the person who'd taught him to play piano in the first place. Fought discrimination every single day of his life from the people who thought they knew what he was because of the color of his skin.

Gloria had never gone through anything remotely like that.

She looked up in surprise as Jerome walked back into the kitchen. He'd changed into a blue shirt and gray trousers. He wore a newsboy cap and held his beat-up briefcase in one hand. In the other hand, he had a small velvet box.

He held the black box out to Gloria. "Here. Maybe you can pawn this for some money."

Gloria stood still and stared at him in wide-eyed confusion. "What . . . ?"

"It's your engagement ring," Jerome said. "I bought it with the advance from the Opera House. *That's* why I wanted to see Ethel Waters at the Cotton Club. They want to have the same sort of thing at the Opera House and they want me to accompany you." He walked over to the piano and set the velvet box on top.

He straightened his cap and picked up his briefcase. "I'll see you at rehearsal. Take some time to think about what you really want, and then we'll decide what to do."

He opened the door and walked out, leaving her alone.

After a few shocked moments, she went over to the piano and picked up the small box. She opened it and stared at the simple ring inside: an unadorned gold band with a tiny diamond.

She'd given his name to Spark only a few days before, with express instructions *not* to let Jerome know that she had gotten him the job. What sacrifices had Jerome made so that she could have this beautiful ring?

She was tempted to slip it on, to see what it would look like on her finger, against her skin. It was the moment she'd been waiting for, uncertain it would ever even happen.

Yet here was the ring.

And Jerome was gone.

LORRAINE

"I think that spot is clean, Raine," Spark said with a smirk.

Lorraine looked up from the bar, startled, and put down the rag. She'd been staring at Hank's backside and wiping down the bar for a good five minutes. "It is *now*."

The last couple of the evening had left an hour earlier—a tired-looking flapper on the arm of an overweight but rich-looking man, stray feathers from the girl's headdress falling in her wake.

Lorraine had stayed to help Hank close the club. She wiped down the bar while he washed and stacked the night's glasses, hosed down and scrubbed the rubber floor mats, and helped the busboys mop the barroom floor. Hank was new, after all, and had never closed before. He might not know what to do and might need to ask Lorraine a question.

And from this vantage point, Lorraine had an excellent

view of Hank's sculpted muscles tensing as he pushed the mop. There wasn't an ounce of flab anywhere on the man. He'd stripped off the blazer he'd been wearing, and now he was working in a white shirt and suspendered trousers. Hot sauce! Lorraine felt like making a mess more often just so she could watch him clean it up.

She tore her eyes away to glare at Spark. "Go do something useful."

Spark pointed at Hank and said, "Listen, I can finish up here. Why don't you go enjoy the rest of the morning with the big six over there?"

Lorraine was suspicious. Spark had never done anything genuinely nice for her. "Are you sure?"

"Go on—I just had a cup of coffee so I'll be awake for a while yet. You look about ready for bed. Maybe Hank can help you out with that." Spark winked clumsily. "Get it?"

"Spark, you are an absolute toad," Lorraine said, but then caught herself smiling.

"Boys!" Spark called to the men, who were wringing out the mops and setting them back in the buckets. "Floor looks good, you can all call it a night!"

A few of the men shouted out goodbyes and walked to the storage room to get their things. Lorraine was delighted when Hank hung back from the others.

"Hi, Lorraine," he said. His dark hair had been fixed with pomade at the start of the night, but now it was disordered in the sexiest possible way. A bead of sweat rolled down his golden neck and under his collar, making Lorraine want to rip the shirt right off him.

"Will you be here awhile yet?" he asked.

"Actually, I'm all done. I just have to get my purse from the office."

"Great!" Hank replied. "I'll grab my hat and meet you out front."

Lorraine nodded mutely. It made sense that she and Hank would walk home together, considering they lived in the same building. But he wouldn't have looked so happy about it unless he was interested in her, too, right?

In the office, she checked her reflection in the mirror over the desk. She wiped her smudged eye makeup until the smudges looked sort of intentional. At least her dress still looked amazing. Hank's sudden entrance into her life had inspired several purchases of some of Paris's latest fashions. This dress had sweet little butterfly sleeves and was made of sheer silk velvet with a floral pattern. A cloth belt was cinched with a rhinestone buckle at the back. She freshened her lipstick—a delicate pink to match her ensemble.

Why wouldn't he be interested in her? She was the cat's pajamas! Nay, the cat's negligee!

◆ ◆ ◆

Hank looked around at the empty streets and darkened windows as they walked. "This is one of the things I officially love about New York. You're free to roam the sidewalks at any time of day or night. Back in Los Angeles, I had to take the trolley whenever I wanted to go somewhere."

Lorraine winced as her heels chafed her feet. A trolley sounded pretty good to her right about now.

He casually slung an arm over her shoulders. "Nice, eh? No one else around, no cars or wagons rolling by—it's like the city belongs to us alone."

Between his arm around her and his use of the word *us,* Lorraine was having trouble not shouting "I love you, too!" into the night air.

She looked up at the sky. The sun wouldn't come up for another hour or two, but it wasn't pitch-black out—the dark was a deep purple. Aside from their footsteps on the pavement, the street was silent. When she walked home alone, the early morning had always seemed desperately lonely. But with Hank along, this early-morning twilight time seemed exhilarating and full of possibility, as if they could do whatever they wanted and no one would be around to stop them.

"It is kind of nice," she replied at last.

When they reached a subway station on Broadway, Hank stopped. "I'm not tired," he proclaimed, a warm smile stretching out across his face. "Are you?"

Honestly? It had been a busy night and she'd barely had five minutes to rest her aching feet. But Hank's copper-brown eyes were like a stiff shot of coffee. This beautiful man didn't want to waste his morning sleeping—he wanted to spend it with her.

"I'm completely awake," she replied.

"Good," he said. "Then I say we go up to Central Park and go out on the lagoon. Afterward, we can get breakfast at this delicatessen my friend Eddie always raves about."

"The boats will be locked up for the night, Hank."

"Passion always finds a way," he said.

Hank was such a risk-taker. How exciting! "You really think so?"

He caught her hand and winked, pulling her down the stairs to the subway platform. "I think *you,* Miss Dyer, can do anything you put your mind to."

◆ ◆ ◆

Lorraine stared at the tall chain-link fence around the boathouse and the lagoon. The gate was chained and padlocked. "This may be a problem."

Lorraine hadn't really loved running through Central Park toward the lagoon in her expensive dress. For one thing, she wasn't the sort of girl who *ran.* Running was for people who didn't mind sweating. And for another thing, she'd had to shuck off her heels and run in her stocking feet, and she didn't even want to imagine what wet things she'd stepped in. But after a few minutes of galloping through the soft darkness hand in hand with Hank, she forgot to be bothered. For the first time in months, she was having *fun.*

Hank shrugged, pulling off his derby and flinging it over the fence. "See? That doesn't look so hard." He wound his fingers into the chain-link and began to climb. Once he reached the top, he swung over and landed gracefully on his feet.

He looked at Lorraine through the mesh. "Are you coming?"

The moment of truth.

She tossed her purse over. Then she took a deep breath, slipped on her shoes—no way was she leaving them here; they cost a week's wages—and wedged a toe into the chain-link. Then the other foot, and up a little farther.

This wasn't so bad! It was like climbing the trellis outside her window when she was thirteen and her mother wouldn't let her go see Terrell Spitznagle, even though Lorraine had explained that she was in love with him. Though come to think of it, Terrell was now fat and balding and about as interesting as a clump of moss on a rock, so maybe her mother had been on to something.

"Come on, slowpoke!" Hank called. "I'd like to make it onto the water before the sun comes up!"

"Excuse me, *you* are not wearing heels," she replied through gritted teeth.

"True, I left those at home tonight," Hank said, laughing.

Lorraine had reached the top. It was a delicate maneuver, swinging a leg over a fence in a dress. A boy wore pants, sure—that was *easy*. But for a girl, there were issues of modesty as well the whole impracticality of rolling a skirt up far beyond the knee.

"Umm," she said, and dropped her leg over the other side, her weight pulling her over, and then it was too late: The hem of her dress was caught on a loose bit of metal.

"Hank!" she yelled, trying not to panic. "I can't get my dress off!"

"The best thing you can do is jump," he said, looking up at her. "I'll catch you."

Ugh. She anchored her feet in the fence, then sprang away and fell. She grimaced at the distinct sound of fabric ripping. *Oh no!* Her beautiful lilac Lucien Lelong was ruined.

But then she was in Hank's arms. He'd caught her effortlessly.

He smiled as he looked at her. "See? That wasn't so bad."

She couldn't help it—she burst into laughter. "Not so bad? I could've broken my neck! And I ruined my dress."

He inspected the damage as he sat her on the ground. Half the hem of the dress had ripped off, exposing the bottom of her white slip. The torn fabric hung limp against her calf.

Hank picked up the frayed edge. As he reached for it, his fingers grazed her leg—they were so warm, warmer than she'd expected, and yet they made her shiver with anticipation. It had been so long since a man had touched her. Since anyone had touched her, really. Even her mother hadn't hugged her when she'd left town.

Hank toyed for a moment with the fabric he held, then dropped it, instead of ripping it further and ravishing

Lorraine against a tree as she'd hoped. His thin but delicious lips formed a playful grin. "I think it looks better this way. You'll start a new fashion trend for sure." He handed over her purse.

Lorraine was sad about the dress, but a few moments in Hank's arms had made it seem less important. "It's just a dress, right?" she said, and hoped he didn't hear the quaver in her voice.

She had been to Central Park on visits to New York with her parents, but she'd never seen the park like *this*. Now that they were over the fence, she could see the moonlight shining off the lagoon. From here it was easy to see the starry sky, framed by the bushy tree branches along the water. She stared up in wonder. "So pretty," she whispered.

"This way," Hank said, already heading off to the old wooden boathouse. There they ran into another padlock, on the two front doors. Hank began rummaging around in his trouser pockets. "Don't worry, I can take care of this."

"Sure you can, Houdini." Lorraine swatted mosquitoes away from her bare arms.

Hank turned away, and she heard clicking noises. A few moments later, the padlock opened and he dropped it to the ground.

Lorraine stared at the piece of metal in his hand. "Why were you carrying that lock pick?"

He tipped his hat. "Why? In case a beautiful young lady needs help breaking into a boathouse for some late-night rowing."

Lorraine loved it when a man came prepared. And had he just called her beautiful? This was swiftly becoming the best date she had ever been on, and the date hadn't even technically started yet!

Hank dragged open the double doors, which creaked like a dying cat in the silent night.

He bowed his head and gestured to the open doorway. "After you."

Lorraine couldn't see much in the inky dark of the boathouse, though her eyes adjusted quickly to the light peeking in through the slatted wooden walls. Flimsy-looking rowboats rested in the water. Everything smelled like mildew. No wonder she'd never come for a boat ride. This was disgusting.

Hank tugged a rope and the doors onto the lagoon swung open. He plucked two oars off the wall and hopped inside one of the boats. As he untied it from its moorings, he said, "You going to stand there all night? Or are you coming along?"

He held out his hand, and Lorraine took it. His hand was bigger and harder than hers, as it should be, and she loved the feeling of her palm against his. Once she was seated, he took an oar in each hand, dropped the shafts into the oarlocks, and rowed them out onto the lagoon.

He rowed hard for a bit and then stopped. The chorus of creaks that accompanied his rowing vanished as he let the boat drift, and all Lorraine could hear were crickets chirping and the gentle lapping of the water.

Lorraine realized her cheeks were sore from grinning. It was beautiful out here, and cool. And . . . *tranquil*—that was the word. As late night bled into early morning and the sky lightened overhead, she felt something she hadn't felt in ages. Peace. Contentment. It was all very strange.

Hank had left his blazer by the fence, and in the growing light she could see his muscles bulge under his thin chambray shirt. How had he gotten into such terrific shape? Lorraine had never seen a bartender who looked anything but unhealthy. She wondered whether the booze bottles were any heavier out in Los Angeles.

"What are you thinking about?" Hank asked, breaking the silence.

Lorraine laughed awkwardly. "Oh, just how beautiful it is out here." She leaned forward a little. "I've never done anything like this before."

"No? Manager of a speakeasy—I would've thought this would be a tame night for you."

"*Tame* would be a good word to describe my other nights," she replied. Then she realized how boring that made her sound. "Not that I don't do *anything,* of course. Just, you know, I don't usually steal boats . . . at five in the morning. But I should more often, because it's fun, really fun." Oh God, she sounded like a halfwit. Here she was feeling more . . . like a regular person, and she suddenly couldn't talk. What was wrong with her?

She pulled her flask out of her purse and screwed off the

top. Liquid courage was exactly what she needed. Before taking a sip, she offered the flask to Hank. "Toast to a successful caper?"

Hank shook his head. "No thanks. I try not to take my work home with me."

Lorraine laughed again. "Me neither!" she lied, leaning over the edge of the boat to pour the contents of her flask into the water. She tried not to grimace at the waste of good gin. "There," she said once it was all gone. "Some little fishies are gonna have a party!"

Hank gave a brief chuckle. "Too bad you don't have any lime to toss their way."

Lorraine's eyes brightened. "Lime, did you say?" She reached into her purse and pulled out half a lime she had wrapped up to take home with her.

Hank's jaw dropped. "Do you always keep lime in your purse?"

Lorraine shrugged and tipped an invisible hat. Then she squeezed the lime into the water. "Of course! In case a beautiful young man breaks into a boathouse for some late-night rowing, and then I offer him a drink but he refuses, and so I pour my liquor into the water."

Hank gave her a look that was difficult to describe, but she was sure the gist of it was: *I'm impressed by you, Lorraine.*

"Touché," he said. "You're a wonder."

Which was such a nice thing to hear that she just giggled in response.

"So tell me about yourself, Lorraine. When did you move to New York?"

She thought for a moment. It felt like a lifetime, but in truth— "It's been about a month or so."

"You're almost as new here as I am!" His face sobered. "So you got the job at the speakeasy pretty quickly, huh?"

Technically, she'd had the job long before she arrived in New York. "Yep."

"You know, you're way too young and beautiful to be running a second-rate gin joint like the Opera House. A sophisticated dame like you should be in college, or getting married, or having a swell time somewhere, not working in one of those seedy places."

The compliments were just too many and too perfect— it was too much fun, as if he'd been reading Lorraine's diary. "Beautiful," "sophisticated," "admired by everyone"—well, he still might say that last one.

Instead, he asked, "How did you get this job?" which wasn't any fun at all.

"Oh, I just kind of stumbled on it. I needed to do something with myself before I start college this fall at Barnard."

"You said you're from Chicago?"

She nodded. "I lived there my whole life. Went to a fancy bluenose school—such a stuffy old yawn—and did the whole debutante thing." She reached over the edge of the boat to skim her fingers through the water. "This one girl at school and I were best friends. But she literally stabbed me in the back."

His eyes widened. "Literally?"

"Well, not literally," she said. "Figuratively."

Hank relaxed. "What did she do?"

"She was supposed to marry this pompous blue blood. But she started sneaking out to speakeasies, got a gig as a singer, and had an affair with a black piano player. When her fiancé found out, he showed up and humiliated her and ran her out of the club. It was awful."

"That sounds rough."

"The worst part was that she blamed *me*. Gloria assumed *I* was the one who told Bastian." Lorraine stopped talking when she realized she'd been using Gloria's name. She was under strict orders from Carlito not to talk about Gloria, *ever*. Nor, for that matter, Bastian. Nor the Green Mill. But she was pretty sure Hank didn't count—what harm could he do to Carlito? He was just a bartender.

Hank reached out to touch her arm. An electric thrill ran up her spine. "That must have really hurt," he said. "That she could believe you'd do that to her after years of friendship."

Lorraine exhaled slowly, hoping he wouldn't take his hand away. "It did."

"What happened to Gloria?"

Lorraine knew she shouldn't say anything more. But it felt so nice that a man was finally showing some interest in her, not as a plaything, but as a person. When was the last time a man had done that?

So she just went for broke. Suddenly she was telling him

about Gloria's engagement party, how she had drunkenly exposed Clara.

Hank's eyes were melancholy by the time she finished. "Oh, Lorraine," he said softly. "I'm so sorry you had to go through all that."

How long had she been talking? She had no idea. The sun was already rising, and the sky had begun shading into a deep and luminous blue. Finally, after years of her being ignored, someone cared what Lorraine had to say. *Take that, Marcus Eastman!*

It was time to make a move. On an impulse, she stood and rubbed her arms. "*Brrr!* It's so chilly! Why don't I sit over there next to you?" She began to move to his end of the boat.

"No, sit back down!" he barked, alarm on his face. "You'll capsize the—"

As he spoke, the boat wobbled. Lorraine windmilled her arms, trying to regain her balance, but it was no use. She fell, sensing as the water closed above her that Hank was going over, too.

The water was cold—shockingly cold—and it ran up Lorraine's nose and into her mouth and tasted like a million unclean things that were all moldy and sitting in the bottom of a fish tank. Hank grabbed her arm underwater, and they both swam to the surface. In the cool air, they coughed and spluttered, and Hank said, "Well!" And then they were laughing.

For a moment, all they could do was cackle hysterically, out of breath and trying to keep afloat. Lorraine wiped water out of her eyes. If there had been any hope of saving her dress before, there certainly wasn't now.

"You are one wild girl," Hank said. His hair was matted to his forehead—Lorraine wanted to lean forward and push it back.

"Gracefulness was never really one of my strongest traits," she replied.

Hank swam to the capsized boat. "Help me flip it back over," he said.

Lorraine joined him, and they both pushed as hard as they could, but the boat only moved away from them.

Lorraine paddled around to the other side. "Maybe we'll have better luck over here!"

"Nah, this thing is never turning back over," Hank said. "I say we just get under it and swim it back to the boathouse upside down."

Lorraine nodded and ducked underwater, then resurfaced inside the shell of the overturned boat. With the sun rising, just enough light streamed in through the water of the lagoon that they could vaguely make one another out. But under the boat it was still quite dark, and almost quiet—she was reminded of what it felt like to hold a shell up to your ear so you could hear the ocean. Only, in this case, all she heard was her own breathing, and Hank's, and the lapping of the water.

Lorraine felt herself blush, and was grateful for the darkness. Surely whatever lipstick and rouge had survived her shift at the Opera House had washed off long ago. Her hair hung in limp ropes.

"You know, I thought you were pretty before, but wow . . . you're really beautiful. No makeup or fancy headdress— you're just who you are." Hank smiled. "Why would you ever want to hide that?"

Lorraine was mortified as she realized that tears were brimming in the corners of her eyes. She had always assumed that insults were the only way a man knew how to communicate his feelings. But here Hank was, being completely honest and sweet.

Hank swam closer. "You're not supposed to cry," he said.

Lorraine had kissed plenty of boys before, but when Hank touched his lips to hers, something about it felt brand-new.

CLARA

Clara concentrated on slathering butter onto her roll.

"Whoever this writer is, he is *eeeeeevil*," Leelee muttered, settling a cloth napkin over her ivory day dress.

Light streamed in through the nearby window, giving Leelee's dark bob golden-brown highlights. Chez Jacques, a cozy but *chic* French bistro on Spring Street, was always packed. The dark-blue-papered walls and jazz playing softly on the Gramophone even in the middle of the day gave the bistro an authentic Parisian atmosphere.

"Oh?" Clara said, leaning over to get a better look at the magazine spread out on the pale blue tablecloth. Leelee wasn't the only one in their lunch party with the most recent issue of the *Manhattanite*. Actually, Coco, Julia, and Nellie were *all* reading the second "Glittering Fools" column.

Everyone but Clara.

"How can they get away with printing trash like this?" Coco exclaimed.

"Isn't it true?" Clara asked.

Coco scowled. "That doesn't mean someone should write about it!"

Clara had to admit it: She was proud to be a part of the *Manhattanite*. The magazine was glossy and smart, and everyone in town was reading it. But even though she was dying to tell them that she was writing for the magazine, she knew better: It was more important than ever to keep her secret, especially now that people were reading and discussing—and outraged by—her columns.

Leelee's plump pink lips turned downward. "He says Edie Burrows's feathered headdress was so enormous that he's 'surprised it didn't jump off her head and fly through an open window.' I thought Edie looked *adorable*."

"She looked like a *crazy* person, Lee," Coco said. The other girls giggled in agreement. "That's one thing the reporter got right. And no way is this writer a man."

"It says *Anonymous,*" Leelee replied, pouting. "How do you know it's a woman?"

"A man wouldn't have such an eye for fashion. And a man could never be so vicious," Nellie said, tucking her curly light-brown hair behind her ear. "This is one cold, calculating bitch."

Nellie Abrams had been one of Clara's favorite old New

York friends—she'd always been willing to say what everyone else was thinking. Nellie wasn't bone-thin like the rest of the girls at the table. She had plentiful curves, which she showed off with the scooped neck of her ruffled peach blouse and a short skirt. Though she wasn't glamorous like Coco or a beauty like Leelee, she had a charisma that was undeniable.

Julia Spence squeezed lemon juice into her glass of water. "Maxie's going to be sore over the way she made fun of him."

At Maxie Gabel's eighteenth birthday party (had it only been two weeks ago?), Clara had given Arthur Spence her phone number. The next day, his older sister, Julia, had called up, eager to reminisce. Clara had always adored the exquisitely pretty redhead.

"I don't even know how the writer saw that!" Coco said. "It was hilarious!"

"Saw what?" Clara asked, knowing full well what the answer would be.

"Apparently," Julia said, "Maxie's mother sews his initials into his underwear. Sounds like the party was oodles of fun."

Coco flipped ash off the end of her cigarette. "It was. But whoever Anonymous is, she makes it sound like all the girls there were too scared to do anything interesting. Until Arthur swanned in and saved the day."

"But isn't that true?" Clara asked. "We were about to leave when he showed up."

"People *know* I was at that party," Coco lamented. "This

column doesn't exactly make any of us there sound . . . you know. Bold. Daring. Lively."

Nellie continued to flick through the pages. "I feel the same way, darling. And what about her snarky mention of the fire Robert Eames set on the balcony at the Webster Hall Garden Party? How did she even know about that?"

Julia tapped her finger on the column. "This girl has to be someone we know."

Clara gave a tiny cough and said, "All I know is that this Anonymous has a real stick up her butt, don't you think? She needs to loosen up and have some fun. What a dumb Dora."

The waiter served their food. Once he was out of earshot, Nellie picked up again. "Lizzy Banks has always hated me, *and* she writes all those stupid short stories. It might be her."

"Wasn't there one with a talking bear?" Coco asked, and she, Nellie, and Clara all laughed.

"A talking bear?" Leelee asked, confused. "That doesn't seem possible. Bears can't talk!" She turned to Nellie and lowered her voice to a whisper. "Can they?"

Nellie ignored the question and turned to Clara. "Lizzy has always liked you. I don't think she ever would've called you"—she paused for a moment, searching through the column—"'. . . spoiled goods that should have been pulled from the shelf ages ago.'" Nellie reached over to grip Clara's hand. "Doesn't that bother you?"

"Talking bears!" Leelee said as she dug into her *salade niçoise*. "Ha!"

The rest of the girls stared at Clara, waiting for her to respond.

Clara merely shrugged. She was glad she'd been smart enough to trash herself in the article and make it seem less likely that she was the author. "At least she's writing about me," Clara said. "The only thing worse than being made fun of is getting no mention whatsoever."

Really, Clara was doing her friends a favor: making them the talk of the town. Any publicity was good publicity.

"I don't know, Clarabella," Coco said. "If it were me and I ever found out who wrote this, I'd put her eyes out with a hairpin."

Leelee abruptly closed the magazine. "So, is everyone enjoying their food?" she asked, her voice oddly high-pitched.

Coco narrowed her eyes. "What is it, Lee?"

Leelee looked from one to the other of the girls, then turned to Clara. "Well, this terrible Anonymous person says Quentin Harkington—"

"Ugh, what a brownnoser," Coco said, groaning across the table.

"He is," Leelee agreed. "Anyway, he's throwing a birthday party for Twiggy Sampson tonight at the Waldorf."

"I know all about it," Clara replied. "Quentin's brother Blake told me about it at the garden party." This, of course, was how the upcoming event had made it into the article in the first place.

Julia nodded. "I'm going with Maxie, Arthur, and Sally. You're all welcome to join us, of course, and I would've invited you sooner, but . . ." She glanced over at Clara. "I assumed you wouldn't want to go."

Clara gave a tight-lipped smile. That would make sense—apparently, Harris Brown (Clara's ex-whatever-you-call-it) had taken up with Twiggy soon after he had tried—and failed—to get Clara back to Chicago.

But Clara *did* want to go: How else would she get material for her column?

Only, she'd be going without a date. Marcus would never understand.

"I already know about Harris and Twiggy," Clara answered softly. "It's fine with me. Really." She waved her hand. "Ladies, I'm in love! With Marcus Eastman. Harris is free to carouse with whichever roundheels he wants. And Twiggy, I hear, is a total lollipop—all sugary sweet and nothing of substance. Besides, this is supposed to be a *fabulous* party. I hear Dorothy Parker will be there."

Coco clapped. "Dorothy Parker! Well, hot damn." Coco had been completely addicted to Parker's dry wit in her old *Vanity Fair* articles, before she'd been so unjustly terminated ("for being too bitingly brilliant," as Coco liked to say).

"When are you going to bring this Marcus around for us to meet?" Leelee asked curiously. "We promise not to steal him away."

Clara said, "Oh, you'll meet him soon," but she felt more than a twinge of guilt.

My old flapper ways are gone, she had promised Marcus, but already they were returning, weren't they?

That afternoon, Clara gazed out at the East River from a bench on the Brooklyn Bridge and ate chocolate ice cream. "So, how was your day?"

Marcus shrugged, taking a lick of his vanilla cone. His gray vest gave his blue eyes a stormy look. "Dandy, I suppose. Just went shopping with Charles Drakeman. He bought a new racket, but I couldn't find one I liked."

"He leaves tomorrow, right?" Clara asked. "I'm sorry I never got a chance to meet him."

Marcus grinned. "Oh, no need to be sorry: you're *going* to meet him. *Then* you can be sorry." He rummaged around in his trouser pocket and pulled out a ticket. "There's an exhibition opening at the Met tonight. It's all about Crusaders' helmets or britches or gauntlets or something like that. The art will be steely and boring, but the food should be fantastic."

"I can't," Clara said. "I already made plans for tonight."

"Plans? With whom? Who are these mysterious figures who fill your hours? I'm not normally the suspicious sort, but I'm starting to feel as if I should be."

It was true: She'd seen less and less of Marcus the more work she did for the *Manhattanite*. They'd shared a few intimate dinners, and they'd gone to see *A Woman of Paris,* a Charlie Chaplin movie that had been marvelous, but every time Marcus had wanted to come back to her apartment, Clara had made up excuses rather than reveal the truth: She needed to work on her column. She was finally successful.

People were talking about her writing, and nothing—not even Marcus's kisses—had ever felt so good.

"It's no one, really," she said now.

"What can be better than Crusaders' steel underwear? What marvelous alternative is luring you away? Maybe I'll drag Drakeman to that, and we can all have fun."

"I'm afraid you can't," Clara said. "I have to go alone."

"Mysteriouser and mysteriouser." Marcus's lips turned up a little at the corners. "You didn't get a job singing with a black band, did you? Because that is *so* last year."

Clara laughed longer than the joke about Gloria warranted. "No, no . . . it's just that I've been working on a little project. I want to try to get a story published in the *Manhattanite*. I've been doing research into the city's red-light districts and the plight of the working girl. I thought a hard-hitting story like that might have a shot at getting the editor's attention."

Marcus stared at her as if she were speaking a foreign language.

Clara took his hand. "I know that sounds sordid and secretive, but I didn't want to worry you."

"Of course I'd worry. Prostitutes run with a violent crowd."

"But I don't need to worry! An old friend from my flapper days has an older brother who's a cop, and he accompanies me on my research. He knows all the right women to talk to, and he makes sure I'm safe."

How easy it was to lie.

Marcus stared deep into her eyes for a moment, then gazed down at the wooden bench. She prayed that he believed her. If he approved of her writing articles like this, it would make it easier for her to eventually tell him the truth about her flapper column.

After a moment, she saw that he looked relieved. "I can't say I like it that you're spending so much time with another man. Nor with loose women." He made a face. "But I have to admit it: I'm proud of you. You're a crusader yourself—just like Lewis Hine. Only a woman has the means of really exposing the sordid underbelly of prostitution in the city. I'm just proud that I'm the lucky fellow who is dating such a forward-thinking woman."

Clara suddenly felt like a fraud. "You make me sound like a saint. But I'm doing this for myself, let's not forget!"

He laughed. "Of course, but still: It's a noble cause. And I had no idea you were so interested in writing!"

"It's kind of a recent interest, but yes." She gave him a small smile. "I think it's what I'm supposed to do."

He settled back against the bench. "They'll eat this sort of thing up at Barnard. You can use this article to get into an advanced journalism class. You'll probably arrive on campus a crusading celebrity!"

"Mmm-hmm." She leaned her head on his shoulder and stared blindly at the water. She doubted her actual *Manhattanite* columns were the sort of thing Barnard would approve of.

"I really am relieved," Marcus said. "I was worried."

"Worried?" Clara asked. "About what?"

"About us," Marcus said quietly. "What else? I've already lost Gloria, who was like my kid sister. I couldn't bear losing you, too."

He turned his head then, and the sunlight glinted off his burnished hair. This was the boy who had convinced her that not all men would stomp on her heart. The boy who'd brought her back to New York in the first place. And how did she repay him? With lies and deception.

She made up her mind to tell him the entire truth soon. As long as she made it clear that she wasn't falling back into her old life, and that all this really was just for a magazine, he would understand.

Wouldn't he?

◆ ◆ ◆

The sparkling teenagers shuffled through the crowd of people waiting to get in. "Make way! Make way!" Arthur cried, and Clara had to laugh at the haste with which people scurried to move aside. It was as though one of them were a film star. Both Leelee and Julia were certainly pretty enough: Leelee a shimmering sylph in white, and Julia snake-hipped and slinky in venomous green silk.

"Clara, my dear," Arthur said, "your public awaits."

For this party, Clara had pulled out all the stops. She looked good tonight. Better than good: She was a knockout.

Her dress was a rich depthless blue that fell in sheer over-lapping layers down to her knees. Pearls wound around her neck in so many loops that they were hard to count, and teardrop pearls hung from her ears. A pair of pearl-colored Mary Janes and a black feather boa completed the ensemble. She looked dark and dangerous and sexy.

Their group passed under the gaudy glitter of the chandeliers in the lobby and packed themselves into one of the elevators. "Make room! Make room!" Arthur cried, shoving himself against everyone and making a nuisance.

"You're not *that* fat," Maxie said, trying hard not to laugh.

"No, but my ego is *gigantic,*" Arthur said.

Clara's friends had finished the contents of Arthur's flask and were starting on Coco's by the time they reached the top floor. The operator dragged the doors open.

This was the kind of party Clara remembered.

There was so much light and laughter and motion that she didn't know where to look. The ballroom seethed with glittering bodies—flappers in their bejeweled best, dancing with young men in white tie, and around the dance floor, men and women squashed tightly into red velvet booths, talking and gesturing and guffawing. At the head of the room, an all-black band in white suits played hot jazz on a tiny stage. Cigarette smoke wafted around the chandeliers and curled against the tall windows.

And there, toward the back—a champagne fountain! Clara grabbed flutes and filled them from the bronze basin.

Then it was onto the dance floor. As they'd arrived, the

band had just swung into "The Black Bottom Stomp." The crowd cheered. Clara raised the hem of her skirt with one hand and held her other arm out, then began to stomp her feet and swing her hips. She could feel herself glowing with frantic energy.

Arthur grabbed her hand, spinning her into his arms and back out again. "You have just the right amount of jump to your jive!"

"Horsefeathers!" Clara exclaimed.

After she'd had one more dance with Arthur, everyone lined up to knock back shots of whiskey at the bar.

"I think I'm okay," Clara said, pushing away the small glass teeming with amber liquid.

Her friends all stared in dismay. "But we're doing it together!" Leelee cried. "All for one and all for . . . wait . . . You know what I mean."

Clara groaned, picked up the shot glass, and drained it.

After another dance, she made her way to the edge of the crowd and leaned against a window. She studied the party-goers, taking notes in her head. The champagne fountain and a brief sighting of Dorothy Parker would make nice details in her column. But Clara hadn't found her column's heart yet.

Behind her, Arthur cleared his throat. He stood with Maxie, Leelee, and Coco, and they each wore the same conspiratorial smile. "Clara, we have something we'd like to show you," Arthur said.

Her friends pulled her to the stairwell, down one floor, and into a corridor lined with hotel rooms. Dozens of party guests crowded the hallway.

"I was asking my friend Jeremy where they got the sensational gin at this party," Arthur explained. "And he told me that they made the gin in this very hotel!"

They had at last reached a particularly large group outside an open door. Arthur extended his arm. "See for yourself."

Inching forward, Clara could see into an elegant hotel room and its adjoining bathroom. A white marble counter, a lightbulb-ringed mirror, fluffy white towels like clouds draped over a silver towel rack. And then there was the main attraction—the large, claw-footed bathtub, filled to the brim with what looked like water.

A long line of formally dressed guests, each with a bottle, flask, or cup in hand, approached the tub one by one. There two tuxedoed men standing beside the tub dipped the containers into the clear liquid and handed them back.

Suddenly Clara was being lifted into the air by Arthur and Maxie and carried forward.

She was somewhere between screaming and laughing when the boys dunked her. She coughed hard and thrashed and got to her feet. She tried to breathe out, and gin leaked from her nose. Disgusting. The gin might have looked like water, but it certainly didn't feel like it—the liquid left a slick film over her entire body. And the gin was *freezing*.

"Good lord," one of the servers said. "Not *again*."

"Classy move," Clara said to her friends, stepping out. She tugged wet strands of hair out of her face and pulled her headband farther down over her forehead. "I will *kill* you all for this," she said in a low voice, though she couldn't help grinning.

It would certainly make for a great story.

◆ ◆ ◆

Ten minutes later, Clara walked back into the ballroom in bare feet, an enormous fluffy white towel wrapped around her. She was still wearing her pearl necklace and headband. Her towel-dress invited questions, and soon Arthur's prank was the talk of the party.

"I saw that dress you had on," one girl said. "Was it ruined?"

Clara trilled out a showy laugh. "Arthur promised to buy me a new one!"

Clara had found long ago that embarrassing situations could be spun into gold with the right attitude. A dapper young man strolled up, praised her new dress as even better than the last, and offered to get her a whiskey and soda to even out the gin. She didn't refuse. Before she knew it, one whiskey soda turned into two. Then she just stopped counting.

And then a familiar voice whispered into her ear, "I should have known you'd be the one swimming in gin."

Clara turned and saw the Cad himself.

Harris looked as polished as ever in his tailcoat and blue silk tie. He'd been little more than a boy during their love affair, but now his face had thinned out a bit. His cocky smile and the devilish glint in his dark sapphire eyes were the same as ever.

Clara was mortified.

Had she run into Harris half an hour earlier, she would have looked stunning and completely put together. But now?

In a split second, however, she made the decision not to be embarrassed. Not in front of Harris. She broke out her brightest grin. "I was looking for a regular bath, but all the tubs were filled with alcohol. Sometimes a girl has to make do."

Harris laughed—a jolly, bubbling noise that Clara had once adored. He stepped closer. "You've got a lot of nerve showing up here after sending me packing like that back in Chi-town." He moved so close that they were practically touching.

To get away from him, Clara would have to barrel through a wall of people or climb over a couple of chairs— risky maneuvers for a girl in a towel.

She looked around. "Where is the birthday girl, anyway?"

Harris pointed to the dance floor. An admittedly very pretty blonde in a low-cut black dress was dancing to a hopping tune. "Good, isn't she? Twiggy dances with the Follies."

"How nice for you. I mean, for her. Now, if you'll excuse me—"

"Clarabella," he said, his fingers trailing down her bare arm. "Why are you still fighting me? I'm free now to do what I want, and you're finally back where you belong. Why don't we go back to the way things were?"

Clara just smiled grimly and said nothing.

Harris looked toward the front entrance to the ballroom. "Where is that Ivy League twit, anyway? The one who was trailing after you in Chicago like a puppy?"

"Oh," Clara said. The large amount of booze in her system had her a little at a loss for words. She stared up into Harris's bottomless blue eyes. Suddenly—and inexplicably—she found it impossible to talk about Marcus, to say that she was dating someone. She wanted, just for a second, to let Harris think she was still available.

"That's over," she said quickly.

"Is that so?" Harris asked. He took her chin in his hand and tilted her face to one side. "Then why is he standing right behind you looking so blue?"

She spun and saw Marcus standing near the entrance. He was still wearing the tux he must've worn to the Met exhibition, and he looked gorgeous, even with the crestfallen expression on his face.

Then all Clara could see was his back, moving away.

"Marcus!" she called, cinching the towel tighter and shoving Harris aside. But when she emerged into the hallway, Marcus was gone.

VERA

Vera looked over the directions to Connie's Inn one more time.

She had allowed Gloria to slip through her fingers not once but twice.

She doubted she'd get a third chance.

She adjusted the belt of her off-white dress as she walked. It was simple, but its dropped waist and pleated skirt flattered her slim figure. Evan had given her some cash to buy it. She didn't like that. Yes, she needed to spend her time finding her brother, not waitressing or dancing in a chorus, but she didn't want to start depending on Evan too much.

It would have been one thing if Evan had been her husband, or even her boyfriend . . .

When Evan had put together that picnic in Central Park, Vera had thought he'd done it because he liked her. *Liked her* liked her. And then he'd talked about her to the guys at the Cotton Club as if she were his girl.

So why didn't he act like it?

He hadn't so much as held her hand since that afternoon in the park, and they hadn't gone on any more "not-date" dates. Vera should have been thankful for that—the last thing she needed was the drama of dating the only friend she had in this city.

But she wasn't grateful at all.

Because she'd realized that she *definitely* liked him.

What girl wouldn't? Vera had never really cared about jazz until she'd heard the gorgeous, mournful tones Evan could tease out of his trumpet. He was talented, handsome, *and* sweet. Maybe now that he was working at the top night-club in the city, he had started to realize how far out of Vera's league he truly was.

She wasn't good enough for him.

◆ ◆ ◆

When she arrived under the narrow black awning of Connie's Inn, she found a line of men and women that snaked down the front stairs to the door of the club. She nudged a tall man with a mustache. "What's the rumpus?"

"They're auditioning today. Are you a dancer?" the man

replied. He looked Vera up and down. "You look like a dancer."

Vera thought fast. "Yep. Do you know where I should check in?"

"You don't need to check in—as long as you've got an audition time, you'll be fine."

"Yeah, but I actually forgot if my audition is at three or three-thirty, so I really need to check."

"Go ask Frank. You can't miss him—big guy with the clipboard."

The door at the foot of the steps was propped open with a slab of wood. The club didn't look so ritzy in the daytime. Chairs were stacked on top of the round tables, and the tables had been pushed against the walls. Vera followed the line of hopefuls all the way through the room, past the pillars at each corner of the dance floor. There a man dressed all in black was teaching a group of scantily clad women some steps on the gleaming, brightly lit wood.

To the right, a muscled white man in a fedora and suspendered trousers checked off items on a clipboard. Frank.

"Excuse me?" Vera asked in her sweetest voice. "I was wondering if a piano player by the name of Jerome Johnson was hired recently."

Frank looked up from his clipboard, startled. "Jerome Johnson? No, he hasn't been here yet."

"Yet?" Vera asked.

"No one by that name has come by." Frank gave her a dead-eyed stare. "What's it to you?"

"I just thought that maybe—" Vera began, her voice cracking a little.

She jumped when she felt a hand touch her shoulder. She turned and saw Evan. He was dressed casually in tan trousers, a white shirt, and a tan blazer, the brim of his brown derby tilted back. She'd forgotten that they'd agreed to meet here after he finished rehearsing at the Cotton Club for the day.

He glanced around the club. "I take it you're not having any luck?"

"No—Jerome never auditioned here."

The trumpet player who'd just finished his audition walked over. "I can't believe it—Evan Montgomery? What are you doing in New York? I thought you were sticking around the Windy City for good!"

Evan shook the older man's hand. "It's a long story, Mike." He looked at Vera. "Vera, this is—"

"Evan Montgomery?" Frank interrupted. "You had a slot for ten a.m. but you never showed."

Evan backed up. "I haven't got the slightest idea what you're talking about. I've already got a gig."

Vera's eyes widened. "What instrument is listed for Evan's audition?"

Frank glanced at his clipboard. "Piano. We're looking for a piano player."

Evan had to be realizing the same thing as Vera: Jerome *had* stopped by Connie's Inn—and had used Evan's name to book an audition. He'd probably used fake names at all of his auditions, which was why it had been so tough to track him down. But he had never shown up. Why?

And then Frank supplied the answer: "I'm not the only one who missed you, neither. There were two scary-looking jamokes asking after you. After a few hours they finally gave up and skedaddled."

So not only was Jerome using fake names, but the Mob was on to his ruse. No wonder he'd never shown up.

Frank glanced at Evan once more. "So let me get this straight: You're Evan Montgomery, but you're not *this* Evan Montgomery?"

"Exactly," Evan said. "That's someone who's been using my name, who we're trying to find."

Frank patted his pockets. "You know, why don't I go on in back and get the audition form the other Evan filled out, and you can tell me who it is if it ain't you."

"That would be wonderful!" Vera said. "The audition form probably has Jerome's address!"

"No problem. But why don't you two wait outside? We're trying to run an audition here. I'll send someone to get you after I've found the paperwork."

"Sounds like a plan," Evan said. "I could use a smoke." He gave Vera a quick hug and her stomach flip-flopped. "I told you we'd find him," he whispered.

As he went out to the street, Vera said, "I have one more favor to ask."

Frank scowled. "What now?"

"May I use your powder room?"

Frank burst into laughter. "Sure thing. There's one back-stage there." He pointed, then shuffled into the office.

◆ ◆ ◆

The restroom was so tiny that Vera's knees banged the back of the door when she sat. But what did it matter? Using the splintered mirror over the dinky sink, she touched up her lipstick and grinned: In just a few short minutes, she would have Jerome's address.

She would be able to see her big brother, to embrace him. To talk to him again after months of silence. To warn him that someone was coming after him.

When she walked out, Frank was still in the office. She listened to a woman sing an off-key rendition of "After You've Gone," and finally Frank returned. He was mopping at his head with a handkerchief.

"Yeah," he said, distracted, "there wasn't much on the form. But here it is." He handed her a sealed envelope.

"Thank you!" Vera said, and she stood on tiptoe to kiss him on the cheek.

He waved her away. "Oh, go on."

Outside, she found the line of performers still there and a few men lounging against the front of the building, smok-ing. But Evan wasn't one of them.

On the sidewalk in front of the club an almost-whole cigarette lay smoldering on the ground. Next to it was Evan's brown derby.

Where would he have gone without her? Without his *hat*?

Vera snatched Evan's hat off the ground and whipped around to face the line of people. "Does anyone know what happened to the man who was wearing this hat?"

No one said a word.

"Oh my God," Vera said, leaning against one of the awning's posts for support. A few people glanced her way, but they didn't stay interested for long. Girls probably acted crazy all the time at these auditions. She couldn't stop herself from quietly weeping.

After ten minutes had passed and there was still no sign of Evan, she suddenly knew: The Mob had kidnapped him. Maybe the two guys Frank had mentioned had stuck around, waiting. And then when Evan had come out and fit Jerome's description . . .

If anyone was going to be kidnapped, it should've been Vera. Evan didn't have anything to do with any of this. He was just a sweet boy who had the misfortune to be friends with someone like her—a girl who brought harm to everyone she cared about.

A woman came and gave Vera's back a few awkward pats. "You all right? I'm Molly."

"Vera," she said. The girl was stunning, with light brown skin and glossy black curls. She was probably just about Vera's age, seventeen or so.

Molly lowered her voice. "A couple of hard-boiled Brunos took him for a ride in a black Packard. One of 'em showed us his gun and told us to mind our potatoes. Said if we was wise, none of us were seeing anything."

Vera almost stopped breathing. "Oh no."

"Yeah, it was kind of scary. And before that happened? The younger one was working me like a drugstore cowboy, trying to get a date. Like I'm going to go meet him at the Ritz-Carlton now."

"The Ritz-Carlton?"

"Yeah. Promised me a fancy dinner. 'I always sup at six,' he said. 'Sup'—what kind of palooka says that?"

Vera wiped the tears from her cheeks. "Only the worst sort."

Molly shrugged. "I thought about going—it *is* the Ritz—but my boyfriend might not have liked it."

"Probably not," Vera said. "But I could go in your place."

"Ha," Molly said. "Serve him right! But you'd better bring some muscle—those guys weren't kidding around."

Vera clutched her handbag close and hurried away. She had just enough time to get back to the boardinghouse, pick up something she'd hidden in the space behind the bottommost dresser drawer, and get to the Ritz before six.

She was glad she'd never gotten rid of Bastian's pistol.

Tonight she might have to use it.

18

GLORIA

Gloria was alone.

She sat at the piano in the apartment, trying to pick out the tune of "St. Louis Blues."

It was well past one in the morning. She hadn't seen Jerome since rehearsal at the Opera House hours ago. Staying out late was how he avoided having to talk to her. They were like two ships passing in the night. They barely spoke. They never touched. And a kiss was out of the question.

Gloria had spent the past week feeling absolutely awful. She wanted to tell Jerome how sorry she was, that the worst day with him was better than the best day without him.

But Jerome didn't make apologizing easy.

Her head jerked up when she heard the key in the lock. She mustered a smile and said, "Hi!"

Jerome hung his hat on the hook and removed his suit

jacket, sat heavily in one of the chairs, and started untying his shoelaces.

"Are you hungry? I could make you a sandwich or something."

Jerome shook his head. He rose from his chair, picked up his shoes, and walked into the bedroom. Gloria slammed the lid on the piano and followed. He was changing into his blue pajamas. One look at his muscular arms reminded Gloria how much she missed the feel of them around her. "I was hoping we could talk," she said quietly.

Jerome sat on the bed, his gaze dark and cold. "It's late," he said, and lay back against the pillows.

"I just wanted to say—" Gloria began, but Jerome rolled toward the wall.

"I'm tired," he said.

"Fine—go to sleep." Gloria stripped down to her slip, turned off the light, and slid into bed. It was strange sleeping next to Jerome while they were in this rut. She wanted more than anything to lean over, to grab him, to break down this invisible wall between them. But she was scared he would pull even farther away.

When his breathing became even, she rolled over and looked at him. There was a full moon outside the blinds, and the silvery light fell softly on his relaxed face. When he was asleep, all his anger was gone. He was again the young man she'd fallen in love with, who she knew deep down loved her, too.

Tomorrow. Tomorrow she would wake up early before

he left for the day, and she would find the words to fix this. But for now she would have to will herself to sleep. For there was nothing worse than being in a bed with someone who had his back turned to you, who didn't want to hold you. It was worse than being in bed alone—a reminder of everything you once had, all that you could lose forever.

◆ ◆ ◆

Gloria was quiet when she unlocked the door the next morning. She had woken earlier than usual to gather ingredients to make an apology breakfast. Who could say no to pancakes and fresh coffee?

Jerome had still been asleep when she'd left, and now she put the groceries down on the kitchen table and slipped off her jacket and her oversized hat. Gathering everything she needed had taken longer than expected—who knew grocery stores were so busy in the morning?—but she was ready to get to work.

Immediately, she could see that something was wrong. Piles of sheet music were missing. And there was no sign of Jerome's clothing from the night before, either.

Jerome was gone.

Not only was he gone, but a quick glance through the dresser and closet revealed that he'd taken most of his clothing.

Dizzy, Gloria gripped the bedpost for a moment to catch her breath, but her heart continued to hammer in her chest.

It didn't take her long to find the note. It was wrapped around a stack of bills.

Glo—

I found a room at a boardinghouse. There should be enough money here for you to get a room someplace. A few of my buddies will be by later to move the piano and get my stuff.

We knew going into this that the relationship would be hard, but I guess it was just too hard for both of us. We can still work together—we both need the money—but I think we should take a break from everything else for now.

I'm sorry.

Jerome

After she'd read it through a second time, her hand almost involuntarily crumpled the note into a ball. How could Jerome do this? After he'd given her that speech about how he'd spent his life fighting for what he wanted? He was supposed to *love* her.

She would never have *abandoned* him—certainly not in a city where he didn't know anyone. So like a musician. All long notes and love songs, but those pretty words and melodies disappeared when times got tough. He'd sneaked out while she was gone. Like a coward.

Well. Gloria would be tough enough for both of them.

She suddenly wished she could talk to Clara. And Marcus—had he moved to the city yet? And Lorraine would've known what to do—she was always so independent. But no—Lorraine would have lied and cheated her way out of trouble. Gloria was at a low point, but she was still better than Lorraine.

Gloria wiped the tears from her cheeks, opened one of the coffees she'd brought back, and walked into the bedroom. In the top drawer of the dresser, beneath her stockings and brassieres, was the LOST GIRL flyer. She unfolded it, flipped it over, and with a pen wrote:

Here I am—Gloria. What do you want?
161 East 110th Street, 4D

Then she folded the flyer, slid it into an envelope, and affixed a stamp to the corner. She wrote *Post Office Box 171* in a clear script across the front and tucked it into her shoulder bag.

She knew this was risky, but she didn't care. She had nothing to lose. Carlito might be behind the flyers, but it might be someone else entirely—a friend, maybe. She had to risk letting Carlito know where she was hiding, just in case he wasn't the person putting up the flyers.

She'd mail the letter, and whatever happened next was out of her hands. She would break the most important rule Jerome had set out for them when they'd arrived in New

19

LORRAINE

Lorraine felt pretty. Desired. Happy.

Finally.

Hank eyed the open crates that filled the office. "Wouldn't it make more sense to do this behind the bar?" Bottles of vodka were arranged in rows on the floor. The usual shipment had just come in, and Lorraine had offered to help Hank count out the inventory.

"It's a privilege to spend time with the manager. You should be grateful!" Lorraine giggled—she found herself giggling all the time now for no reason other than that she was with Hank.

A groan came from behind the desk. Spark lowered his newspaper. "Could you two pipe down? I'm trying to do the crossword here." He coughed.

So Hank technically *could* have counted these bottles by

himself. And it *did* make more sense for him to do it behind the bar. But ever since he'd kissed her in Central Park, being in a room that didn't have Hank in it had become pretty much impossible. Lorraine had to be where Hank was, and she couldn't be out in the bar right now: Gloria was rehearsing.

Lorraine had been so afraid Hank would be like other boys. They always made excuses the day after late-night necking sessions: They'd been drunk! They'd been bored! They'd been out of their minds! Or worst of all, they ignored Lorraine completely.

But the morning after her kiss with Hank, he'd shown up at her door with coffee and croissants. Since that night in Central Park, he'd called her honey four times and darling twice.

Lorraine was longing to ask him if they were officially going together. But this was the closest thing to a real relationship she'd ever had. She wasn't about to screw it up by actually *calling* it a relationship.

Spark folded the newspaper, stood up, and stretched. "I should go check up on our new piano player. Make sure he's working well with the band."

Lorraine's head jerked toward Spark. "Wait—*what?* You never even told me you fired Felix!"

Spark made a great show of rolling his eyes. "You *told* me to. I asked the new singer, and she suggested this black kid she'd worked with, Jerome. I hired him a few days ago—a week, maybe."

Jerome had been at the Opera House for an entire week—and Lorraine hadn't sent word to Carlito! "Since when do you hire *anyone* without consulting me first?" she asked. "I'm your boss! I can make or break you, Spark!"

Hank cleared his throat and said, "Sixteen, seventeen, eighteen bottles of vodka."

"I mean . . . never mind about the making or breaking stuff. Obviously, I would never hurt you, you're very dear to me. Like my own child—except you're older than me, and . . . well, you know what I mean. I just like to be *informed,* you know?"

"Well, geez, *boss,*" Spark said. "You always scram when the band practices. Figured you didn't care."

Lorraine peeked out the window to the barroom. Sure enough, there was Jerome, pounding out scales on the piano. She couldn't see him all that well through the two-way mirror, but she would have recognized him anywhere—by the sure way his long fingers skimmed over the keys, if nothing else.

And there was Gloria on the other side of the stage, shuffling through sheet music and talking to Bernie, the trumpet player. "We have to send a wire, pronto," Lorraine said.

Spark sighed heavily but turned back to the desk. He picked up the pad of telegram forms and a pen, then looked at her. "All right, shoot."

"Uh, it should say 'I hired him.' Scratch that. How about 'A second bird is in the cage'?" No, that still wasn't much of a code. "I've got it. It should read, 'The canary has found a blackbird . . . to play the piano.'"

Spark looked up from the pad. "Are you opening some kind of bird shop on the side or somethin'?"

"Just get someone to take the telegram over to Western Union," Lorraine snapped. "And do it yesterday."

"All right, crazy lady, I'll go get Joe to do it."

After Spark had shut the door behind him, Hank looked at her, concern obvious in his eyes. They were brown like hot cocoa, which made Lorraine think about being warm in front of a fire with him, maybe with a blanket wrapped around them. It would be the dead of winter, and they would have been dating for months while she attended Barnard, and she would say witty things to Hank about Descartes and Plato, and Hank would laugh and start unbuttoning her blouse, and wasn't that what life was all about? Wasn't it?

"Lorraine?" Hank asked. "Is something wrong?"

Lorraine sighed. How to begin to explain this stuff to him? She didn't want her dealings with the Mob to scare him away. She just wanted to kiss him some more. And maybe bring him to a party at Columbia in the fall so that she could show him off in front of Marcus Eastman. "No, it's just—" she was beginning, when the door swung open.

It was Puccini. "Hi there, Raine," he said in his eerily jolly tone. "Why don't I come in?"

"I, uh— Of course, come in." She hated how unnerved she sounded.

Puccini stepped into the office. He wore a green, oddly shiny suit and a striped tie. His fat fingers clutched the edges of a glass jar filled with chocolate bears. He always bit the little bear heads off first. "You want one? The dark chocolate ones are my personal favorite."

"No, thank you."

"What's wrong, doll face?" Puccini asked. "You seem surprised to see me."

"I'm just not used to seeing you here during the day." The owner rarely arrived at the speakeasy earlier than eight. Lorraine liked it better when Puccini was somewhere else, doing whatever it was he did: hurting people, she supposed, if not killing them. He was a gangster, after all.

"Yes, well, I came in today—earlier than usual—especially to have a little chat with *you,*" Puccini replied. And then he smiled.

Oh God, it was creepy. Lorraine knew that smiles were supposed to be reassuring, but a smile from Puccini made her think of a cat sizing up a wounded bird. "That's just," she said, "great."

Hank was suddenly completely focused on his bottle-counting, as though "One bottle, two bottles, three bottles" took every ounce of brainpower he had.

"Carlito is in New York," Puccini said in a low voice. "Have you heard from him?"

Lorraine nodded, even though she'd had no idea Carlito was here. But somehow, things had all worked out. Her job was done—she'd hired Gloria and Jerome, gotten them into

the club at the same time. And now Carlito was here. *Phew!*
"I know," she replied. "I won't be working here too much
longer—not now that Carlito is in town."

Puccini's grin transformed itself into a scowl. "I don't
know what made that punk kid think you'd be a good manager. Look at this! What are you thinkin', unloading the
shipment in the office?"

"Sorry, boss," Lorraine said, her voice cracking. "We
didn't unload by the bar because, uh, the light's better in here
and I thought we could read the labels better, avoid another
whiskey sour incident."

Puccini stared at her. "Fair enough. But hurry it up. You
know what happens at the end of an opera, right?"

Lorraine smiled a little. Freedom from this place was so
close she could taste it. "The diva gets a standing ovation?"
she said with a nervous laugh.

Puccini didn't smile back. "No. She dies."

Lorraine put her hand to her chest. "Am *I* the diva?"

He nodded. "So let's make sure this isn't an opera. You
understand?"

"Perfectly, I understand perfectly."

He patted her arm. "Now there's a doll." He looked
around at the crates and picked up his jar of chocolate bears.
Then he walked out, humming a classical tune in a deep
baritone.

Lorraine slumped against the desk, breathing hard. She
jumped when Hank put his hand on her shoulder. "Raine,
are you okay?"

"Sure! I'm fine! Totally fine!" she replied. After all, Puccini's threat would never come close to becoming a reality. She had Gloria and Jerome right out there in the barroom, and it wouldn't be too long before Carlito was on his way.

Hank looked at the closed door. "I didn't realize Puccini was such a monster. Why do you work for a man like that?"

"Hank, you don't understand. I have to."

"You don't have to do anything you don't want to, Lorraine."

She let out a harsh laugh. "Oh yeah? Who'll protect me? My invisible white knight in shining armor?"

Hank laid his large hand over hers. "*I'll* protect you."

Lorraine looked down at the scarred desk top, lost in the tingly feelings of his touch. "Okay, well, if we're done counting these," she said at last, clearing her throat, "we can leave the ones for the bar on the desk. The rest of the crates go into storage. I'll show you where that is."

He hefted a crate and carefully followed her down the hall, all the way to the last door on the left. She yanked the string on an overhead light, illuminating a tiny room piled high with liquor. Most of the bottles were in crates, though a banged-up bookshelf held several loose bottles for easy access.

"Maybe we should swipe a bottle for the next time we break into Central Park," Lorraine said. "I know you don't like to take your work—"

Hank interrupted her by reaching over and pulling her lips to his. After a minute with his large hands wrapped around her back, she felt sad when he pulled away, but she supposed all good things had to end sometime.

"That would be great," Hank said. "Though maybe we should buy our own bottle. Wouldn't want to get my girl into any more trouble." He picked up his crate. "Now, where should I put this?"

His face was calm and impassive, as if he hadn't just called Lorraine *his girl*. Had she imagined it? No, no, she definitely hadn't. Hank had called her his girl! As in his girl*friend*! She broke into a smile that felt too big for her face. It was a smile a million Puccinis couldn't steal from her.

"Lorraine?" Hank asked. "Instructions?"

Lorraine pointed to the top of a pyramid of crates. "Can you reach up and put it up there?"

Effortlessly, Hank lifted the crate high. As he did, the bottom of his jacket rode up, and Lorraine's breath caught at what she saw on his hip: a leather holster, not unlike the one Carlito always wore. And it wasn't empty.

"What are you doing with a gun?" she almost shrieked. "You're not a gangster, are you?" She didn't know whether she could take finding out that the one decent man she'd ever met was yet another member of the Mob.

Hank put down the crate and took her in his arms. "No, Raine, of course not!" He kissed her quickly. "It's for self-protection. I just get nervous, being surrounded by mobsters every day." He smiled. "But this joint ain't so bad—aside from selling booze, it seems to be on the up-and-up."

Lorraine almost laughed at his naïveté. "Hardly!"

Hank cocked his head. "What do you mean?"

She lowered her voice. "You know Ernesto Macharelli?"

"Of course—Al Capone's right-hand man?" Hank said. "But he's in Chicago."

"Not entirely. He and his son are bankrolling this joint!"

"Huh, Ernesto Macharelli laundering his money in New York City. Now, how does a girl like you have information like that?"

Lorraine and Hank stepped apart as Spark walked into the room without knocking. "We got kind of a problem," he said.

Lorraine waved him off. "What I do with my employees is my business."

Spark snickered. "Aw, I don't care about that. I was talking about the singer and the piano player? They ain't exactly getting along. I think one of 'em is going to walk."

"We can't let that happen!"

"I was thinking maybe a word from you might help."

"Me?" Lorraine coughed violently. "No! What they need is a bonus! Go out there and offer them a bonus."

Spark glared. "What they *need* is the fear of God in 'em."

Lorraine pushed Spark toward the door. "Do it."

"Whatever you say," he answered, backing out of the room.

"What's going on?" Hank asked once Spark had left.

"I can't tell you," Lorraine said, and dropped her gaze.

She was wearing nice shoes. Pale-blue heels decorated with beaded flowers that were trimmed with rhinestones. "I mean, I'd like to tell you, but I really can't. I mean, I shouldn't. Unless you really want to know. And then I can tell you, but you've got to give me your most— No, I can't."

Hank shrugged. "Okay, that's fine. I'll go get the rest of the shipment."

"Fine!" she said. "You don't need to twist my arm."

Lorraine told Hank the part of her story she hadn't told him out on the water in Central Park: how Carlito had set her up with the job so that she'd trap Gloria and Jerome. "Jerome murdered Tony—probably in cold blood—and that killing started this whole mess."

Hank's eyes were wide when she finally finished. "Lorraine, you need to—"

The door creaked and Spark burst in.

"Don't you know how to knock?" Lorraine yelled. How dare he interrupt such a private moment? "Why do you think God invented doors? Or knuckles?"

"I'm sorry, Raine, but apparently they don't want their bonus, because the girl just ran off in tears."

"*What?* You idiot!" Lorraine screamed. "Go get her *right now!*"

Spark huffed and walked out nowhere near as quickly as he should have. Lorraine stormed out right behind him. What if Spark couldn't catch Gloria? She had promised to deliver *both* of them to Carlito. And gangsters didn't play around where broken promises were concerned.

She burst into the barroom and plowed straight into someone. "Watch where you're—"

He looked thinner and hungrier than he had back at the Green Mill, and his features were sharper at the edges. He was still beautiful, though—at least, beautiful for a black man.

"Pardon me," he said, giving her the polite but uninterested smile people gave to strangers.

Jerome didn't recognize her.

He had only ever seen her at the Green Mill, where she had looked very different. Now, because she'd been supervising the booze shipments since the morning, and her shift would be over before evening, she wasn't really glammed up. Instead of a flashy sequined number, she was dressed in a simple blue Patou day dress.

And, since Hank had made his under-the-rowboat comment about how nice she looked without makeup, she had started wearing less.

She opened her mouth to say something and found herself coughing.

"Are you all right?" Jerome asked. Before she knew it, he had sat her down on a bar stool. "This lady here is choking!"

Hank was suddenly there, striking Lorraine on the back. She coughed violently and leaned into Hank, trying to ignore the skinny, hungry reality of Jerome beside her.

Hank looked up at Jerome. "You should go. You really don't want to be here right now."

"What?" Jerome said.

"I'm serious. Get out of here. Now."

"You don't need to tell a fellow three times," Jerome muttered, and marched to the stairs.

In despair, Lorraine watched him go. If she told one of the boys to run after him now, there might still be a chance of catching him. But she couldn't get her breath to speak up.

Whenever she'd imagined Jerome in her head, she'd seen a hardened criminal. A killer with cruel eyes and a scowling mouth. But Jerome didn't look like a coldhearted killer. Not in the way Puccini and Carlito looked like killers. Their eyes were flat and dead. But Jerome—hungry as he looked, his eyes had the glint of life in them.

Someone handed her a glass of water.

Bernie, the trumpet player, cleared his throat. "So, uh, is rehearsal over? We can't do much without a singer *or* a piano player."

Lorraine nodded vigorously. "Yeah, you all should head home. Just practice a lot before Saturday. Zuleika's debut should be the best thing our audience has ever seen, got it?" She took a drink of water so that she wouldn't have to talk anymore.

Puccini strolled out onto the barroom from the office. "Rehearsal's over so soon?"

"It is," Lorraine said, and took another drink of water.

At that moment, a group of men came down the stairs. At

the front was Carlito Macharelli, looking debonair in a black pin-striped suit, a fedora's brim bent over his dark eyes.

"Carlito," Puccini said. "Wasn't expecting you so—"

Carlito raised a hand. "We'll catch up in a minute, Puccini." He slid over to the bar. "If it isn't Miss Dyer," he said, looking her up and down. "Don't you clean up nice in the big city."

"Thanks," Lorraine said, shivering. "You look nice t—"

"You're gonna talk to me now, punk, and you're gonna get this idiot girl out of my hair. She's makin' a mess of my club and I'm sick of it!" Puccini said, loosening his tie.

"Calm down, Puccini," Carlito said in his usual smooth voice. "I'm sorry to saddle you with such a dumb Dora. You have no idea how much my father appreciates this favor. Though I don't think he'd be so pleased if he knew how your crew botched the Grokowski job last month."

Puccini looked as she'd never seen him before: terrified. "I don't see how that's got anything to do with this," Puccini said.

"You wouldn't," Carlito said, patting his shoulder. "Puccini, please: Just keep her a little longer, eh?"

Puccini glared at Lorraine. "All right. But she's making her curtain call here, understood? *Finito.*"

As soon as Puccini shut the door of his office behind him, Carlito said, "May I have a moment, Lorraine?"

"Sure," Lorraine said, and he sat down next to her at the bar. "I'm guessing you received my telegrams."

Carlito looked surprised. "No, actually. I was just tired of waiting around and figured I'd drop in to check on you. What's the update?"

Lorraine smiled. "Gloria and Jerome were here together!"

"Great!" Carlito said, rubbing his hands on his thighs. "Where are they now?"

Lorraine let out a nervous laugh. "That's the thing. They *were* here, but now they're . . . gone."

"Gone?"

"Gone," Lorraine repeated, nodding.

There was silence for a moment, and then Carlito screamed, "They're *what*?" His arm snapped out and he grabbed Lorraine by the sailor collar of her dress. Behind him, Lorraine saw Hank coming forward, but she flicked a hand at him to leave her alone—he would only make matters worse.

"You're telling me that you had the two of them right here and you let them slip away together?" Carlito asked, dragging her close so that their faces were almost touching.

"They didn't technically leave *together*," Spark contributed from behind the bar. "The singer ran out about twenty minutes ago, and then the black boy left about ten minutes later."

Carlito stared hard at Lorraine. "You couldn't find an excuse to keep even *one* of them here?" He pushed her away, and she fell off the stool.

"Hey!" Hank said, but Carlito glared at him and he didn't say anything more.

Lorraine tried to get up, but Carlito's shiny black shoe came down on the hem of her dress. For the first time since he'd arrived, Carlito was smiling.

"Oh, Raine," he said, fingering the silver pistol at his hip. "What *am* I going to do with you?"

CLARA

It was the afternoon after the party, and Clara was a wreck.

"So you see, it was all for the magazine," she said, stirring cream into her third coffee of the day. "I'm still the same person, Marcus."

Marcus flipped through the copy of the *Manhattanite*. It was the issue with the first of her "Glittering Fools" columns. She had begged him to meet her at Lindy's for lunch so that she could explain why she had lied to him and gone to Twiggy Sampson's birthday party.

He'd reluctantly agreed.

Marcus finally pulled his eyes away from the magazine, but only to look at the large slice of strawberry cheesecake sitting between them. "Don't you want any?"

Clara usually adored Lindy's cheesecake, but today her stomach turned at the sight of it. Instead, she reached across the table and put her hand on Marcus's arm. "What are you thinking?"

Marcus pushed the magazine aside. "I just don't know why you kept this a secret from me."

She traced the edge of her coffee saucer with her spoon. "I didn't think you'd approve. I worried that you'd think I was falling back into my old life."

"And back into Harris Brown's arms?"

"Marcus, I told you—nothing was going on. That was the first time I'd seen Harris since Chicago. I was just saying hello."

"Clara," Marcus began, taking her hand, "I believe you. And I was being honest when I told you I was proud of you and your writing. It's a courageous thing, putting your work out in the world. I love it that you dare to try. And I love you."

Then his smile faded. He wasn't going to let her off easy. "But I *am* worried about the effect of all these parties on you. Why not go to Barnard and get a *real* education instead of some fly-by-night reporter job, gossiping about a life you've worked so hard to put in your past?"

"But that's just it, Marcus," Clara replied. "That flapper world is the same, but *I'm* different."

"Are you? You got about two hours of sleep last night. And from the way you've been picking at your food, I'm betting you've got a hell of a hangover."

"Guilty as charged."

"And isn't there a tiny part of you—the merest bit, the smallest part—that is glad you've got the magazine as an excuse to fall back in with your old wild crowd?"

"Of course not!" Clara said, but she had hesitated—only a moment!—and Marcus noticed.

He glanced down at the magazine. "I thought that when we came to New York, we'd . . . I don't know, have a life *together*. But sleeping all day, partying all night, saying what's clever instead of what's true . . . *Manhattanite* or no, there are *real* consequences to living that way, Clara."

"I know, but—"

"I thought you wanted to be different," Marcus continued as though she hadn't said anything. "I thought you wanted a better life—one that didn't center around boozing and puking and sequined dresses and speakeasies." He paused. "I thought you wanted a life with me."

"I do," Clara said emphatically. Marcus was the best thing that had ever happened to her—he'd showed her that it was possible to love again after so much heartache.

"No, you don't. You wouldn't be pulling these kinds of shenanigans if you did. That's not how you treat someone you love, Clara. It's just not."

Clara gazed at the other happy couples, the mothers and fathers and children eating lunch, the waitresses strolling around with soft drinks on round trays, all of them exactly who they appeared to be. But Clara? Who was she?

How ironic: When she had lived her life doing what men

expected of her, she had lost herself. And now that she was finally doing something that was entirely her own, she was losing the man she loved.

"Come with me," she said, almost without thinking. "Be my sidekick."

"That's not the point," Marcus said. "I used to like partying, too, but I've seen the downside. What happened to you, what happened to Gloria and Jerome . . . to Lorraine. There comes a time when you need to get serious about something." He sat up straight. "I'm serious about school."

Clara narrowed her eyes. "And I'm serious about my writing."

"Good," Marcus replied. "Then study writing at Barnard. Go after something more than twenty column inches about some ditzy flapper's birthday bash. This kind of stuff won't last." He lifted the magazine for a moment. "There are some witty lines in here, Clara. You have real talent. You could do so much more."

"This is just how I'm getting my start," Clara answered.

"It's easy to say that now. It won't be so simple five years down the line when you're an established gossip columnist with editors lining up to pay you for drivel." He pushed himself up out of the booth. "If you want to write, write about something that matters. If you want to write trash, then find someone else to love, because I won't be waiting around."

Maybe they *were* silly and frivolous, but Clara was proud of her columns. She put a lot of work into them. And people talked about them. They were *good*. Was it wrong to feel pleased about writing something that people actually *enjoyed* reading, rather than something they read because they wanted to look smart and sophisticated?

Parker would never say these things to her, Clara found herself thinking. Parker believed in her, in what she was doing. At least that was something.

Marcus laid some bills on the table. "I have to go to this charity gala at Sherry's tonight at eight—my mother's on the board of the Chicago branch. I'd love for you to be my date, though I'll understand if you've got other plans."

He smoothed his hand over his amber hair, then pulled on his straw trilby. Clara sighed. Her writing was important, but was a society column really more important than Marcus?

She put that decision out of her mind for now. Marcus was offering an olive branch, and she knew she would regret it if she didn't grab it. She forced herself to smile. "I'll see you there."

"Good," Marcus told her. "Because I'm not only serious about school, Clara. I'm serious about you."

After he'd left, she let her pretend smile disappear.

◆ ◆ ◆

This was hell.

About the only thing Clara had said all evening was "thank you" when complimented on her champagne-colored dress. The flowing skirt came down to her ankles, and the loose sleeves that draped to her elbows were hardly flapperesque. The dress was lovely and safe. All the matrons at the party loved it.

Marcus was in the corner of the room, laughing over an anecdote that could in no way be that funny. Not in a million years.

Between them was an obstacle course of linen-covered dining tables, each with a set of oldsters in tuxedos and ball gowns loudly guffawing and smacking their lips as they ate hors d'œuvres and drank lukewarm lemonade.

It was already ten o'clock—Clara wanted out of there. She'd been hoping to stop by the office to drop off edits on the Twiggy Sampson story. Parker usually stayed at the office until midnight—he was more of a workhorse than Clara would've guessed.

Finally, Marcus caught Clara's eye. He looked beautiful in his tux, clean-shaven, every strand of hair Brilliantined perfectly in place. "Having fun?" he asked. For the second during which his eyes met hers, this was the most fantastic party she'd ever attended.

"Sure. I could use actual food, though. What do you say we blow this shindig and grab a real dinner?"

He shook his head and went off to talk to yet another middle-aged society woman.

"Well, *I'm* hungry," she called after him. She spotted a waiter carrying a tray of shrimp and headed that way.

In her rush, she almost took down a young woman in a

silky red gown. "Oh, I'm so sorry," Clara said, catching the woman by the elbow. On anyone else, the gown would have been too loud for polite society, but with her large hazel eyes and flawless skin, this girl looked like a fashion plate.

But her beauty wasn't what was surprising—Clara had seen this girl at the Green Mill. "Forgive me if this sounds strange, but have you ever been to Chicago?"

The girl smiled and, if anything, became even more beautiful. Her features were familiar: large eyes and mouth with a tiny nose, a wispy blond bob, sooty black lashes.

"A few times." The girl extended her hand. "Maude Cortineau. Nice to meet you." Maude cut her big eyes back and forth, then pulled a delicate little flask from her red clutch. She took a swig, then held it out.

Clara accepted the flask and took a quick sip. "Thanks. So how'd a party-loving girl like you end up at a boring event like this one?"

"By accident!" Maude gave a gurgling little laugh, and Clara realized that she was completely splifficated. "I came to New York with my boyfriend but got dragged to this by my aunt—she's on the committee."

Clara looked out on the room. "So which one's your boyfriend?"

Maude hiccupped. "Oh, Carlito wouldn't be caught dead at this sort of party."

"Carlito? The gangster's son?" Clara asked, her mind racing. This girl probably knew a lot about the Mob under-world.

Maude nodded. "That's my boy. The Big Cheese."

"Oh, he's so handsome," Clara said. "Why aren't you off with him?"

"He's working right now," Maude whispered. "He's here to 'clean house.'" She took another swig from her flask.

Clara tried not to show her excitement. "That sounds *very* mysterious."

"It is! Well, not really—someone killed one of his gang." Maude fished a cigarette out of her purse. "People think it was the Green Mill's piano player, but that's because Carlito is ashamed that it was a girl—some crappy torch singer who only sang the one time before her husband came and dragged her off. She's got a new gig at the Opera House now." A waiter walked by. "Ooo, look, finger sandwiches. I love those. Anyway, nice meeting you, Cora."

Maude walked off after the finger-sandwich-bearing waiter.

Gloria, *her* Gloria, had killed someone? Clara's first instinct was to laugh. But that certainly explained why Gloria had left town in such a hurry. If Jerome had been in danger, nothing would have stopped her cousin from protecting him.

Clara found Marcus talking to a decrepit old woman who looked as if she'd been roused from the grave for this party. Clara pulled him over to the corner of the room.

"That was rude, Clara," he protested.

"Just listen to me for a minute," she said, quickly relaying everything Maude had just told her. "And to think I was just trying to get a juicy story out of Maude."

Marcus caught Clara's arm in a firm grip. "Clara, you *cannot* write about this. Give me your word that you won't. Gloria will be arrested, Jerome will be killed. God, *you* might even be killed, too."

"Of course I won't," Clara said. "I . . . wasn't even thinking of that."

But now she *was* thinking about it.

Wasn't Marcus being a little hypocritical? He gave her this high-and-mighty speech about writing something more than society drivel, and now when she'd found something truly serious, he was basically forbidding her to write about it? That didn't seem fair. There would always be real consequences to writing these kinds of stories—that was what made them news. There would be people she might hurt, grim truths she would bring to light that might better have been left buried. It seemed that nothing she did in her writing career would make Marcus happy.

Clara swallowed. What would a real journalist do?

◆ ◆ ◆

Fifteen minutes later, Clara breezed through the front door of the *Manhattanite* offices. A black janitor was mopping the lobby floor. He tipped his hat to her and kept at his work. She flashed her press pass at the desk guard, got into the elevator, and rode it to the fourteenth floor.

She wasn't disappointed when she saw light seeping out from underneath Parker's office door. She knocked lightly. "Parker? It's me, Clara."

"C'mon in," he called.

Clara had been here a fair number of times now—she'd written three "Glittering Fools" articles, including the Twiggy Sampson story, and she met with Parker to receive her assignments and her edits afterward. But those meetings were always during the day.

Parker was sitting in front of his typewriter with handwritten pages scattered around him and a nearly empty mug of coffee. Instead of his usual impeccable suit and tie, he just had on a white shirt and nondescript trousers. Daytime Parker was handsome and stylish, but Clara was surprised to find that nighttime Parker was downright sexy.

From the way he was staring, it didn't seem as if he minded the way Clara looked, either. "Where are you coming from? Couldn't be work—a flapper wouldn't be caught dead with a hemline that low."

"You don't like it?"

"I didn't say that. You look sensational." He gestured with his coffee mug. "I'd offer you a cuppa joe, but this is the last of it. I've been drinking for about three hours."

Clara laughed. "You'll be up all night! Too much caffeine."

Parker blinked. "Isn't it normal to stay up until six in the morning?"

Clara gave another laugh. "No, I don't think it is."

"Ah well. I guess I need a woman around to tell me these things."

Clara didn't know how to respond, so she awkwardly pulled her article out of her bag. "I thought I'd drop these edits off. Sorry I didn't get a chance earlier."

"It's fine." He looked at the clock on the wall. It was ten to midnight. "And technically you're still on time, so thank you for that. Let's go over this."

She hadn't been expecting Parker to review her work in front of her. "Now?"

"Why not?"

Clara knew she should go home and get some sleep. But Parker had never wanted to go over edits together before. So she walked around the desk and sat next to him. Their chairs were close; their legs were almost touching.

Clara leaned back regally in her chair and laced her fingers behind her head.

"What are you doing?" Parker asked.

Clara grinned. "Just seeing what it's like—you know, sitting behind the desk instead of in front of it."

He laughed. "Keep going at the rate you are now and you could be sitting here someday. Although I don't know how you'd expect your reporters to remember any edits you give them, not with those big blues of yours to distract them."

She blushed. "You really think I could be an editor?"

"Sure. You've got an eye for what matters in a story, and you're not sentimental. You've got a flair for sharp language. And you're willing to work hard for what you want instead of accepting marriage to some Harvard millionaire. Not that the fellow wouldn't be a lucky man . . ." He trailed off, his green eyes radiant. "Is there a, uh, lucky fellow in your life?"

"I, um . . ." *Yes, there* is *a lucky fellow and his name is Marcus!* her mind screamed at her. But the words wouldn't come. "You're getting awfully personal, aren't you? I thought you were all work and no play."

A strand of his wavy dark hair fell into his eyes. "I love to play, as long as I have a good partner."

Clara's stomach started to swirl. She felt guilty for not telling him about Marcus. But things were complicated. "Let's get started."

Clara felt a bit of a rush as Parker read over the column. He laughed in the right places, and his cuts made her writing sharper than it had been before.

"A gin bath!" Parker said. "Really?"

Clara only burst into embarrassed laughter. It was nice to joke with someone, the way she and Marcus used to.

After about forty-five minutes, Parker rubbed his temples and said, "All right, I think we're done here. Good work." He picked up a photo of Twiggy that would run alongside the article. "I'll tell you this much—she has nothing on you, doll."

A silence settled between them, and Clara stood up. The

compliments were nice, of course, but it was time to leave—before anything happened that she'd regret. "I should probably go."

Parker stood up as well, trailing behind her to the door. "I guess I'll go wrestle with the coffeepot," he said. "I've got an idea for a story and I don't want to lose it."

Parker would never judge her for staying up all night to write her stories. Unlike Marcus, he would encourage her to follow every exciting lead she came across. "You know . . . I got information on what could be a great story."

"Oh? You want to pitch it to me?"

"I'm not sure if I can," Clara said, suddenly feeling nervous. "I have some, uh . . . *moral* questions about writing it."

He leaned closer. "What do you mean?"

"The story involves someone close to me. And publishing it could possibly hurt her. What do you think I should do?"

"I'm a journalist," Parker replied. "The only morality that matters to me is the truth." He took her shoulders in his hands. "What about you?"

She could see in his eyes that he wanted to kiss her. His fingers trailed over her shoulders, under her hair, and toward the nape of her neck. Before she had even thought of what she was doing, her own hands had settled on the soft white linen of his shirt. She could feel his trim torso through the cloth, only a thin layer of material separating her skin from his. She could feel her chin tilting upward, her lips parting in anticipation.

Then Marcus's face flashed into her head.

She jerked away. "I have to go." She clumsily slung her purse over her shoulder. "Have a good night."

Parker started to speak, but Clara was already out the door, in the elevator, watching as the doors closed and she was alone with her thoughts, the warmth of his breath still lingering on her cheek.

VERA

"Welcome to the Ritz-Carlton, miss," the doorman said. "Mr. Demartino is waiting for you in the dining room." The doorman was only a little older than her and looked a bit like Evan, making her stomach lurch.

Vera had never been inside such a luxurious hotel. And clearly, the hotel had never seen a young black woman in an evening gown. Vera was quite conspicuously the only black person in the joint who wasn't dressed like a maid or a bellboy.

"Thank you," she said. She had never had more than a couple of dollars to her name; she'd never received anything but hostility from the sorts of folks who stayed in fancy hotels like this one.

Her black heels sank into the scarlet plush carpeting. The entire lobby glowed with money and refinement, and she could feel the rich white people's eyes boring into her with each step she took. Past the elevators were the restaurant's gold-handled glass doors.

If Vera hadn't been so worried about Evan, she might actually have enjoyed herself.

Inside, the maître d' at the podium scowled. Then his face split into a broad, cold smile. "You must be Mr. Demartino's *special guest.*"

Vera nodded. What did he mean by *special guest*?

The maître d' picked up a menu. "Right this way, *mademoiselle,*" he said in a fake French accent.

Vera followed him to a table at the back of the restaurant. Of course the gangster would've warned the Ritz staff that he was meeting a black woman for dinner. That was why they were welcoming her instead of slamming the door in her face.

Men with guns and power tended to have that kind of effect on people.

But tonight the tables were turned. Vera had a gun in her purse and a mission, and nobody—especially not some two-bit mobster—was going to stop her from rescuing Evan.

Demartino was sitting at the farthest table in the restaurant. He had a huge booth all to himself. He looked as if he was in his early twenties. His massive body looked uncomfortable in a formal suit—this man belonged in a plain shirt and pants with suspenders.

"You're not the gal I asked out earlier," Demartino said, but his confusion quickly changed into a sick grin. "Though

I'm not complainin'. You're an even choicer tomato than the other one."

That was exactly why Vera had worn her most expensive sleeveless black dress—a gift from an admirer at the Green Mill. It was a Madeleine Vionnet, and the sheer silk chiffon felt luxurious against her skin. She'd accessorized with the (real) pearl necklace her father had spent ages saving up to buy for her mother and a matching (fake) pearl headband.

Vera returned Demartino's smile. A jagged scar started between the middle and index fingers of his right hand and ran up under his cuff. She'd never met him, but she knew this gangster's nickname from the Green Mill: Hatchet. He was a high-level goon of Carlito's.

So that was who'd snatched Evan.

"Molly's boyfriend didn't want her out with another man, even one as handsome as you," Vera cooed. "So I volunteered to come in her place." She sat and leaned her elbow on the table. "It works out pretty well for everyone, since I've got a favor to ask."

Demartino lit a cigarette. "Whatcha need? Some dough? Daddy's got you covered, baby lamb."

Vera ignored the fact that a lamb actually *was* a baby sheep, so it made no sense to refer to her as a baby lamb. "I need you to take me to Carlito Macharelli."

He snorted. "Oh, that'll be a good one to tell my buddies later. Ha! Take her to Macharelli," he said to no one in particular, dragging heavily on his cigarette. "Ha! Too funny. You're a hoot, baby lamb. A regular owl."

Vera didn't laugh. "I'm serious."

After a moment, he stopped laughing. His smile got bigger. "No way." He straightened his jacket. "Now, if ya ain't here to have a good time with me, I'm off ta find someone who will."

"Wait!" Vera said.

"Sweetheart, I'm doing you a favor," Demartino said. "Carlito don't take kindly to anyone demanding anything— not even good-looking dames like yourself. He may be young, but he's tough, and he's got a lotta muscle behind him. Baby boy's got a big daddy, and even I don't mess with that. Now scram." He started to scoot out of the booth.

"But Carlito's here to find Gloria Carmody and Jerome Johnson," Vera said coolly. "And I know where they're holed up."

Demartino slid back into the booth. His face looked a little panicked. "What do you know about that?"

"You grabbed the wrong person this afternoon. Evan? He doesn't know anything. *I* know where Jerome and Gloria are living," she lied. "But I'll only tell Carlito myself." She stared at Demartino until he looked away. "You still want me to scram?"

"Why would you want to tell Carlito? I'm a hell of a lot friendlier."

"It's Carlito or nobody. So what's it gonna be?"

Demartino lifted a hand to flag down the waiter. "I need to use your telephone."

The waiter nodded. "Right away, sir."

"What's your name, doll?" Demartino asked.

"Vera," she replied.

"Wait here." Demartino followed the waiter out of the restaurant.

Vera's hands shook. She pressed them flat on the table. What if he was just calling some goons to come take care of her? He was the only lead she had. How else would she find Evan?

She sighed in relief when Demartino returned with the waiter. "Get a cab for me and the lady. We're going to Rick's Steakhouse, midtown."

◆ ◆ ◆

Rick's Steakhouse was packed, the small tables pushed tightly together and a fog of cigar smoke filling the room. There were no women in sight—every guest was a man in a flashy suit. Several of the men had scars on their faces, and even the ones who didn't had the look of hardened criminals. Carlito and his men must have picked this place as their base of operations while they were in New York.

"Hey there, honey!" one man yelled at Vera when she passed. "I was just gonna ask for some coffee with my dessert—guess now I don't have to!"

Vera clutched her beaded purse a little closer and tried to ignore the catcalls as Demartino led her to the back of the restaurant.

A group of four men were playing poker around a square table and smoking cigars. The one with a mountain of red chips in front of him was none other than Carlito Macharelli himself. His hair was slicked back, his gray suit perfectly tailored, and his face starkly handsome in the arrogant way of someone who is never told no.

Carlito smiled at Vera when she and Demartino reached the poker table. "Well, well, look who's in the Big Apple. It's one surprise after another in this town." He elbowed the man on his left. "First Joey here nabs the *wrong* guy auditioning under the *right* name, and then the sister of the guy we *are* looking for comes a-calling. We're catching everybody but the one person we actually want. Joey, be a gentleman, why don't ya?"

The man scrambled out of his chair.

"Have a seat, Vera," Carlito said. "Hatchet, how about you get us a couple of drinks? And how about the rest of you give us some privacy?"

The other men drew their chairs away, leaving only Vera and Carlito at the poker table. Once they had both been supplied with drinks, he gave her a long, hard stare. "You're looking for your brother, aren't you? I don't believe for a second that hooey Hatchet said about you knowing where Jerome and Gloria are. If you knew, you would've left town with your brother and his gal right away, taken 'em somewhere far away from where I might find 'em."

Vera had picked up her drink; now she set it on the table

without taking a sip. "What makes you think I wouldn't turn them in to you? I might get a nice reward out of it."

" 'Cause you ain't that type of girl," he said. "But you obviously know more than you should. So how about you spill the beans before one of my guys here spills your blood all over the back alley?" Vera put all her willpower into not shuddering at his words. "No one's noticed you missin' from Chicago 'cept for that nice father of yours. I should pay him a visit when I get back to Chicago, pay my condolences—"

"Stop!" Vera said. The image of her father's face had been too much. She pointed at Carlito. "You may play at being the big, tough gangster boy, but you're only twenty. Barely old enough to grow a mustache. Nobody would listen to you at all if your daddy weren't standing next to *him*—Al Capone. So don't try and get all tough on me. You ain't nothing but a spoiled brat."

"You don't really think you're going to walk out of here, do you?"

Vera took a deep breath. "I'll get straight to the point," she said. "I was on the docks the night Sebastian Grey was shot." She didn't give herself any time to gauge Carlito's reaction. "We both know that you and my brother are next on the killer's list."

For a second, Carlito's eyes registered shock. Then they went back to their normal dead quality. "You're making no sense, doll."

"Don't play me for a fool, Carlito," Vera said. "You ran

because you two were set up. Bastian got iced, and I'm here to tell you that the torpedo, the hired gun, is in Manhattan, looking for you. But I can deliver *her* to *you*. I know who she is."

Vera was no closer to knowing the identity of the assassin than she had been in Chicago. She had nothing real to offer Carlito in exchange for Evan—so she needed to make this lie convincing.

She ever so slightly opened her purse, her fingers grazing the silver pistol.

"It's pretty simple, really. Forgive my brother, let go of your grudge, and give me my boyfriend back."

Carlito smirked. "*Boyfriend?* Since when is my old trumpet player in love with you?"

Vera figured it was smarter to refer to Evan as her boyfriend. As Gloria had proved, a person in love would do anything. "I know the killer is here because I saw her following Gloria Carmody two weeks ago. And then I saw her again earlier today." Vera let out a full-throated laugh. "Oh, and by the way? I know that Gloria actually was the one who killed Tony." Carlito coughed at this bit of news. "So why don't you just drop this thing about my brother already?"

Carlito sat in an angry silence. He fussed with his chips, stacking them again and again.

From the corner of her eye, Vera saw something glitter. She looked over: Another woman was in the steakhouse after all.

Maude Cortineau was perched in a chair against the wall, smoking a cigarette. When Maude noticed Vera looking at her, the blond moll glanced down at the floor. But it was clear she'd been listening to Vera and Carlito's entire conversation.

How had Vera not noticed Maude before? The sequined, sea-foam-green dress was hardly inconspicuous. But Maude seemed to have a talent for disappearing into the background.

"Gloria may have pulled the trigger, but they were both responsible," Carlito said finally. "And I can face this killer on my own, especially if she's just a dame. Thanks for that scrap of information—seems like the only bit you've got." He swirled the ice in his empty glass. " 'Cause, see, while you have no idea where Jerome and Gloria are, *I* do. They work for me, not that they're wise to it. They've both got gigs in one of my clubs.

"No one'll believe the truth about Tony from a girl like you. Especially if you're dead. So be careful what kind of tone you adopt with me."

It wasn't fair! She had come all the way from Chicago, had risked so much, and somehow Carlito had already won. "Fine," she said. "Just let me have Evan and we'll leave."

Carlito chuckled. "Oh, I don't think so, Vera. In fact, I don't think I'm going to let you go at all." He nodded at a few of the men sitting at the surrounding tables. Suddenly they stood and created a wall of muscle behind her chair.

Vera reached into the purse in her lap and pulled out Bastian's pistol. She pointed the barrel at Carlito's head. She could feel the men crowding her chair move back.

"Let him go. *Now,*" Vera said, proud of the strength in her voice.

Carlito stared at her with his mouth slightly open.

Vera switched off the safety on the gun.

Something shifted in Carlito's eyes; he knew how serious she was. He looked over her shoulder at one of the men. "Okay, Eddie—you go and untie him."

Vera kept the gun trained on Carlito while a rotund bald man walked to the corner of the restaurant by the men's room. He opened a heavy wooden door to reveal a tiny closet. In with the brooms and mops was Evan, tied to a chair with a gag in his mouth. He had a black eye and a scrape on one cheek.

Vera gasped.

Gag removed and ropes untied, Evan stumbled a little as he stood and took in the sight of his ex-bandmate's little sister pointing a gun at the son of one of the most powerful Mob bosses in Chicago. "Oh my oh my oh my," Evan said.

Vera didn't move the gun from its aim at Carlito's head. "Stand up. You're taking a walk with us." Carlito got to his feet, and Vera pushed the pistol into his back. The room was completely silent—thugs were standing and sitting, awaiting Vera's next move. "*No one* follows us. Unless you want to explain Carlito's death to his dad."

The men backed against the walls, clearing a space so Carlito and Vera could walk out of the steakhouse with Evan behind them.

Outside, Vera led Carlito to a black phone booth. "Call us a cab."

Carlito gritted his teeth. "I'm going to enjoy cutting that smug smile off your face."

Vera cocked the pistol's hammer. "Do it!"

He fished a nickel from his pocket and talked to an operator, and eventually a Checker cab pulled up at the curb.

Vera stood between Evan and Carlito, her right hand inconspicuously pushing the gun into Carlito's spine. "Where you off to?" the balding cabby asked.

"Just a minute," Evan said. He reached over to pat Carlito on the shoulder, then opened the door of the cab. "Thanks so much for taking us out after the show tonight, boss." Evan climbed into the car.

"And offering to pay for our ride home!" Vera said with a smile. "That was just so sweet of you."

Carlito turned his dark glare onto Vera.

She prodded him again with the gun. "About ten dollars should do it."

"Ma'am, unless you live in New Jersey—" the cabby began.

"Ten dollars," Vera said again.

Carlito fumbled around in his pocket, muttering something that sounded like "dismember your whole family," then handed Vera the cash.

"Thanks, hon," Vera said. She slowly took the gun away from his back and flattened it against her thigh. "It's always nice to see old friends—sorry to cut this short."

Vera climbed into the cab next to Evan. "Just drive, please," Evan said to the driver.

As the cab took off, Vera looked out the window and saw Carlito staring after them. Once they were far enough away so that he was just a speck in the distance, she felt her entire body tremble. She leaned against the sticky brown seat, breathing hard.

Evan pulled her into his arms. "It's all right, Vera, we're all right."

She dug her head hard into his shoulder. "I'm so glad you're okay. When I came out of Connie's today and you were—"

"It's okay." His hand smoothed her hair. "I was so worried they might have someone waiting for you, too. Not that they would've been able to do anything." He gave a low whistle. "I always knew you were smoking, Vera, but I didn't realize you were packing heat."

She lightly touched the dark bruise around his eye. "You're hurt."

He covered her hand with his. "I'm *fine,* thanks to you." He moved her hand so that her palm skimmed his lips. "Really, thank you." Then he chuckled. "So I'm your boyfriend? That's what you told Carlito."

"Well, you told your band at the Cotton Club that I'm your girl."

She could feel his breath on her cheek. "I do talk about you an awful lot. I can't help myself." He tucked her hair behind her ear. "I think I'm in love with you, Vera," he said, the words rushing out. "Or at least . . . in a whole lotta like."

Vera couldn't help it—she was glowing. But there would be time for canoodling later. Right now, she had to focus. "Evan, I'm in a whole lotta like with you, too. But we need to find my brother *now*. You heard what Carlito said—he could get Jerome and Gloria anytime he wants. I don't think he was bluffing."

"Turns out I may have an idea about that," Evan said.

"You've got a lead?" Vera said. "Well, don't keep it to yourself—spill!"

"When I was in that closet, that scrawny girl, Maude, took pity on me. When Carlito and his guys were out, she talked the boys into letting her feed me."

"She fed you?" Vera felt a weird pang of jealousy. "Put food in your mouth?"

"Not exactly. She brought me a steak sandwich and untied my hand so I could eat. And then while I ate, she talked up a storm at me. I tell you, it was like a different kind of torture."

Vera laughed. "I remember her."

"Anyway, she wanted to know if I'd ever met one of Gloria's old friends—this girl Clara—at the Green Mill. Seems Maude had bumped into Clara at a party here in New York. And she was mad because Clara hadn't mentioned she'd appeared in Maude's favorite magazine."

"Which is?"

"Some rag about flappers in New York called the *Manhattanite*. Apparently somebody wrote about how Clara is damaged goods and how she should stay in Brooklyn Heights."

"Really? Did Clara know where Gloria was?"

"Maude didn't really discuss that with me. I was done eating, so she tied my hand back up and took her bag-o'-bones self and her magazine back outside."

But simply knowing that Clara lived in Brooklyn Heights wasn't much to go on. "Did you get her last name? Or where exactly she lives?"

Evan frowned. "Vera, I was in a closet. Tied up. Blind."

"Okay, okay—I hear you." Vera sighed with relief. Maybe everything would work out. "Let's get a copy of this *Manhattanite* magazine."

Evan put his arm around her shoulder. "You're not tired after all that? You're amazing."

Before she knew it, he'd leaned in and kissed her. At first her eyes went wide with surprise, but then she closed them and enjoyed the moment. For a few seconds, Jerome, Gloria, Carlito, even the mysterious assassin—all of it left her mind. Her whole world was Evan's lips.

Evan pulled back. "I've been wanting to do that ever since that day in Central Park," he said, leaning his forehead against hers.

She couldn't help smiling. "Yeah? I've been wanting you to do that ever since before we left Chicago." She looked back in the direction of the steakhouse. "I guess we'll have time to do *more* of that after we find Jerome and Gloria. If we find them."

Evan squeezed her hand. "We will, Vera, don't worry."

"Thanks." She kissed him again. "And, Evan?"

"Yeah?"

"I think you're pretty amazing, too."

GLORIA

Gloria tried in vain to close her suitcase.

She opened the case again and pulled out her tattered day dresses, leaving the pricier garments she'd brought from Chicago: a beaded black Chanel dress, a silky green blouse from Paris that matched her eyes exactly, a headband made entirely of artfully intertwined pearls.

She wadded the cheaper dresses in an empty record crate at her feet. All the 78s and the Victrola were with Jerome, wherever he was staying—along with his share of the rent. Even with the gig at the Opera House, she couldn't afford this apartment on her own. The money Jerome had left her would get her—at most—a room at a boardinghouse, like the one they'd stayed in when they first got to the city, before they found this place. Not that she'd be safe here even if she *could* afford it.

What had she been thinking, responding to that flyer? "Here I am." Such a dumb move. Her mother might have suspected she was in New York, but there was no way she could pay someone to go around town putting up flyers. She didn't have the money—she had been cut off by Gloria's father. And since new flyers kept turning up, the possibility of their being linked to Bastian had been eliminated.

So now Gloria was leaving. Her only hope was that by the time Carlito sent his goons, she would already be safely set up somewhere else.

Someone knocked on the door.

Gloria's heart fluttered. Who could it be? Jerome had a key, and anyway, he wasn't coming back.

Carlito!

The knocking came again, this time hard enough to rattle the door in its frame. Gloria looked frantically around the apartment for a place to hide.

Maybe she could just sit here quietly and they would go away. She silently sat on a chair, watching the door. If she could wait them out, she could escape the back way. Not that the flimsy lock would stop a determined person for long—

The door wasn't locked.

She stood up. Maybe she could shoot the bolt home without the thugs on the other side noticing. Maybe she—

The doorknob turned.

Gloria's breath caught in her throat, her feet frozen to the floor.

The door swung open, and her fears were confirmed: Two

burly black men in blue boilersuits stood outside, their bulk completely filling the doorway. One man had close-cut hair, while the other was bald. The bald one crossed his muscular arms and looked down at Gloria.

"So you been here all this time?" he said in a deep baritone.

The other one said, "You know why we're here."

Gloria let out a shaky breath. She put her hands out, palms up. "I will go peacefully," she said. "I am ready for the worst."

Both men stared at her as if she were a crazy person, and the one who had hair looked as if he was trying to stifle a laugh.

"Uh, lady," the bald one said, "we're just here for the piano."

Gloria blinked, then thought back to the note Jerome had written to her: *A few of my buddies will be by later to move the piano and get my stuff.* She had completely forgotten.

She jumped up and pulled the door open wider. "Sorry about that. I was, uh, expecting someone else."

The men walked over to the piano, the bald one pushing a dolly in from the hallway. Gloria stood back by the kitchen table. "Do you two want some water, or maybe some coffee?"

Maybe she could get some information about where Jerome was staying. She was still angry with him, of course—the only words they'd exchanged at the Opera House since he'd left had been spiteful ones. But she couldn't help wanting to know where he was, whether he was all right.

Whether he missed her.

The men shook their heads. "Nah, we're fine. We just need to get this downstairs." They took a few minutes to wrap the piano in thick gray blankets and then tipped it sideways. There was a soft confusion of chords. They strapped it to the dolly, tipped it back, and rolled it toward the door.

"So, where exactly are you taking this thing?" she asked. "Not too far, I hope. It looks heavy!"

The bald one glanced back. "We'll be okay."

Gloria followed the men out of the apartment, leaving the door open. They were easing the piano down the stairs gently, taking the steps one at a time. She leaned over the railing. "Could you please tell me where Jerome is staying?" she called. "I just want to know how he's doing."

The bald one grunted as he continued to step carefully backward down the stairs. "Don't you worry your pretty little head about Jerome."

The men turned the piano on the landing and moved out of sight.

Jerome had told his friends not to tell her where he was? What baloney! She dashed back into the apartment and donned her floppy hat and coat. Then she hurried down the back stairway, crossed the tiny lobby before the men with the piano had reached it, and, for the first time ever, went out the front door.

A large white truck was parked outside with RON'S MOVERS painted in bold letters across the side. The back of the truck was open and a ramp was extended, awaiting Jerome's piano. Without pausing, Gloria broke into a gallop and ran up the ramp.

Phew! There were plenty of places to hide in here: The truck was packed with stuff. She pushed past a couple of boxes and a lamp and found a big black chest. She crawled inside, then folded up her floppy hat and used it to prop open the lid of the chest.

A moment later, the truck sagged on its springs and she heard the men grunting as they pushed the piano up the ramp.

"That Jane back there was *crazy,*" one of them said. "A real dewdrop." The other just laughed. Gloria heard the heavy tread of boots, a clatter as the ramp was unhooked and slid into the truck, and then the closing of the truck's doors.

After what felt like an eternity (though it had probably only been twenty minutes), the truck stopped. The back doors opened and the men climbed inside. "Just a little more elbow grease and we'll be done," one said. They rolled the piano down the ramp.

When she could no longer hear their voices, Gloria climbed out. There was no one around; the coast was clear.

She hopped to the sidewalk and adjusted her dress. They'd gone much deeper into Harlem than she had ever ventured—152nd Street and St. Nicholas Place. Unlike on her street, where elderly men and women sat on chairs outside their buildings, this block was completely deserted.

In front of her was a gray boardinghouse with sagging

steps and a wooden stoop that sorely needed a new paint job. This must be the place.

Gloria pushed open the door and found a foyer as old and dirty as the house's exterior. There were cracks in the ceiling and the faint odor of mothballs. A scruffy old cat that looked as gray and dirty as the rug on the floor let out a faint meow.

A middle-aged black woman sat behind a desk, smoking a cigarette. Her eyes narrowed. "You get lost?"

Gloria stood tall. "I sincerely hope not," she said in the deep voice she'd once used to mimic her teachers at Laurelton Prep. "I'm looking for a Jerome Johnson. He used to work at my club downtown, and our till is eighteen dollars short. This is the address we have on file for him."

It was the best story she'd been able to come up with while crouched in the back of the moving van. Her now-dirty day dress wasn't the right attire for a club manager, but she couldn't worry about that.

The woman barely shrugged. "He's in Five F, go on up."

Gloria hadn't expected it to be *that* easy. As she made her way tentatively up the stairs, she worried that she would bump into the movers. But she didn't hear them until the last flight. She could hear the dolly's rusty wheels rolling down the hallway.

She peeked around the corner. The men had stopped outside an unvarnished door marked 5F and knocked. It opened, but Gloria couldn't see whom they were talking to.

Whoever it was stepped out into the hall, and Gloria nearly fell over: It wasn't Jerome.

It was a black girl her own age.

She was pretty, with big brown eyes and a short burst of curly dark hair. Her sleeveless canary-yellow dress was cheap, but a girl with her slim figure and light brown skin would have looked good in anything.

"If you could just put it against the right wall, that would be great," the girl said.

"Sure thing, Marcie," one of the movers said.

"He'll be back at six," the girl said.

The men rolled the piano into the apartment and Marcie followed, shutting the door behind her.

Where had Jerome met this Marcie woman? And how could he have found her in the few days since he'd moved out? He worked fast. Or maybe Marcie was the reason he'd left in the first place.

A short, hiccupping sob escaped Gloria's lips as she stomped down the stairs. She didn't glance at the woman behind the front desk as she burst out the door and onto the street. She staggered down the block and eventually came upon a subway station.

Once she was seated on a bench, waiting for a downtown train, she began to cry. She had barely faced the fact that she and Jerome had broken up, and he'd already found some-one else.

Gloria's relationship with Jerome—her love for him, the way he'd taught her to sing, how she had come into her own because of him—was the most important one she'd ever had. It mattered more than her relationship with her father and mother. And certainly more than her relationship with Lorraine, or with Clara, or even with Marcus—they were all only friends.

But with Jerome there was heat. There was passion. Even when they were angry with each other, or when money was tight, she'd always figured she and Jerome had their love. And that it would always keep them together.

But clearly that wasn't how Jerome felt.

Maybe he was happier now. He would never have to hide his relationship with Marcie or feel awkward about introducing her to his friends. He'd gotten what he wanted— someone who understood him in a way Gloria never could.

She boarded the train and was glad to find the car practically empty.

Why had Jerome given up on her so fast?

◆ ◆ ◆

As she turned the corner toward her old apartment, she saw three police cars parked along the curb. The street was crowded with people who'd come out to see what the ruckus was all about. Two uniformed officers were standing on the stoop, talking to her frazzled-looking landlord.

The flyers! She'd completely forgotten.

It had never entered her mind that the police could have been behind the flyers. But it made sense: The police had figured out that she killed Tony and had used the flyers as a way to lure her into their clutches.

She turned on her heel and walked back the way she'd come.

How could she have been so stupid? The charade she'd used to get into her apartment had not only allowed her to live secretly with Jerome—it had helped hide her from the police.

She and Jerome had been so careful for months, going through such complicated ruses, using fake names and never telling their address to prospective employers, never entering or leaving the apartment together.

And now, thanks to Gloria, all of that had been in vain.

The Lost Girl had finally been found.

LORRAINE

Lorraine wanted to hit someone.

Specifically, she wanted to hit Thor, the nasty little midget who was currently telling her off.

"Naw, this set list is all wrong," he said in his thick Windy City accent. "Who wants to hear a buncha slow songs at the beginning of the night? Redo it."

Lorraine walked over to the table where the pint-sized gangster sat. She held her hand out for the clipboard. "Fine. I'll write a new set list."

"Not so fast, doll," he said, sneering. "Before you do this, you gotta get someone to take those posters back to the printers. They'll look better with red lettering."

She raised her eyebrows. "But between her hair and her dress . . . isn't that kind of a lot of red?"

Thor puffed on his stogie. "Oh, you think so? How about I call up Carlito, see what he thinks about splashing some *red* around here? I think he'd like the idea just fine."

Lorraine snatched the clipboard. "Fine, I'll get Jimmy to do it."

"Attagirl. And get that old codger to mop the floor again. I want to be able to see my reflection."

Lorraine counted to ten in her head. And then she made herself smile. "Why, sure thing, Thor." She wished she could just ignore everything Thor said, but he was Carlito's right-hand man, and her safety depended on keeping Thor happy.

He grunted. "I don't know what you're so happy about. Me, I'm never happy. Life is a vale of tears, Lorraine. And when I'm done with you, you'll appreciate that."

The day after Jerome and Gloria had slipped out of Lorraine's grasp, Thor had shown up at the Opera House.

"What are *you* doing here?" she'd asked him.

"I work here now," he'd said.

"Not if I don't say so. I'm the manager!"

"Not anymore, sweetheart." He'd beamed at everyone else in the room. "Say hello to your new *general manager*. Lorraine, why don't you run and get me a coffee?"

"Let me guess," Lorraine had asked. "Small?"

That day she'd gone home with an enormous coffee stain down her dress.

Thor had immediately taken full advantage of his new position. Suddenly nothing could be done in the club without the "Thor stamp of approval." As per Carlito's orders, Thor kept an eye on Lorraine at all times.

Sure, Lorraine disliked Spark. And she practically hated Puccini. But that was nothing compared with the way she felt about Thor.

Thor seemed to take great joy in taunting her and bossing her around. "And please tell me you were smart enough to stock the special brandy for when Frankie Balzini comes in with his new moll?"

Lorraine blinked as she stepped behind the bar. "I'll go get it."

She pulled Jimmy out of a poker game with Spark in the office and sent him off to the printers. Then she handed the set list to Spark—for once he didn't even complain. At last, she carried the expensive bottle of liquor back to the bar.

Hank brushed Lorraine's fingers with his as he took the bottle from her, giving her a sympathetic look.

Lorraine knew she must've looked tired and haggard, but Hank was his usual unkempt-in-the-sexiest-possible-way self. Today he wore dark gray slacks and a pale blue V-neck sweater. His practically black hair was getting a little long and kept falling into his eyes. But it didn't look sloppy: it looked adorable.

The truth about how Lorraine had come to work at the Opera House hadn't scared Hank away—if anything, he'd become more devoted than ever. He stopped by her apartment every morning to walk her to work, even on days when he wasn't working. He kept trying to convince her to quit her job or go to the police, promising he would protect her.

Not that Hank's knight-in-shining-armor act wasn't sweet—it was. But it was also kind of stupid. Lorraine could only imagine what Carlito would do to her if she tried to back out on the deal now. Thor had tried to fire Hank the day he arrived, but then he'd seen how quickly Hank mixed drinks and had allowed him to stay.

"Who's Frankie Balzini, anyway?" Lorraine reached for a lowball glass from a tray and went back to drying.

"Only one of the top bootleggers in the city—a good buddy of Owney Madden." Thor took another puff on his cigar. "Raine, how about you get me a shot of that brandy? I'd better sample it before Frankie does, make sure it's top-notch. In fact, better make it a double."

Hank cleared his throat. "I can get that for you, boss—"

"I told *Lorraine* to do it," Thor growled. "You go on upstairs and help the boys unload the shipment. Dryin' dishes is woman's work, anyway."

Lorraine wanted to wring his neck. She'd never dried a dish before now!

Hank reached under the bar to squeeze Lorraine's hand, then crossed the barroom and walked up the stairs.

Thor hopped onto one of the bar stools. "If I didn't know any better, I'd say that bartender's carrying a torch for you."

Lorraine felt her cheeks redden.

"I can't imagine why," Thor went on, smacking his lips. "You've got some nice gams, I'll give you that, but even you know you need about ten pounds o' paint to make that mug look presentable."

She handed him his drink. "At least I can ride all the rides at the carnival."

Thor pushed the glass right back. "Don't be stingy, sweetheart." He wove his fingers together and cracked his knuckles. "So the canary and her spade boyfriend are coming in for her debut tomorrow night, right?"

Lorraine nodded. "Yep, at eight."

Thor grinned. "Now, *there's* one choice bit of calico. Though I doubt she'll look so good once Carlito's through with her."

Lorraine stopped drying. What was Thor talking about? "Carlito would never do anything to Gloria," she said. "It was the piano player who killed Carlito's partner, not the singer. *He's* the one who's gonna get it."

Thor barked out a little laugh. "You really don't know anything, do you? I'll let you in on a little secret." He lowered his voice. "Jerome wasn't the one who took Tony out—it was that little bluenose."

Lorraine's blood went cold in her veins. "I don't believe you."

Thor took a sip of his brandy. "Carlito covered it up—imagine how it'd look if word got out that a seventeen-year-old *girl* knocked off one of his top guys?"

"So—so what is he going to do once he catches them?"

Thor shrugged. "Who knows? But the boss has got big plans." He chuckled and then ran the flat of his hand across his neck, miming the slashing of his throat.

Lorraine looked away in horror.

Thor knocked back the rest of his drink. "Well, I'm off to the little boys' room," he announced, jumping off his stool.

Lorraine waited until he'd disappeared into the men's room. Then she dashed up the stairs and found Hank in the alley outside. "I need to talk to you," she said. "I've only got a minute before he tracks me down. It takes him forever to get up those stairs, what with those tiny things he calls legs."

Hank cocked his head. "What's up?"

She relayed what Thor had just told her. It had never—not even for a second—dawned on her that Carlito would want to physically hurt Gloria.

Lorraine was a lot of things—she knew that. She could be a bitch, a drunk, a doormat, a backstabber . . . sure. Was she proud of all those things? No. But a girl did what she needed to do. She wasn't a *killer,* though. She wasn't an accomplice to murder. And no matter how bad things had become between them, Gloria Carmody had been her best friend for most of their lives. Whatever bad things Gloria might have done, she didn't deserve to be killed for them.

"Carlito promised me he was just going after Jerome, that he was only going to rough him up and send him away. He promised me he wasn't going to kill anybody—that's why I took the job!"

Hank rolled his eyes. "And you *believed* him?"

Lorraine dropped her face into her hands. "Yes!" she cried hopelessly.

Hank put a hand on her shoulder. "You don't need to worry, Raine. I'll help you."

Lorraine shook him off, angry tears welling up in her eyes. "What can you do? You're just a stupid bartender!" Her eyes widened as she heard the words come out of her mouth. "No, no, I didn't mean you're stupid—but you *are* a bartender."

Thankfully, Hank didn't seem offended. Instead, he just gripped her shoulder tighter. He was so strong! "We can warn them. You've got their address, right?"

The door of the club banged open. Thor stood there, angry, his face red. "What are you doing out here?"

Hank held up a cigarette. "Just came out for a smoke, boss."

"Get back in here, Lorraine," Thor commanded, his expression unchanging.

As Lorraine turned to follow Thor inside, Hank started talking again. "Actually, boss, I've got to run over to the butcher's to pick up those special steaks the Balzini party ordered."

Thor glanced back. "Make it quick."

"They'll need a manager's signature." Hank gave his million-dollar grin, holding the door open for Thor and Lorraine. "I know the butcher is awfully fond of Lorraine. They usually knock down the price if she tags along."

Hank really must have had a lot of experience with gangsters: Their inherent cheapness when it came to business always won out above all else.

"All right." Thor crossed his arms, then sighed. "But don't you take any wooden nickels, Raine—you understand?"

Lorraine nodded, glad that in addition to being a sweetheart *and* absurdly handsome, her boyfriend was clever. Maybe bartenders were smarter than she'd thought.

◆ ◆ ◆

Lorraine stared up at the ugly brown building. "Eew. Are you sure this is it?"

Hank pulled a slip of paper out of his pocket. When they'd run to Lorraine's office to get her purse and hat, Hank had copied down the address they had on file for Gloria. "Yep, here we are. She didn't list an apartment number, though, so we're just gonna have to ask around."

Lorraine clutched Hank's arm as they walked up the steps. How wonderful it was to walk on a man's arm, even with all the terrible things going on. At six feet, two inches, Hank made Lorraine feel ladylike instead of like a too-tall ugly duckling. She imagined what it would be like to have him by her side at Barnard, how all the other girls would swoon over him (of course they would, he was swoon-worthy!) and then want to be her friends. And Lorraine would wear glamorous clothes, and Gloria would be safe, and safely out of Lorraine's life, and Hank would maybe go to school himself and stop bartending—well, he would mix her drinks at home—and the two of them would get married and have beautiful babies. And get nannies to take care of the babies.

What a grand new life that would be!

But first she had to clean up the mistakes of the old life.

In the lobby of the shabby apartment building were a few people—Italian factory workers and young families passing through, and two men talking by the stairs.

Hank tapped one man on the shoulder. "Sorry to bother you," he said, "but we're looking for a friend of ours. Her name's Gloria Carmody. She has short wavy red hair, green eyes, very pretty?"

Lorraine tried not to bristle at the fact that Hank had called Gloria pretty.

The man tugged on his mustache. "She young like you, yes?" he said in a heavy accent. "I see her here, there."

Lorraine grinned. "Wonderful—do you know which apartment she's in?"

Her face fell when the man shook his head. "No, I only ever see her here, in lobby," he replied.

The other man pointed at a door. "Always seems to be heading to the basement. Nothing down there but the boiler room."

Gloria had dumped her perfect life so she could sing in a speakeasy and fall in love with a poor black man, and now she was living in a boiler room? The girl did some crazy things.

Lorraine followed Hank down a rickety set of wooden

stairs to a dirty cement-floored basement. Piles of unidenti-fiable objects covered with tarps filled the room, with only narrow spaces between them. Lorraine sneezed as their feet kicked up dust, and she tried not to touch any of the sooty pipes that snaked through the room. "I hate dirty things," she said.

Hank appeared to be looking around for something. "Jerome and Gloria both listed this building as their address, right? But everyone we saw in the lobby was white. No way would the landlord let a colored boy live here. And from what the tenants were saying, it doesn't sound like Gloria lives here, either." He picked up a canvas bag he found on the floor and looked through it. "Aha!"

"I don't really think you should be going through people's things," Lorraine said.

"What if Gloria only *pretends* to live here? This building is right on the edge of Harlem. Say she and Jerome live in one of those buildings, and Gloria sneaks through this one and into a black building through the back? A colored landlord wouldn't take any more kindly to her living in his building than the landlord in this building would take to Jerome."

"Sounds far-fetched." Lorraine wanted to tell Hank that he should stick to bartending and leave the detective work to someone else, but she bit her tongue.

"Not if she has a good disguise," Hank said, tossing the canvas bag to her.

Inside were a long black coat and black gloves. Lorraine

checked the label on the coat—it was from the House of Beer in Paris. Quality goods. Exactly the sort Chicago Gloria had owned. "There's nothing here that would cover her hair."

Hank shrugged his big, beautiful shoulders. "She probably keeps a hat in there. Maybe she took it with her."

He opened the back door and went outside. Walking to the ragged fence at the back of the lot, he started pushing on each wooden slat. A scarred piece of wood swung aside at the gentlest poke. Lorraine followed him through the wide gap in the fence.

They found themselves in the backyard of a building that was in even worse repair than the one they'd left. Two older black women narrowed their eyes at Hank and Lorraine as they walked through the back door, but made no move to stop them. Lorraine had spent her life looking at and through colored people in the exact same way that she was being looked at now—it felt strange to be on the other side of that look.

Gloria had lived *here*—in this dump? "What now?" Lorraine whispered, wincing at the scraggly grayish carpeting beneath her brocade pumps.

"I doubt they live on the first floor," Hank replied, deep in thought. "Why go to all this trouble if Gloria was going to hit all the foot traffic coming from the lobby? If I were trying to hide, I would live on the top floor."

"Why?" Lorraine asked, intrigued by Hank's detective

skills. "Not that I don't love the view from a penthouse, of course."

"Let's say someone was able to find out where they were but didn't know the apartment number. They'd start knocking on doors on the first floor and work their way up, right?"

Lorraine shrugged. "I guess so."

"So let's start at the top and work our way down," Hank said, heading toward the stairs.

Lorraine groaned and trudged after him. They eventually reached the top floor, which turned out to be the fourth. She tried to catch her breath and watched as Hank knocked on the nearest door.

A young black man looked as surprised as Lorraine when he opened the door. "Yes?" he asked warily.

"Hello, I'm Paul Seymour and this is my fiancée, Betty," Hank said, slinging his arm over Lorraine's shoulder. "We're getting married soon and we were wondering if you'd be willing to play the piano at our reception."

The man blinked. "I'm sorry, sir, I think you got me confused with somebody else."

Hank was all flustered embarrassment. "Oh, I am so sorry! Aren't you Jerome Johnson?"

The man shook his head. "The piano player? Naw, that music comes from over in Four D."

Hank smiled back. "I must've written the address down wrong. Thanks."

Lorraine stared at Hank as they walked down the

hallway. "Did you used to act out there in California, too? What else do you do that I don't know about?"

"What can I say? I'm a man of many talents." They stopped in front of 4D. "Are you ready?"

Lorraine exhaled. Now that they were finally here, her stomach was knotted into nervous coils. Surely Gloria still hated her. But Lorraine would just have to force Gloria to listen. For her own good.

She nodded. "I'm ready."

Hank rapped on the door; a moment later a young man answered. A white man. He was dressed far too well to be living in a place like this, in a navy blue suit, and his dark hair looked as if it had been trimmed by a professional barber. The man didn't say anything—he just crossed his arms.

"Uh, we're here to see Jerome Johnson," Lorraine said nervously. "Or Gloria Carmody. Or both, really."

The man gave a crisp nod. "Wait here." He closed the door.

"Who's that?" Hank whispered.

"I've never seen him before."

A moment later the door opened again. The man waved them in, reminding Lorraine of a butler. "Please come inside."

Lorraine looked around at the dingy apartment, noting its peeling wallpaper and the tacky fact that the door led straight into the kitchen. The oak dining set screamed "flea market," and the doors on the cabinets looked as if they were ready to fall off their hinges.

Lorraine couldn't imagine Gloria—model-student, well-mannered, diamonds-and-lace Gloria Carmody—in this apartment. Lorraine felt a guilty lump welling in her throat. How much must Gloria have loved Jerome to put up with these hobo-camp living conditions?

The only other person in the room was an older man sitting in a chair by the window. His bronze hair was shot through with silver, as was his mustache. He was dressed in an impeccable gray suit that probably cost more than a year's rent on this tiny apartment.

Lorraine took a quick, short breath as the man turned toward her.

"Why, Lorraine Dyer," he said. "You have a lot of explaining to do."

CLARA

When life gives you lemons, sometimes you need to stash them in the icebox and make a martini with olives instead.

Clara patted her short golden hair as she turned onto Tenth Street.

For once, she wished her hair were long enough to twist into a sophisticated knot at the nape of her neck. Her boyish party-girl bob clashed with her outfit, but otherwise she looked the part of a real journalist: Her burgundy blouse and black skirt were fitted enough to be flattering but conservative enough to look professional. She even had a notebook and a pencil in her purse.

It was nice to have something to be excited about when nothing else in her life seemed to be going right.

Things were still rocky with Marcus.

They'd meet up, and Marcus would give her suspicious

glances as if he expected her to break out a flask and start dancing on the nearest table. On evenings they didn't spend together, he'd ask painfully detailed questions about her plans as though he didn't believe a single word she was saying.

He'd lost faith in her, and she was slowly trying to rebuild his trust. But it wasn't exactly sexy to feel as if your boyfriend were a copper keeping watch over your every move.

And Marcus didn't even know that she'd almost kissed Parker.

At the blue-lettered sign for Saunders' Furniture, she turned down a narrow alley, following Leelee's directions to the Opera House, and quickly found the large steel door under the bare bulb.

The wall was plastered with old posters pasted one atop another, but the newest one caught Clara's eye: a stylized portrait of a beautiful woman with a flaming red bob and green eyes, standing next to a piano. It advertised the up-coming debut of "the scorching singer hot enough to make the Devil himself blush": Zuleika Rose.

When Maude Cortineau had slurred that Gloria had a gig at the Opera House, Clara had assumed Gloria was working as a waitress. But no—she was headlining under a made-up name. The girl had gumption!

Marcus would never forgive Clara if she wrote this story, but she wasn't here for either Parker or Marcus. She was here to warn Gloria about Carlito. If, in the process, she figured out an angle on Gloria's story, all the better.

She rapped hard on the door.

"Sorry, toots, we ain't open yet," a boy said, poking his head out. His expression softened as he looked Clara up and down. "I mean, what can I do for you?"

She gave him her full-wattage smile. "I'm Clara Knowles, a reporter for the *Manhattanite*. I've heard you're opening a fantastic new show here and I was hoping to do a story on it."

The boy's eyes flicked from the press pass to her legs. "I ain't used to newshounds bein' pretty little Janes. The band doesn't rehearse today, though. Show debuts tomorrow night."

Clara pushed herself through the doorway. "That's fine— I'd much rather get a feel for the place before reporting on the band. Maybe talk to the manager?"

"Okay," the boy said. "Follow me."

◆ ◆ ◆

It wasn't long before Clara was sitting at one of the Opera House's round tables, sipping seltzer. The speakeasy was more or less deserted this early in the day but was one of the grandest she'd ever seen. A very good-looking bartender had come out through a door near the bar to pour her seltzer, but then he'd left the way he'd come. The only other person in the place was a grumbling old man pushing a broom over the hardwood floor.

The place looked plush and had a red-tinted den-of-sin

theme. Even though they were in a huge basement, it didn't feel like it—the ceilings were high and dark and the stage looked as elaborate as at any theater on Broadway. This would have been a good gig for Gloria, if only Carlito hadn't been behind it.

Clara needed to get information out of Spark—an odd-looking man with wispy brown hair, wearing a boater and a red-and-white-striped vest, who'd introduced himself as the person running the club. "So, have you been open long?" she asked.

Spark shrugged. "We just changed the name to something swankier. We've been around for a while." He thought for a moment. "But how about you just say in your article that we're new?"

"Of course," Clara said with a girlish smile. "Where'd you find this Zuleika"—she glanced down at her notepad—"Rose, is it?"

"The way you find most of 'em. We put out an ad. She auditioned."

"You're not worried about running a no-name singer when places like the Cotton Club and Connie's have got big stars like Bessie Smith and Nora Bayes?"

"Naw. I picked Zuleika out myself," he said, puffing out his skinny chest. "That girlie can wail. No shame in bein' the one to discover a first-rate torch."

"You hired Zuleika?"

"Yes indeedy."

"So you're the top dog around here?"

Spark sat up a little straighter in his chair. "You could say that."

The man with the broom sputtered a laugh. " 'Cept you'd be lying," he muttered under his breath.

"You close your head, Rod," Spark warned.

"Wait, so you're *not* the manager?" Clara asked, looking from Spark to Rod.

"I most definitely *am*—" Spark began, his neck turning red.

"He doesn't make any decisions," Rod continued in his gravelly voice. "Miss High-and-Mighty does. Or *did,* up until a few days ago."

A woman manager at a speakeasy? Clara certainly hadn't been expecting that. "Could I maybe have a word with *her*?"

At just that moment, the door next to the bar swung open. A tall girl with a dark bob walked out, her large hazel eyes glued to a clipboard. Her profile was severe but not in an unattractive way—she reminded Clara a little of Coco. The girl had a coltish figure that suited her white smocked dress perfectly.

Spark stood up, visibly annoyed. "Hey, boss, this lady here from the *Manhattanite* wants to know the rumble on Zuleika and her band. I'd answer her questions myself, but I got some important work I gotta go finish."

The girl glanced at Spark as he passed. "If you're talking about the crossword puzzle, good luck coming up with an exotic bird that starts with Z."

This woman was the boss? As Clara took in the girl's features, she felt the blood draining from her face.

Lorraine Dyer.

The clutchingly desperate girl she'd left back in Chicago.

The girl who was madly in love with Marcus Eastman.

The girl who'd tried to ruin Clara by exposing her to the world.

Clara gripped her pencil so tightly that it snapped in two.

Minus the raccoonlike makeup and the frantically grasping manner, Lorraine looked spiffier than Clara had ever seen her. Almost a woman. A moment ago, Clara had thought Lorraine seemed graceful—elegant, even. But Clara couldn't forget that voice. Or that birdlike head darting forward on the thin neck. How was Lorraine a part of this? Could it be a coincidence that Lorraine was somehow managing the club where Gloria was singing?

Lorraine sidled up to the table. "Hi, nice to meet you," she said, jotting something on her clipboard. She didn't bother to look at Clara. "Of course the new show is going to be spectacular. Zuleika Rose is the cat's pajamas, the cat's meow, the cat's paw and tail and whiskers and— Oh, she's the cat's everything, really."

"Lorraine," Clara said.

Lorraine glanced up briefly but showed no sign of recognition. "I've never met Zuleika personally," she went on. "Of course, very few have. She's like a night owl. Or just a regular owl, I suppose. But anyhow, I've heard her sing and she doesn't hoot. She yodels like a real canary, let me tell you—"

Clara stood and said, *"Lorraine!"*

Lorraine's eyes got so big that Clara could see the whites all the way around her dark irises. Gone was the confident speakeasy manager—Lorraine was the insecure prep school outsider all over again.

"Clara?" Lorraine asked in a gasp. "Clara *Knowles*?"

"In the flesh."

"Oh God, oh God." Lorraine fanned herself and panted so heavily that Clara worried she would swoon.

Clara put her hand on Lorraine's arm. "Is there somewhere more private we could talk?"

Lorraine stared at her in silence, then said, "Yeah, yeah, uh—follow me."

Spark chose that moment to return. "Wait—you two know each other? How?"

"Oh, go blow a horn," Lorraine said rudely, motioning for Clara to follow her.

"Just remember, Thor's comin' back from his afternoon poker game soon!" Spark called after the girls as they passed behind the bar and into a cramped, empty office. Lorraine closed the door behind them.

"Clara, what are you *doing* here? Don't you know that this place is run by *mobsters*? It's dangerous!"

"I could ask you the same question," Clara said, plopping down in the chair in front of the desk. "Does Gloria know you're the manager here?"

Lorraine bit her bottom lip. "No."

"What kind of game are you playing?" Clara asked, raising her voice just slightly. "Did you know that Carlito owns this club? This isn't another one of your catty pranks, Lorraine. This is the *Mob*. Gloria's in *real* danger."

"You think I don't *know* all that?" Lorraine wailed, her voice rising to a shriek. "Who are you to come barging in here, telling me what to do? This is my club!" She rolled her eyes. "Sort of."

"Tell me you're not working for Carlito."

Lorraine slumped into the chair behind the desk, tears running down her cheeks.

"What did Gloria ever do to make you hate her that much?"

"I was angry," Lorraine answered. "Gloria betrayed me— she believed I went behind her back and told Bastian about her stupid affair. But I didn't! That wasn't me! I swear!"

Clara reached across the desk and put her hand on Lorraine's. "I believe you."

"My reputation was completely ruined, and Gloria didn't do a thing to help. She was too busy running off with mobster-killing black men. She was supposed to be my best friend, but she turned the world against me."

"If there's anyone you should be upset with, it's *me,* not Gloria," Clara said. "*I* lied to you—all of you—and I took the man you loved away. All Gloria did was believe you talked behind her back . . . and you've got to admit that's not really a stretch."

Lorraine sniffled. "You asked why I hate her and I told you. Carlito offered me a job here if I would help him find Gloria and Jerome. So I did. And now I'm in love, so you can keep Mr. Marcus Eastman all to yourself in whatever love nest you two are sharing like some pair of diseased birds. Case closed, Miss Reporter."

Clara slammed her hands down on the desk. "Who *are* you, Lorraine Dyer? Who turns over her best friend to a certain death just for some kind of idiotic revenge?"

"But I'm not—"

"This is going too far, Raine. Jerome isn't the one who killed that gangster—Gloria is. And the reason she killed that guy? Because he was going to kill *them*. It was self-defense. Carlito is going to *kill* Gloria. But none of that matters to you, does it?"

Lorraine gawped. "How do you know about Tony? I only . . . I only just found out. I didn't know before." Clara could see the old insecure girl—the one from Laurelton Prep, the one who still loved Gloria Carmody—peeking out. "I swear."

"Look, you've done some terrible things," Clara said, "but you're not a bad person. We all make mistakes. It's how you fix them that counts."

Lorraine said, "I'm way ahead of you. I *am* going to fix things. I have a plan—"

"What, like your plan to humiliate me back in Chicago?" Clara snapped. She'd been an idiot to think she could appeal to Lorraine's better nature—it didn't exist.

Clara grabbed her purse and stormed out, ignoring Lorraine's attempts to call her back. She almost knocked over an overdressed midget on the stairs and was too worked up even to find that strange.

◆ ◆ ◆

Clara was still angry when she entered her apartment in Brooklyn.

She slipped off her heels, set her purse on the kitchen table, and walked into her bedroom, where she found Marcus sitting at her desk. It was strewn with notes she'd written before she left for the Opera House—the details about Gloria's situation with Carlito.

From the look on Marcus's scowling face, it was clear he'd read all of it. "I cannot believe you would do this."

"I wasn't going to publish it. That's just for me, so I could practice—"

"I don't believe you!"

She backed out of the bedroom, shaken. Marcus had never raised his voice to her.

Marcus followed, the notes crushed in his hands. "I'm going to find Gloria. I've got to save her before your selfishness gets her arrested or killed." He tossed the pages into the trash. "Why I ever believed you'd changed, I can't imagine." He grabbed his jacket off the back of a chair and strode toward the door.

"I don't want to see you again," he said, his hand on the

doorknob. "But then, I haven't really seen you all summer, anyway. Not the Clara I fell in love with."

With that, he slammed the door behind him.

Clara sat with her elbows on her knees, trying not to cry but unable to stop herself.

Then she heard a knock. *Oh, thank goodness*. He'd come back.

She wiped her eyes and swung open the door.

But instead of Marcus, she saw a striking black girl. The girl was wearing a simple but pretty yellow dress. Something about her looked familiar, but Clara couldn't put her finger on what. A handsome black man with a black eye stood beside the girl, looking dapper in a tan suit and blue shirt.

"May I help you?" Clara asked.

"I certainly hope so," the girl said. "I'm Vera Johnson. Jerome's sister."

This was all too much to handle. "Oh my," Clara said softly, her knees going weak. "You and I really need to talk."

And then she crumpled to the floor.

25

VERA

Clara Knowles was so much more glamorous than Vera remembered.

Vera remembered Clara's coming with Gloria to the Green Mill. Back then, Clara had seemed like a refugee from Victorian times, looking as if she'd been dressed by her grandmother.

But *this* Clara would have been at home on the cover of a magazine, modeling the latest fashions. She was some kind of beautiful. Swanky and stylish and radiating the kind of smarts that made her look sexier than any eighteen-year-old had the right to be. Her face looked just as perfect, aside from the fact that her mascara was running a little.

Or rather, that was how she *had* looked. Now she was passed out.

"Hold her head," Vera said to Evan, who'd caught Clara

when she'd swooned. Vera went inside and wet a dish towel in the kitchen sink. Then she mopped Clara's forehead with it.

Slowly, Clara's eyes fluttered open.

"Are you okay?" Vera asked.

"I'm fine now. Thank you," Clara said. She woozily got to her feet. "Um, come in. Please."

The living room was sparsely furnished with a blue sofa and an armchair, two lamps, and a lovely mahogany coffee table.

Clara collapsed into the armchair. "And you are?" she asked, turning to Evan.

"Evan," he said. "An old bandmate of Jerome's."

"I see," Clara said. "I'm sorry about just now. It's not you—it's just, well . . . It's been an eventful day. How'd you find me?"

"Well, it's a little complicated," Vera began.

◆ ◆ ◆

Vera hadn't even realized how long she'd been talking— about what had happened back in Chicago, about the assassin and Bastian and Carlito—until she glanced at the clock. It was getting close to five in the afternoon. "We saved time and just went to the offices of the magazine and talked to a handsome fellow there."

There was only one handsome fellow at the *Manhattanite*. "That would have been Parker," Clara said.

"That's him. Once we explained that we'd known you back in Chicago, he gave us your address and phone number. We tried calling, but you weren't home."

"I was out looking for Gloria."

Vera leaned forward. "That's why we're here—we've *got* to warn my brother and Gloria about Carlito."

"Hmm," Clara said, frowning. "All I really know is that Gloria is working as the singer at the Opera House. It's a speakeasy downtown." She got up to pull a notepad out of her black purse. "I'll write down directions. Gloria and Jerome are supposed to perform there tomorrow, but it's a trap set up by Carlito Macharelli and"—she grimaced— "some awful person we used to know in Chicago."

Clara tore off the sheet of paper and gave it to them. "I'm not really sure what to do except go there and warn her and Jerome."

"Then that's what we'll do," Vera said.

Clara frowned. "It's a whites-only club, I'm afraid. You won't be able to get inside."

"Who said anything about getting inside?" Evan said. "Way I see it is that they're going to have to take Gloria and Jerome *out* of there. And we'll be waiting."

Clara hesitated. "I'm not sure you two have the muscle to slow down a bunch of gangsters."

"And who said anything about it being just us two?" Evan said. "Me and Jerome? We know a lot of people. And we take care of our own."

As they walked out of Clara's brownstone, Vera looked long-ingly at Evan, at the way the summer sun bounced off his dark skin.

"What are you staring at?" he asked playfully.

She stopped in the middle of the sidewalk. "Things are about to get really messy." She thought of Bastian's dark blood seeping into the planks of that faraway dock, of Evan himself tied up and gagged in a closet. "Things already *are* messy. Jerome is my brother, Evan, and I have to go and save him. But you . . . you could leave right now." She swallowed and looked at their intertwined hands. "You came with me to New York, and that was more than enough. More than I had any right to ask for."

"No way," Evan said. "You saved my life back there. I owe you. Besides"—he tucked a strand of her hair behind her ear, and his fingers lingered on her cheek—"I don't *want* to leave. I belong here, with you."

Part of Vera wanted to lean into him, to be as close as pos-sible to this beautiful boy. But another part didn't want him to feel how hard her heart was beating. How she felt about Evan—the wild craziness of their connection—was brand-new territory.

"Whatever happens," he said, "I'm going to be here for you."

Then he kissed her. Their lips touched, and it was so passionate and intense that Vera could hardly breathe. Whatever happened at the Opera House tomorrow, there was no guarantee there'd be more moments like this. So she just gave in and kissed him, holding him and trying to make up for lost time.

26

GLORIA

Gloria had never dreamed a speakeasy would become her port in a storm.

But as she descended the Opera House's spiral staircase, the knot of dread in her stomach loosened a little. Since seeing the cops outside her apartment, she'd walked around the city with the constant fear that someone was following her. The only place where she felt safe was the Opera House—there, at least, no one knew who she really was.

Unable to go back to her apartment, she had spent the night in an around-the-clock diner. A waiter had been kind to her, letting her nod off now and again and keeping an eye on her. In the morning she'd walked around Central Park until she was exhausted, finally sitting on a bench near the Metropolitan Museum. Once evening rolled around, she freshened up her dress as best she could and went to work.

Spark and Hank the bartender both nodded hello as Gloria climbed the steps and went through the stage door. Tonight was her big debut, and all she was planning to worry about was singing her heart out. Everything else could wait for another day.

For a moment, she thought back to her debut at the Green Mill—the lights, the buzz, the onlookers in their fancy clothes drinking out of mismatched mugs and teacups, waiting and listening just for her. She remembered the exhilaration of standing in front of a microphone and digging deep into her soul and seeing what she was truly made of. There was nothing like singing.

Well, there was *almost* nothing like singing.

Being in love, Gloria thought—that was pretty special, too.

The women's dressing room was at the end of the hallway, past a foul-smelling lavatory and a mirror hanging over a small table. Gloria sucked in her breath when she saw Jerome standing outside the door. He hadn't changed into his suit yet—he was still wearing a blue checkered shirt and tan trousers.

Jerome looked tired, too. Still, somehow, in a way that only he could pull off, he managed to look more sexy and bohemian than weary and hungry. But Gloria worried: Was he eating enough? Getting enough sleep? Was he happy?

Then she remembered Marcie. Suddenly Gloria didn't feel so bad. And she certainly didn't care whether he was happy.

"I didn't think you'd come," she said. He'd skipped a rehearsal—some of the guys in the band had said he was out looking for a new gig.

"I didn't think *you* would come." Jerome's lips were tight, his jaw clenched. "Band doesn't work without a piano player, but we would've been just fine without a singer."

"I don't usually quit things once I commit to them. Unlike you. What do you want, anyway?"

Jerome hooked his thumb at the door behind him, directly across the hall from the women's dressing room. "This ain't the Green Mill, sweetheart—you're not the only one who gets a room to prepare."

"Don't call me sweetheart," Gloria said, her voice rising. "Don't ever—"

"Uh, excuse me?" Spark had come in from the stage. Along with his usual straw boater, he wore a long black coat with tails that seemed to engulf his body. "I'm just checkin' to see if you two need anything."

"Trust me," Jerome said, crossing his arms, "nothin' you offer will be good enough for this one. Some girls are too highfalutin for their own good."

"Oh, please! Some men are too full of themselves and proud to ask for help when they *obviously* need it."

"I never rejected your help!" Jerome said.

"Right, just so long as I didn't help *too* much. You'd rather just let us starve to death. At least your pride would be intact."

"Heh, heh," Spark said, straightening his red polka-dotted bow tie. "I see you two are getting along well! Let me know if you need anything."

Gloria huffed. "It'd be nice to have a hot lemon tea, something to clear my throat."

"But be careful," Jerome said to Spark. "She might take a sip and decide it's *too* hot. Then she'll get mad at you for giving her *exactly* what she wanted."

Gloria glared. "At least I'm brave enough to say what I want. Unlike some people."

"Don't do this girl any favors, Spark," Jerome shot back. "She'll only rip your head off for trying. Just like a praying mantis. Lady is lethal."

"And you shouldn't talk to *him* at all," Gloria snapped. "Tell this wet blanket anything serious, and he'll run scared. Boo-hoo!"

Gloria twisted the knob on the dressing room door and opened it. "Oh, golly! Look at me, walking inside my room without having to put on a disguise first!"

"There's no disguising that whiny voice!" Jerome replied. "Maybe you could get me something that would block out her yammering, Spark."

"You won't be able to hear it from *Harlem*!" Gloria shouted, throwing up her arms. "Maybe you should do us all a favor and go back there."

"Maybe I will—"

Spark raised his hands into the air. "Will you two give it a rest already? You sound like my parents, for God's sake. I don't care if you get along or not—just be out on that stage and smiling at ten o'clock."

"Of course," Jerome replied, breathing heavily. "*I'm* a professional."

"I am, too!" Gloria yelled. "More professional than you, piano man!"

But Jerome had already shut the door to the men's dressing room behind him.

Gloria groaned and walked inside the tiny space that was the women's dressing room. The hardwood floors were filthy, but the large mirror with its border of lights came straight out of her singing-to-packed-crowds fantasies. A silver bin on the vanity held tins of powder and rouge, eye pencils in varying shades and thicknesses, and several tubes of lipstick.

Gloria sat in front of the vanity, pulled off her white cloche hat, and checked her hair. She slashed eye pencil along the edges of her eyes and the tiniest bit on her brows, then smudged on a smoky bit of kohl to make the green of her irises stand out. A dash of red lipstick made her lips look more kissable.

At the thought of kissing, a sigh escaped her. How could Jerome make her so angry, yet fill her with the desire to jump into his arms at the same time?

She inspected the clothing rack. There were silky and sequined numbers that must have belonged to previous singers. Spark had given Gloria a box of safety pins and said, "Meet your seamstress. If you got something spectacular at home, you go right ahead and bring it in. Otherwise you're going to have to make do with one of these numbers."

She removed a silk crêpe dress from its hanger. It was such a pale shade of pink that it looked almost white. Pearly white beads decorated the bodice and waistline. Gloria pulled on the sleeveless chemise that went under the dress, then the dress itself. She fastened the sides and smiled into the mirror.

Even though her heart was broken and her purse was nearly empty and she had nothing much to call her own—she had this job.

A chance to sing. A tiny bit of glamour.

However many wrong turns she'd taken in the past year, she'd kept one promise to herself: She'd become a complete and utter flapper. An independent woman.

A knock at the door, and then Spark's voice: "I brought some lemon water for you two lovebirds. Try not to kill each other—at least not until after the show."

Slipping her feet into white satin peep-toe heels, Gloria walked into the hall.

Jerome chose the same moment to emerge. Now he was dressed in a gray suit, a burgundy shirt, and a gray tie, his shoulders looking broad and masculine in the gray jacket. It wasn't fair that he still got to be so damned good-looking when they were no longer together.

Jerome looked more elegant than Gloria had ever seen him. He looked like a man.

They arrived together in front of the table where a pitcher of water was sitting next to a single glass.

"Oh," Gloria said. "You go ahead and take it."

He nudged the glass toward her. "Naw, I'm not the one who has to sing."

She could feel the corner of her mouth turn up. "Who only brings one water glass, anyway?"

Her heart hammered when he smiled back. "Well, between you and me, I'm not sure the cheese is still firmly on Spark's cracker."

"You think he's really crazy, or just tanked?"

"Crazy. Though maybe he also gets drunk before he dresses himself in the morning."

"God, I hope so. How else to explain his fashion sense?"

Then they were laughing.

Gloria tried to remember how long it had been since they'd done something as simply enjoyable as sharing a joke.

"How could you leave?" she asked softly. "I tried to apologize so many times . . . but you just wouldn't listen."

"I didn't want to give you the chance. If I let you apologize, I wouldn't have been able to go. Without me around, you actually have a shot at a normal life. You were right—you're the one who has to jump through hoops and settle for less to be with me. A man from your . . . background could offer you so much more."

"What about that girl Marcie staying at your boarding-house?"

"Wait—how do you know about Marcie?"

"I kind of stowed away on the moving truck yesterday." At the look on Jerome's face, Gloria added, "I was worried!

And this Marcie girl was in your room, telling the movers where to put your piano."

He laughed. "Marcie Beebe? She's Reverend Beebe's daughter—she helps her father run the boardinghouse. She was just helping out while I was gone."

"And you never . . . with her?"

"You really think I would do that to you?" Jerome asked, looking hurt. "That's the thing with you, Glo—you make so much out of nothing, always jumping to conclusions. Like you did at the Cotton Club, thinking I was talking to Evan and Vera behind your back without hearing me out. Why can't you just trust me?"

"I'm going to work on that, Jerome. But we're still going to fight sometimes. That's what couples do. And for better or for worse, in sickness and in health, onstage and in disguise, they stick together."

Jerome broke into a smile. "That sounds a lot like marriage vows."

Gloria knew her own smile was every bit as goofy as Jerome's. "Hold that thought," she said.

In the dressing room, she rifled through the contents of her shoulder bag and pulled out the black velvet box. She'd been carrying it around, meaning to return it to him, but now she was glad she hadn't. Even holding it made her hands tremble as she thought about what was inside.

In the hallway again, she held it out to Jerome. "You need to do this again, the right way."

Jerome opened the box and removed the gold ring. "Such a little thing makes such a big difference."

"It's not a little thing, Jerome."

Oh, how it shimmered in the light!

"Is that how it works?" he asked. "You ordering me to propose?"

Gloria was about to backtrack, to apologize, but then Jerome went down on one knee right there in the hallway.

His hand shook a little as he took her fingers in his. "Gloria Rose Carmody, I love you. I didn't know what love was till I met you, didn't know that I had it in me to care so much for someone else. I don't want to be anything I'd have to be without you, and I don't want to ever be far from your side. These past few days have been miserable."

Gloria was going to have to redo her makeup if he went on much longer. She couldn't hold back her tears.

"I love you, and I love you, and I love you so much." He was weeping, too, but in the happiest way possible. "Not only are you beautiful and kind and true, but you have the most amazing singing voice I have ever heard, or ever will hear. Make music with me for the rest of my life. Please. Will you marry me?"

Gloria didn't even have to think before gasping, "Yes!"

He slipped the ring onto her finger. The delicate gold band with its tiny, sparkling diamond looked more at home on her left ring finger than Bastian's gaudy iceberg ever had.

Then she was in Jerome's arms, and he was spinning her

in circles. His lips found hers and they stayed locked that way, her hands gripping the back of his neck hard, pulling him closer, but never close enough. His grip was even stronger, clutching her hair, wandering over her neck, shoulders, and back with an almost desperate urgency. He pressed his chest hard against hers, and she could tell he wanted what she did: to be so close that nothing could separate them ever again. She hadn't even realized how much she missed him until right this second.

Too soon, he pulled away. "Now all we have to do is find someone to actually marry us. Where it's not against the law. Or going to get us killed."

She cupped his cheek with her hand. "We will, Jerome, don't worry."

He took her hand and kissed the back of it, staining it with the red lipstick smeared on his mouth. "All right, Miss Rose. You better go finish getting ready for your debut."

After one more quick kiss, Gloria returned to the dressing room. He loved her! Only her, as she loved him, body and soul. They would be together. Whatever obstacles they faced, they would face them together. She fluttered her fingers and looked at the tiny glinting diamond on her ring. She was his and he was hers and who gave a damn about her makeup?

But there was a show to perform, and they needed the money.

So she set to work fixing the lipstick that had been

completely rubbed off, wiping and repainting her eyes. But every few minutes she'd forget herself and smile and cry and mess up her makeup all over again.

She was doing her lips for the fourth time when there was a knock at the door. "This is very unprofessional behavior, Mr. Johnson," she called as she opened it. Her smile slipped away when she saw not Jerome's handsome face, but Spark's ugly one.

"Sorry to bother you, Zuleika, but apparently you've already got fans. Some black girl wanted to come back to see you. We couldn't let her in, of course, this bein' a classy joint. She left, but she came back with this." Spark lifted a pink hatbox Gloria hadn't noticed he was holding. "It's a present. Girl said it was a memento from the Green Mill, one you'd need for your Opera House debut."

Once he'd left, Gloria placed the hatbox gently on the vanity as if it might explode.

The box had to be from Vera.

Gloria pulled the lid off, bracing herself for whatever was inside. But it was just a hat. A large, ugly black hat not unlike the much-hated hat she'd worn as part of her between-buildings disguise. But this hat was cheap. Certainly it wasn't the kind of hat she'd normally expect to receive as a gift.

There had to be a note.

There was an abundance of white tissue paper in the box. She dug through it and found a sheet of lined notebook paper. The handwriting on the note looked like a neater, more feminine version of Jerome's.

Gloria—

Look out. You may need this to protect yourself and my brother. You've done it once before, and I know you can do it again if you have to.

—V

Gloria read the note twice, then looked again at the hat-box. She pulled piece after piece of tissue paper out of the box until her fingers found something cold and hard.

She knew what she held before her hand made its way out of the box.

Bastian's old silver pistol. She'd wished for the gun here in New York. Now she had it.

As she felt the weight of the weapon in her hands, all she could think about, all she could remember, was aiming it at Tony and pulling the trigger. How quickly it had happened—everything had been a rush, too loud and too chaotic.

Then nothing at all.

Vera must have taken the pistol after Tony's death.

But why did Vera think Gloria needed the gun now?

◆ ◆ ◆

There was another knock on the door. Gloria hitched her skirt up and tucked the gun into her garter. "Coming!"

Nothing could have prepared her for the unwelcome sight of her former best friend.

Lorraine Dyer.

Gloria recoiled. "You!"

Lorraine looked better than Gloria remembered. Her black tiered dress was too short to be flattering, but it was merely bold, rather than prostitute-in-training. A black feathered headband sat perfectly over her hair, and elegant silver earrings dangled from her ears. Lorraine's face had once been one of Gloria's favorite things: it had meant comfort, trust, and a lifetime of loyalty.

But that was before Gloria had realized that Lorraine, her most cherished friend, was nothing but a jealous, conniving *bitch*.

Gloria went to slam the door in Lorraine's face.

Lorraine blocked it with her foot. "Wait! Gloria, I know you're still mad at me, but I promise you'll be happy to see me in a minute."

"You are the *last* person I want to see right now. Why are you here?"

Lorraine waved her hand in dismissal. "Way too long a story to tell right this minute. *Ve-ry* long. Tedious, really. I'll explain later, I promise. But look who's here." Lorraine stepped aside. "Your dad!"

Standing behind her was Lowell Carmody.

The red hair Gloria had inherited was being overtaken by gray, but she would've sworn he looked exactly the same since the last time she'd seen him in Chicago, before he'd run off with that chorus girl and abandoned Gloria and her mother. Before he'd ruined everything.

All Gloria could do was look from Lorraine to her father in silence.

Lorraine smacked her lips awkwardly. "Okay, I've gotta go! Curtain in fifteen, Gloria!" Gloria vaguely wondered how Lorraine knew her curtain time, but her father standing in front of her was the more immediate problem.

"May I come in?" Mr. Carmody asked.

Gloria opened the door wide. She'd never expected to have her first conversation with her father in months while she was dressed this way, about to perform a show in a speakeasy.

She couldn't help noticing that he smelled faintly of cigars and peppermint. So painfully familiar. She felt herself collapsing inside. She missed her father, missed having someone to take care of her. She didn't always make the best choices on her own.

"Daddy," she said in a whimper.

Her father moved in for a hug. It was so hard to stay angry at him! She hadn't even known how badly she'd craved her father's embrace until she was in his arms.

"Wh-what are you doing here?" she stammered.

"Listen, sweetheart, I know I haven't been the best father lately. But your mother and I have been so worried. You think it's okay to just disappear?" He crushed her against him. "We both want you to come home."

"Home," she repeated. Being dragged back to Chicago was part of the reason she hadn't wanted to contact her father in the first place.

He must have understood. "If you don't want to go back to Chicago, you could come live with me. I've been looking for you ever since Beatrice said she thought you might be in New York. I've hired private eyes; I paid a company to hang flyers all over town. And seeing what you're doing now, it— it— There's no sugarcoating it, Gloria. This life of yours horrifies me. It's not what any daughter of mine should be doing—hanging around in these sorts of establishments, cavorting with these kinds of people. It's not how your mother and I raised you."

"You?" Gloria asked. "You're the one hanging the flyers?"

"I would have done anything to find you," Lowell Carmody said. "I've always wanted the best for you."

Gloria could feel herself being swayed by her father's words. But she had to remember everything he'd done. "Even when you tried to force me to marry Sebastian Grey? Am I just supposed to forget that ever happened, how difficult you made things for me, for Mother?"

"It was a confusing time. I was making a new life with Amber—"

"Right. Your exotic dancer."

"She's a performer," Mr. Carmody said through gritted teeth. "I'd expect you to understand that, seeing how you're dressed."

"Don't get all high and mighty with me. You show up here with Lorraine *Dyer* after hanging up a few flyers and expect me to run back into your arms?" Gloria backed away, blotting the damp skin underneath her eyes with a tissue. "No way."

Mr. Carmody slicked back his hair with his hand. "Gloria, I was under the impression that you *loved* Bastian. I was wrong. It's only now that I've found Amber that I realize how important love really is. I want you to find what I have—I want you to marry someone you really love."

Her father *loved* Amber? It was a possibility Gloria had never even considered—to her, their relationship had never been about love. A rich older man, a sexy younger woman—it was the oldest story in the world. Could it be possible that her father meant what he said—that he wanted Gloria to marry for love?

"I'm so relieved to hear you say that, Daddy, because . . ." Gloria extended her left hand to show off the gold engagement ring. "I'm in love, Daddy."

"So soon? Who is this boy, Gloria?" he asked, his voice low and intense.

Just then the door opened. Jerome walked in. "Sorry to bother you, Glo, but—"

Gloria pointed at Jerome. "It's him! He's the one I love, Daddy."

Lowell Carmody's face became as red as his hair. He took hold of Gloria's arm and pulled her as far from Jerome as the tiny room would allow. "Absolutely not!"

Mr. Carmody had never been a violent man, but for the first time, his expression scared Gloria. "If you even *think* about going through with this ridiculous marriage, I will completely cut you off! Again!"

"But, Daddy—" Gloria began.

"Curtain!" Spark called through the open door. "Get in your places, everyone!"

Gloria yanked her arm out of her father's grasp and took Jerome's hand. Without a second glance at her father, she led Jerome out of the dressing room.

Lowell Carmody could claim till he was blue in the face that he'd changed. But when it came down to it, he still cared more about his image than he did about Gloria. Some father.

She squeezed Jerome's hand as they walked down the hallway.

"Are you okay?" he asked her softly.

The feeling of Jerome's hand—the warmth of his palm, the smoothness of his fingers—calmed her. "I am now," she said. "Let's go blow the roof off this joint."

LORRAINE

Never judge a book by its cover.

People always said that as if it were some great piece of wisdom, but Lorraine had always lived by the opposite idea. Looks were important, and she had always admired pretty things: the delicate cut of a pink diamond, the gleam of a fresh strand of pearls. Adorning oneself with beautiful things made one beautiful, didn't it?

Yet the outsides of things—well, they could be deceiving. That was a lesson Lorraine had learned ten times over—with Marcus, with Bastian, with Clara, certainly with Gloria, and now with Hank.

Dear, sweet, sexy Hank, who had kissed her under a rowboat and let her think he was her boyfriend.

How could she have been so stupid?

"Hey, watch it!" one of the barbacks shouted at Lorraine as he rushed past with a crate full of whiskey.

The Opera House was more tightly packed than she had ever seen it. The posters had done their work: the cream of New York society was there for Zuleika Rose's debut. Laughing crowds of glittering people filled the floor—men puffing on expensive-smelling cigars, women dancing in place, the fringe on their sparkling dresses swaying. Most of the booths against the wall were filled with groups of middle-aged businessmen in flawless black suits and bowlers, save for Polly Adler, the buxom madam of several brothels, who was sandwiched between Puccini and Dante in one of the back booths, puffing on a cigarette. In the next booth over sat Thor with four Chicago mobsters Lorraine recognized from the Green Mill.

A sweet, lilting tune poured out of the Gramophone set up next to the stage. With the soft music and the smoke clouding the air, the atmosphere felt dangerous and romantic. Just yesterday Lorraine would've been trying to convince Hank to abandon his bar duties for one short turn on the dance floor.

Now she could barely look at him.

Hank and Cecil were both behind the bar, slinging drinks as quickly as they could. Lorraine joined them and tried to help, handing bottles of vodka and whiskey and gin as the bartenders called for them.

Inside she was dying from heartache. But on the outside she was listening to the instructions Hank whispered to her.

"It's getting to be time, Lorraine," he said in a hushed voice.

Lorraine handed him a couple of shot glasses. "Got it."

There would be time for more crying—and drinking—later. Right now was about trying to save Gloria and Jerome from a tragic fate.

Hank dug around in the shelves behind the bar, pretending to look for something. "Just to make sure we're crystal clear on how this will go down. We want as few guns on the floor as possible. Tell the midget and Carlito their gang can collect Carmody and Johnson out in the alley after the show. Say the idea is not to upset the patrons." Hank grabbed a bottle of sherry from the top shelf. "Don't tip your hand. You have to be as cool as a cucumber."

"I'll be cool, don't worry," Lorraine said. "I'll be downright freezing!"

Hank frowned. "Yeah. Just talk as little as possible—that's probably the safest thing."

It was as if he had stabbed her in the heart with a corkscrew.

Lorraine looked gorgeous tonight—she knew she did. Her black dress bore a striking resemblance to the gown the model was wearing on the cover of this month's *Vogue*. Lorraine's eyes were smoky, her lips vamp red. The black feathered headband and silver chandelier earrings added that last little bit of sparkle.

But all her effort was wasted on Hank, whose eyes didn't

show a trace of his old devotion. Instead, they looked condescending. Just the way someone else used to look at her— *Marcus,* she realized with another pang. *Why do boys always seem to look at me like that? Like I'm nothing?*

"Was it really all a lie?" Lorraine asked quietly. "You don't have any feelings for me?"

"Come on, Lorraine. I already told you—this is work for me. Besides, look at yourself. You've got no moral center, babe, you're just a dizzy opportunist." Hank turned back to the bar to take more drink orders.

Lorraine dug her nails into her palms. She'd wasted enough tears on Hank in the past twenty-four hours. After they'd found Lowell Carmody in Gloria's old apartment and arranged for him to come to Gloria's debut, Hank had told Lorraine they needed to have a talk.

Turned out he wasn't just a bartender after all.

He was an FBI agent.

He and his team had been after Carlito and Puccini for a while. Hank had gone undercover and had been using Lorraine.

Hank listed the many crimes he'd seen Lorraine commit—aiding in the sale and distribution of alcohol, concealing Tony Giaconi's murder, and . . . oh, a bunch of other things Lorraine had stopped paying attention to. Long lists had always been hard for her to follow.

She was thunderstruck by Hank's confession. He didn't love her? He didn't even *like* her?

Suddenly her image of herself strolling around the Barnard campus had been replaced with a vision of herself doing hard time. She couldn't go to jail!

No, the only way Lorraine was going to get out of all of this with a clear record was by doing exactly what Hank told her tonight. Carlito and Puccini would think they were about to nab Gloria and Jerome, but Hank and his FBI buddies would bag Carlito and Puccini instead.

And she was going to help make it happen.

Lorraine ran a well-manicured hand through her hair and gave Hank one last wistful look. Even though she knew he was nothing but a lying scoundrel, she still wanted him to like her. How messed up was that?

Just then, the Gramophone stopped and the gold velvet curtains parted. The show was about to begin! The members of the band were in matching gray suits. The man called Jonesy held the mouthpiece of his saxophone to his lips, and the lead horn, Bernie, raised his trumpet. The bassist, Rob, sat to the left, bow in hand over the strings of his upright, and Jerald the percussionist twirled his drumsticks. Jerome sat poised at his piano, the dark, vibrant heart at the center of this group of white men onstage. Anticipation hung in the air, thick as the smoke that filled the dim speakeasy.

And then Gloria walked out. The crowd hushed and then burst into applause.

She looked absolutely gorgeous. The white beads on her dress gave her an ethereal glow. The pale pink dress was almost too innocent, more befitting the blushing ingenue Gloria had once been. But her red lipstick was sultry, and the slit running up the side of her dress was incredibly sexy. When Gloria had sung at the Green Mill, she'd been full of nervous energy that the entire audience could feel. But this Gloria was sleek and cool—the ideal bluesy vixen.

The trumpet played a mournful introduction; Gloria took center stage and turned her green eyes toward the audience. When she opened her mouth and began to sing, it was as though she were singing to Lorraine—and everyone in the room—personally.

> *Once I lived the life of a millionaire,*
> *Spending my money, I didn't care;*
> *I carried my friends out for a good time,*
> *Buyin' bootleg liquor, champagne, and wine.*
>
> *When I began to fall so low,*
> *I didn't have a friend, and no place to go;*
> *So if I ever get my hand on a dollar again,*
> *I'm goin' to hold on to it till them eagles grin.*

Gloria and Jerome had been practicing, but they'd *never* sounded this good. Even the scattered clusters of young girls who'd been talking as the band began to play shut up in a hurry.

In the past six months, Gloria had grown up. Her voice

now was filled with all the hurt and longing that singing the blues required. Her loss and loneliness poured over the audience, and not a single person could look away. Lorraine was thunderstruck: What had Gloria gone through that made her understand true sadness so well?

When Jerome rattled off a solo, Gloria leaned against the piano and watched him play. When she began to sing again, she gazed directly into his eyes. It was scandalous in so many ways—but they were all the right ways.

Oh God, Lorraine thought. *This is going to be a hit! The Opera House is going to be a huge success with this duo!*

And then she remembered. This show was going to be a one-night-only engagement.

When the song ended, the applause was thunderous. Gloria and Jerome launched straight into another tune—this one more upbeat. Women grabbed their dates and dragged them to the center of the club to dance.

"She's a helluva lot better than I remember," a raspy voice said. "It's almost a shame we can't keep her."

Lorraine glanced down and saw Thor standing next to her. His flinty eyes glared at her from under his black bowler hat. He barely reached her waist.

"Ain't it, though?" Lorraine said. "So, uh, where's Carlito? I would've thought he'd be here by now."

"On his way," Thor said. "And be a little louder, why don't ya? Don't think everyone in the room could hear you."

Where had Lowell Carmody disappeared to? Lorraine

scanned the audience for his bright hair and eventually saw him standing close to the bar. His arms were crossed and his face was red. He seemed more timid than she would have imagined, but perhaps he was just shocked. She couldn't exactly blame him. And then she saw another familiar face and had to steady herself against the wall.

Marcus Eastman was leaning against the bar, nursing a drink.

Marcus! Eastman!

It had been so long since she had seen him, since she had obsessed over him and tried to get him to be her boyfriend. She had given up on that dream, but it was still shocking to see him. What was he doing there? He had to be there with Clara, right?

Lorraine could feel her stomach somersault. "I've gotta go check on something at the bar," she said, not sticking around to see Thor's reaction. She sidled through the crowd to the bar and tapped Marcus's shoulder. "Well, look who's here."

He turned around and was even more beautiful than she remembered. Those gorgeous cheekbones, smoldering blue eyes, the sexy curve of his lips. No dimples, though, since his usual joking grin was nowhere to be seen. Maybe he and Clara had split up: He did certainly look a little blue.

"Lorraine? What on earth are you doing here?"

"Long story," Lorraine replied. "What about you?"

Marcus's eyes flicked to the stage; then he laughed. "My story might be even longer. You having a good summer?"

"I'm not sure 'good' is the adjective I'd use."

"Yeah, me neither." His too-blue eyes met hers. "*You* look good, though."

Marcus Eastman was giving her a real, live compliment? "Thank you." She tucked her hair behind her ear. "Where's Clara?"

He gave a sad smile. "I don't know where she is." He picked up his drink and took a sip. "Maybe we were all a little hard on you, Raine. I'm not saying you dealt with it well, but . . ." He swallowed hard. "It's awful being lied to."

Lorraine felt a sharp poke in her midsection and looked down to see Thor standing next to her. "Time to look alive, kid."

Lorraine turned and saw Carlito Macharelli on the stairs. She glanced back at Marcus. "I've gotta go," she said. "Good to see you, though."

Marcus tipped his head. "See you at school in a few weeks, Raine."

Lorraine smiled to herself and walked away. Several of the men and women on the floor turned to stare at Carlito as he and his three associates entered the club. Lorraine wasn't sure whether the girls recognized Ernesto Macharelli's son from the papers or just thought he was handsome in that deliciously grim, throw-me-over-your-shoulder way.

Carlito did look particularly sharp tonight in an ivory suit and black shirt. And those intensely dark eyes were irresistibly sexy and mysterious. Only someone who knew him as well as she did would recognize his expression—he was out for blood.

"Scram," Carlito said to the men already sitting in one of the booths. He extended his hand toward Lorraine. "Ladies first."

All too quickly Lorraine was trapped, sitting between Carlito and Thor, the red leather hot and sticky against her bare arms. *Stay calm, stay calm, stay calm.*

Maude Cortineau squeezed in after Carlito. She looked sensational in a dark-blue dress, a matching headband, and strand upon strand of silver beads.

"You really packed them in tonight, didn't you?" Carlito asked.

Thor made a face as if he were in pain—he was smiling, Lorraine realized. "Yep," he said. "You should see the cash box—beautiful stuff. Everyone seems to be lovin' the band."

Lorraine pitched in: "Thor was just saying how it was a shame Gloria and Jerome couldn't stick around. Since they're so good, you know."

"We're all set to catch the canary and her fella," Thor said. "We'll be waitin' for 'em by their dressing rooms after the show."

"No!" Lorraine said.

Carlito, Thor, and even Maude all turned to look at her.

"*No?*" Carlito repeated, a menacing smile teasing his lips.

Lorraine gulped. "I just thought your men were gonna catch 'em out in the alley after the show. A big parade of goons dragging them out will be pretty obvious, don't you think? This place is hopping. We don't want to upset the patrons."

Carlito scooted closer. "I don't remember when I started taking orders from you, Raine. Is there somethin' you're not tellin' me?"

Lorraine started breathing fast. "Not at all, I—"

"Boss?" a voice called.

Carlito looked up at the mustachioed man standing next to the booth. "What?"

"Probably nothing," the bodyguard said in a deep voice. "But we noticed a pretty blond girl movin' toward the targets. Should we stop her?"

Carlito, Thor, Maude, and Lorraine all slid out of the booth. Almost immediately, Lorraine spotted Clara pushing her way to the stage.

Good old Country Clara looked like a Hollywood starlet. Her sleeveless gold-and-silver dress had a boldly graphic teardrop design, and Lorraine immediately was jealous. Clara looked fabulous. A sharp-looking man with wavy dark hair followed her hesitantly through the crowd.

"Signal Tommy to grab her. But let's not leave anything to chance," Carlito said. He pushed through the EMPLOYEES ONLY door that led backstage.

Thor took off along the edge of the audience. His small stature made it easy for him to move fast through the crowd, and he reached the stage before Clara did.

He bounded up the steps at the side of the stage, ran along its lip, and launched himself at Clara. But Clara saw him a moment before he leaped, and dodged right. His body struck the floor with a muffled thud.

When she saw Thor, Gloria immediately stopped singing.

Lorraine didn't know what to do. Should she run to help Gloria or try to catch Carlito? Hank's stupid plan was falling apart. She stood frozen, a spectator like everyone else.

Jerome grabbed Gloria's arm, and as Clara finally reached the stage steps, the two of them pushed past the confused musicians in the band toward the wings, all the while waving at the audience as though this were part of the show.

But then everyone stopped in their tracks.

Carlito walked out from the wings. The gangster shoved aside Bernie, who dropped his trumpet with a loud clang. Thor clambered back onstage, his hair a mess and his jacket askew. Gloria and Jerome stood center stage with Thor on one side and Carlito on the other.

And then someone blew a whistle.

It was Hank. Suddenly a half dozen men on the dance floor flashed FBI badges, while others stormed the stage. More agents came down the club's staircase, blowing whistles and holding pistols aloft.

And then all was chaos—women shrieking, glass shattering, people throwing drinks to the floor and surging toward the exit. Lorraine just stepped back against the wall and let it happen.

"Carlito Macharelli!" Hank yelled as he approached the stage. "You're under arrest!"

Carlito stood proudly in the spotlight, staring out into the club. "Under arrest? What for?" he asked calmly. The microphone broadcast his voice. "I just came out to see the show. Like the rest of these good people." He jerked his thumb toward Jerome. "This is the boy you should be arresting. He shot one of my men back in Chicago."

The audience gasped.

Jerome stepped forward. "It's true. I shot and killed one of his men."

Lorraine stared at Jerome. Here was a man who was willing to go to jail for a crime he didn't commit, just to protect a woman. He really did love Gloria—more than Lorraine had thought a man could ever love a woman. The way Lorraine herself wanted to be loved.

And she had betrayed them both.

CLARA

Clara's jaw dropped at Jerome's lie.

"It's true. I shot and killed one of his men."

She already knew how much Gloria loved Jerome—her cousin had given up a life of chandeliers and champagne for him. Gloria had suffered the scandal of a white girl falling for a black boy. She'd even *killed* for him.

It seemed Jerome loved Gloria every bit as much in return.

"I'm impressed," Parker whispered in Clara's ear, startling her. "I never expected you'd have a story like this up your sleeve."

Parker didn't look the least bit concerned about the doomed lovers onstage. Instead, he was a hungry wolf, thrilled by the hunt. The man really *didn't* have any morals. All he saw were stories. And Clara was turning out to be just like him.

She was still working out how to respond when she heard Gloria clearing her throat. "Jerome didn't kill anyone. He's lying, to save me." Gloria took a deep breath and stood up a little straighter. "I was the one who shot Carlito's man."

The crowd buzzed: "These singers all work with the Mob, darling—you can't expect them to be the least bit respectable." "Has she killed anyone else?" "Does she have a gun on her now?" "Sexy, talented, *and* she can shoot a pistol—boys, I think I'm in love."

But most of the audience, like Clara, just stared at the stage in stunned silence.

"It was in self-defense. He was going to kill both me and Jerome," Gloria continued. "But that doesn't change what happened. The gun belonged to my fiancé, Sebastian Grey. I have it right here." She reached under her dress and withdrew a silver pistol from her garter.

There were more gasps, a few screams, and Spark yelled out, "She's got a gun!"

Someone touched Clara's shoulder. She turned and saw Lorraine and a wan-looking blond girl in a dark-blue dress.

"Relax, it's just me," Lorraine whispered. "So skittish—you'd think our best friend was confessing to a murder or something."

"Maude Cortineau," Clara said, recognizing Carlito's moll.

"You didn't even tell me you were in the *Manhattanite*!" Maude said. "I love that magazine!"

"You should meet my date," Clara said. "He's the magazine's editor, Parker Richards." She looked around but didn't see Parker, only more and more FBI agents flooding the club and shouting out that no one was to move. "Lorraine, was *this* your plan to help Gloria?"

Lorraine made a more-or-less motion with her hand. "Sort of." She pointed at the good-looking bartender-turned-FBI-agent. "See, that's Hank. We were dating until—"

There was the deafening sound of a gunshot.

Half the women in the club screamed. It took Clara a second to realize she'd been one of them.

"Drop your weapon!" the man whom Lorraine had called Hank shouted. The room grew silent.

A series of clicking noises filled the air as all the agents unholstered their guns, pointed them at Gloria, and cocked the hammers.

"Drop your weapon!" Hank repeated.

Gloria laid the gun at her feet and raised her hands. "It wasn't me!"

On the left side of the stage, Carlito Macharelli coughed. He coughed again and fell to his knees, his mouth open. He'd been holding his right hand over his chest. When he moved it and looked down, a red stain blossomed on his white lapel. Carlito stared at the growing stain, confused.

"Carlito!" someone yelled. A short, fat man rushed forward, his cartoonish features contorted not so much in concern as in fear.

"That would be Puccini," Lorraine whispered to Clara. "He's the owner."

Carlito watched as Puccini lumbered up the steps to the stage. "I . . . ," Carlito said. "You . . ." His eyes rolled back and he slumped to the ground.

"Oh my God, oh my God," Lorraine muttered over and over till Clara was ready to slap her.

Gloria and Jerome had moved to a corner of the stage with the musicians, as far from Carlito's body as they could get. Gloria's face was pressed into Jerome's chest and his arms were around her back.

Puccini knelt down beside Carlito. The chubby gangster looked terrified. "Spark!" he yelled.

There was a commotion at the stairs, where the gangly would-be manager Clara had met was arguing with an FBI agent. "You really think I'm gonna let *you* out?" the agent asked Spark. "No one here is moving a muscle, *especially* not you."

"Who fired his weapon?" Hank shouted.

No one said anything.

"In that case," Hank said, "no one leaves this hellhole until we've searched it top to bottom." He waved his gun hand. "Everybody take a seat on the floor."

Parker suddenly appeared and grabbed Clara's hand. His face was pale and damp. He wasn't the slick journalist anymore—he was afraid for his life.

Just like everyone else. No one in the crowd was wasting

time with gossipy whispers anymore. Everyone was looking left and right, to the mahogany bar, to the booths, and back to the stage, searching for the source of the gunshot. For the gun that could go off again any second.

Someone cried out, "Let me *go!*" and there was a rustling from the wings. A moment later, two burly FBI agents led a woman onto the stage.

What Clara saw surprised her: The woman was a stunner, an older beauty with flawless skin and a glossy platinum-blond bob. Her sleeveless red dress was a little on the long side, but it was sheer in more places than it wasn't. This was Carlito Macharelli's killer?

Doubtful.

But as the woman squirmed, Clara caught sight of an empty leather holster strapped to her thigh. Maybe there was more to this sheba than met the eye.

The agent on the woman's right held a black gun out of reach—it was bigger and bulkier than Gloria's little pistol. The kind of gun a person needed know-how to use.

Hank climbed up onstage and looked down at the glamorous blonde. "Ruth Coughlin. What brings you to New York?"

The woman spat in his face. "I ain't telling a bull like you a damn thing."

Hank calmly took out a handkerchief and wiped his cheek. Then he handcuffed her.

Ruth showed off teeth that were just as gorgeous as the

rest of her. "Just take me to the station already. You can play all the games you want with my lawyer."

So this was the woman who'd murdered Bastian, who'd followed Gloria, who'd been out to kill Jerome, and who had killed Carlito. But why?

The two agents led the woman through the crowd and up the stairs, and Hank supervised as agents handcuffed Puccini and Spark, who cried fat, blubbery tears into his ugly bow tie.

The cops didn't handcuff Jerome—instead, they put the cuffs on Gloria. Then they led her out of the club, Jerome following close behind.

"Gloria," Clara called out as she passed.

Gloria looked back for a second and somehow managed to smile. "Clara! What are you—"

"This ain't a social hour," the agent said, forcing Gloria to keep walking.

"Come see me, okay?" she called over her shoulder. "And bring me a shawl? I hear the slammer's pretty cold."

There was a moment, just as Gloria reached the top of the stairs, when she locked eyes with a handsome older man in a brown suit. There was something oddly similar about their features, which made sense: The man was Clara's uncle. Gloria's father.

Wasn't he going to do something? Say something? His daughter was in handcuffs, for goodness' sake! She had just admitted to killing a man!

But Lowell Carmody just averted his eyes and walked away.

And then Gloria was out of sight.

Maude placed a hand on Clara's shoulder. Oh God—she'd want to talk about the *Manhattanite*.

But instead Maude grinned and clapped. "I'm free!" she squealed like a little girl.

Clara, Lorraine, and Parker all gave each other confused looks. *What?*

Maude giggled again. "It's terrible about Carlito dying and all that, but I've been trying to figure out how to get away from him for ages. Now I don't have to worry about him tryin' to kill me!"

"Oh . . . ," Lorraine said. "Well, good, then . . . I guess."

Maude sighed. "Everyone I date ends up dead, you know? I was gonna leave Carlito for Bastian Grey. Say what you want about him, but he was a classy guy. And single! But then he got killed." Maude's voice broke. "So I had to come here with Carlito." She smiled again. "But I guess it all worked out in the end, huh?"

"Maude Cortineau?" a man's voice said. It was Hank. He was even better-looking up close, with his messy almost-black hair, smooth tanned skin, and light brown eyes. "We'd like you to come with us to the station. We want to ask you a few questions about Carlito."

Hank gave Lorraine a curt nod as he led Maude away. "Good work, Raine." He paused. "Have fun at Barnard next year."

Clara turned to Lorraine. Lorraine was watching Hank

climb the stairs with a familiar expression on her face: It was the wistful way she'd always looked at Marcus. "So, you and Hank . . . ?" Clara asked.

Lorraine let out a bitter laugh. "Oh, you know me. I never seem to get it right when it comes to men."

"Did you know this was going to happen?" Parker interjected.

Clara wanted to pretend that she had. That she had some sort of in with the FBI and had stores of knowledge about the Mob. But it was time to be more honest in her work and in her life. "I only knew a little."

"Well, whatever you knew, good work. How do you know the singer?"

"She's my cousin."

"Your cousin? That's great—we can work the personal angle. Now we head over to the police station and try to get some of these agents to talk to us." He looked around. "Think there's a telephone around here? Maybe I could get our photographer to meet us there. That FBI agent Hank and the singer would look great on our splash page."

Clara hesitated. Didn't Parker have any compassion for Gloria after what had just happened?

She stepped away. "You want to tag along to the police station?" she asked Lorraine. "I could use a friendly face."

"No thanks. I need to get far away from the Opera House and everything that goes with it." Lorraine tugged nervously on her earrings. "Could you tell Gloria I say hi, though? And that I'm sorry? And that she was amazing tonight? Did I mention that I'm sorr—"

Clara patted Lorraine's arm. "I will. And, Lorraine . . . good job tonight. I'm actually kind of impressed."

Lorraine's eyes softened. "Thank you, Clara. It was nice meeting you, Parker." Lorraine turned and walked away.

"Clara?" a voice asked as she and Parker were about to leave.

She turned her head, and there he was.

Marcus.

Clara had to squelch the desire to give him a hug. He was not hers to hug anymore.

"Marcus," she said with a small smile. "Hi."

Marcus's eyes flicked to Parker and back to her. "Who's this?"

"He's my editor," Clara said quickly.

Parker extended his hand. "Parker Richards, editor of the *Manhattanite*. You must be proud of everything your friend's accomplished, huh?"

Clara's heart seemed to stop for a moment at the way Parker called Marcus her friend. Parker had no idea who Marcus was because Clara had never mentioned him. She'd never mentioned having a boyfriend, even when Parker had asked her about it.

Marcus stared at Parker's hand, then turned to Clara, his blue eyes cold. "So *this* is why you wanted to be a journalist."

"Marcus, that's not fair. It's not like that."

"You want to talk to me about what's fair?" he asked, his

voice rising. "Well, you've got a helluva story now, Clara. I hope your typewriter keeps you warm at night." His mouth twitched. "And your new beau."

Marcus stomped up the stairs. Clara stared, unsure of what to do. A voice in her head was screaming *Go after him!* She could explain about Parker. Marcus wouldn't have gotten so jealous if he didn't still love her, right?

Parker tapped her shoulder. "You all right?"

"I'm fine," Clara replied. "C'mon, Parker. Let's go up top and see what's going on outside."

Clara felt guilty about letting Marcus down once again. But there was one thing Marcus was definitely right about: This was a helluva story.

◆ ◆ ◆

If Clara thought the scene inside the club had been chaotic, it was nothing compared to what she found outside. The alleyway was filled with people—FBI agents she'd expected, but outnumbering them six to one were black men and a few women. Most of them were dressed to the nines and carried instruments in cases—they were musicians, she realized. Someone out on the street was blowing a horn, and the plaintive sound wended its way into the alley.

"Who are all these people?" Parker asked. "Why are they here?"

"A parade?" Clara guessed.

"Clara!" a voice called, and from the crowd came Vera

Johnson and her handsome trumpeter boyfriend, Evan. Vera looked stricken. "Is he all right? Jerome?"

"He's fine, Vera," Clara said. "I think they're bringing him out—" Before she could finish, the girl threw her arms around Clara and crushed her in an embrace.

"Oh, thank you!"

"I didn't do anything!" Clara said once they'd parted. "Though it looks like you were ready to do something."

"We couldn't muster the cavalry," Evan said, shrugging, "but we did the next best thing: Everybody we know and everybody *they* know in the industry. Figured Carlito and his gang couldn't shoot *all* of us. We figured we could over-power them with a big enough mob. There can be power in numbers."

And then Jerome was there, walking down the alley be-tween two agents.

Vera flung herself at him, practically knocking him off his feet. The agents stepped back and reached for their weapons, but Jerome just waved them off and said, "It's my *sister*, guys."

Jerome pulled Vera into a tight hug, and she sobbed into her brother's chest. "I'm so sorry, Jerome," she said, the words muddled by her tears. "For everything you've gone through. I'm just so glad you're safe."

"Shhh," Jerome said, "of course I'm safe. Why wouldn't I be?"

Vera looked as though she wanted to answer the question

but had no idea what to say. She seemed so young, so frightened; she reminded Clara how young they all were. Publishing articles? Chasing after mobsters? Capturing killers? What normal seventeen- and eighteen-year-olds did these sorts of things?

If nothing else, Clara thought, *let it never be said that I haven't lived an exciting life.*

For the first time in a long while, Clara felt truly alone. But she wasn't scared. Instead, she felt exhilarated, fresh, and new. Life wasn't always about love—that was the old way, when a girl lived solely for her man. Nowadays life could be about promise, about work—about a girl's finding something she was good at and following through.

She was done trying to be the woman Marcus or Parker wanted her to be.

She was going to be the woman *she* wanted to be.

This story was just for her.

GLORIA

CARLITO MACHARELLI KILLED AT
SPEAKEASY OPENING!

CHICAGO DEB SHOWS MOBSTER WHO'S BOSS!

FORBIDDEN LOVE, GANGSTERS, AND MURDER:
A NIGHT NEW YORK WILL NEVER FORGET!

It had finally happened: Gloria Carmody was a star.

She carefully clipped articles from the *Times,* the *Post,* and the *Wall Street Journal*. New York papers weren't the only ones covering her story—the reporters in Chicago had been all over it, too. Several made trips to New York just so they could interview the teenage aristocrat who'd fallen in love with a black musician and shot a gangster. The *Tribune* and the *Evening Journal* had both already run more than one two-page spread about her.

That was how she learned about Ruth Coughlin and how Ruth's boss, Al Capone, hadn't been too happy about Tony Giaconi's murder. Al Capone had just managed to get Chicago under his thumb. How would it have looked if word had got out that Capone couldn't control his own guys? That one of those guys got knocked off by a black piano player and a deb? So Capone sent Ruth to clean up Carlito's mess. She took care of Bastian first on the docks in Chicago. Then she went after Carlito, Gloria, and Jerome in New York.

Gloria set the articles aside and opened the black scrapbook Clara had brought her as a gift.

The magazine article that took up the first few pages always made her smile. Clara's photographer had taken about a million pictures of Gloria, Hank, and the other agents after they arrived at the police station. Gloria looked like a frightened little girl in some and a backtalking criminal in others.

But in the photo Clara and Parker had chosen for the article, Gloria's face had just the right mix of righteous anger, pride, and bruised glamour. She looked like a white light next to the group of dark-suited FBI agents.

GLORIA CARMODY FIGHTS FOR LOVE
By Clara Knowles

Eighteen-year-old Gloria Carmody is a flapper extraordinaire, the embodiment of all that the daring modern girl strives to be—with all that modern girl's tarnished dreams and dizzy exuberances, all her accidental sins and passionate mistakes. Gloria has dared to live without society's approval. She's gambled everything so that she can be the one thing that matters most to her: true to herself.

In Chicago, she rejected a picture-perfect society marriage to pursue the taboo love of piano player Jerome Johnson. That's not all she went after—she also snagged a job singing the blues at a top Chicago club, the Green Mill. She courageously defended Jerome's life and her own against the gangster Tony Giaconi, shooting him dead when he threatened her. And when, six months after her crime and in another city, Gloria at last had to face her punishment onstage at the Opera House, she didn't shed a single tear.

And yet she is sitting in a jail cell, awaiting trial, instead of out on the street, living her life to the fullest. How can we, as a society, condemn a girl for protecting herself against a man sent to kill her and her lover—

Gloria was grateful for the article. It was the first story about her case to appear, and it set the tone for everything that followed. Instead of depicting her as a notorious criminal, the press hailed her as "the new woman"—a leader for flappers and other strong-willed women to follow.

Only, she didn't feel like much of a heroine right now. Everything in this place was gray—the brick walls, the sheets on her cot's too-thin mattress, and the steel desk bolted to the wall. Sometime soon, the Chicago police would show up to take her to a more permanent cell in that city. There would be a trial, then most likely prison for life.

For the past three days, Gloria had felt as if she'd done nothing but answer questions—from the police, the FBI, the hordes of reporters. Then there had been visits from her friends. Clara had come every day, sometimes with her editor and sometimes without.

"Hopefully my articles will get you out of there soon," Clara had said earlier that day, leaning against the bars of Gloria's cell. "No offense, Glo, but gray is *not* your color."

"Don't worry, Gloria," Parker had said. "With everything Clara's been writing about you, the judges in Chicago will award you some kind of medal before they let you spend another second in prison." He'd given Gloria a tight smile—she figured he was being casual to calm her nerves about staying in a holding cell.

Truthfully, Gloria liked Parker: He seemed even more intelligent than he was attractive, and that was saying something. But she kept hoping Clara would turn up with Marcus instead. Gloria had been very happy to see Marcus the day after her arrest, but he hadn't been his usual jokey self without Clara.

"Marcus, what happened between you and Clara?" Gloria had asked.

He'd smiled a watery shadow of a grin. "Who cares about my depressing tales of lost love? You've got bigger problems. Figured out how to tunnel outta here yet?"

Lorraine had shown up just as Marcus was leaving. "So, anyway, I'm so, so sorry for what I was going to do, I didn't think Carlito would hurt you, I just—"

Gloria put her hand up. "Stop. I will never forgive you for

what you did to Clara back in Chicago or what you tried to do here. You were ready to let Carlito *kill* me and Jerome just because I was mad that you ratted out my affair to Bastian? Because I was angry with you for making such a show about Clara at my party?"

"Carlito *said* he wouldn't—"

"No one is that stupid, Raine, not even you." Lorraine was silent. Gloria sighed, and then said, "But like it or not, you saved Jerome's life and mine. So . . . thank you."

Lorraine grinned. "Anytime, *ma chérie*. So . . . has Hank asked about me?"

◆ ◆ ◆

Gloria had been allowed one tearful telephone call to her mother. She'd expected her mother to be angry—about her running away, about Jerome, about Tony, about all of it— but Beatrice had been nothing but happy to talk to her little girl again. Beatrice had arrived in New York a few days earlier and had spent every moment working every connection she had to get Gloria out of jail.

Gloria hadn't heard from Lowell Carmody yet, and she didn't really expect to. Her father had been ready to cut her off when he found out about Jerome. Gloria was pretty sure that on the disapproval ladder, gangster-killing was at least a few rungs above a black fiancé.

Her chest tightened at the thought of Jerome.

Along with Vera and Evan, he'd been barred from visiting her even once since she'd been arrested. It was so incredibly unfair. Gloria and Jerome had spent their last month together in New York fighting over their impossible future. And just when they'd decided to make the impossible possible, to go up against the world with only each other as allies, to do everything that love was about, they'd been torn apart.

She sat up quickly when she heard footsteps in the hall.

Agent Hank Phillips appeared outside her cell. At the Opera House, Gloria had thought Hank was twenty or twenty-one. But in his black suit and tan trench coat, with a few days' stubble on his chin, he looked a little older, maybe twenty-four or twenty-five. Of course, he'd have to be at least that old if he was an FBI agent.

"Hey there, princess," he said, smiling. "Still pasting up that scrapbook of yours?"

Gloria shrugged. "Not like I've got much else to do."

"Now, that's where you're wrong." He pulled a pack of cigarettes from his coat pocket. "Want one?"

After days of snarky insults, Hank was being weirdly nice. Still, Gloria hadn't had a cigarette in ages. She stood, and Hank lit two cigarettes. He handed one to her and she took a puff. She ended up coughing. "These things aren't good for a person."

Hank crossed his arms. Lorraine had told Gloria how Hank had tricked her. Gloria didn't have a lot of love for Lorraine, but the trickery made her dislike Hank even more.

"I've got a proposition," he said. "You can sit here in jail, or you can do something for us."

What sort of help could the FBI want from her?

"It's not *you* we're after, Gloria," Hank said. "There are bigger fish to fry. And we can use you to get to them. I've talked to some folks on your behalf, and we've come up with a deal: If you help us, you go free. If you don't, well . . ." He took a drag from his cigarette. "But it's not gonna be easy. This'll probably be the hardest thing you'll ever have to do in your life."

Gloria glanced back at her scrapbook, thinking of the last few lines of Clara's article.

So, girls, take heed. Whenever you feel as if you're really pushing the limits, think of Gloria Carmody. Think of all she's been through and push further, push harder. Fight for what you want, for the people you love. Be a true flapper—be fearless.

Gloria certainly didn't want to spend the rest of her life in jail. She wanted to be with Jerome, to make music with him onstage and in life. And she had better live up to her own example, right?

She looked down at her left ring finger, wishing she'd been allowed to keep that one bit of sparkle in this cell. She'd only worn the ring for a few hours, but already her finger felt wrong without it.

The hardest thing she would ever have to do in her life?

She had already killed a man, fled her childhood home, lived in poverty, had her heart broken, and been arrested and sent to jail.

What could be harder than that?

Then Gloria realized: living a life without Jerome.

That would be the hardest thing.

She put a hand on her hip and stared Hank straight in the eye.

"What do you need me to do?"

Jillian Larkin's fascination with flappers and the 1920s began during her childhood, which included frequent home screenings of the classic Julie Andrews/Carol Channing film *Thoroughly Modern Millie.* She lives in New York.

Young. Wealthy. Defiant. Beautiful. Dangerous.
It's 1923 . . . and anything goes.

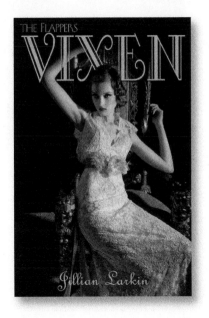

Don't miss a single second.

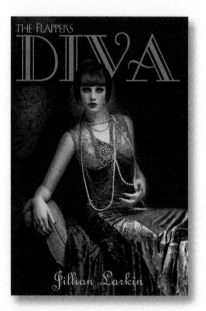

Find out what happens next when

DIVA

goes on sale in 2012!

For the latest Flappers news, visit
theflappersbooks.com.